Penguin Books
Carry on, Jeeves

Pelham Grenville Wodehouse was born in 1881 in Guildford, the son of a civil servant, and educated at Dulwich College. He spent a brief period working for the Hong Kong and Shanghai Bank before abandoning finance for writing, earning a living by journalism and selling stories to magazines.

An enormously popular and prolific writer, he produced about a hundred books. In Jeeves, the ever resourceful 'gentleman's personal gentleman', and the good-hearted young blunderer Bertie Wooster, he created two of the best-known and best-loved characters in twentieth-century literature. Their exploits, first collected in *Carry on, Jeeves*, were chronicled in fourteen books, and have been repeatedly adapted for television, radio and the stage. Wodehouse also created many other comic figures, notably Lord Emsworth, the Hon. Galahad Threepwood, Psmith and the numerous members of the Drones Club. He was part-author and writer of fifteen straight plays and of 250 lyrics for some thirty musical comedies. *The Times* hailed him as a 'comic genius recognized in his lifetime as a classic and an old master of farce'.

P. G. Wodehouse said, 'I believe there are two ways of writing novels. One is mine, making a sort of musical comedy without music and ignoring real life altogether; the other is going right deep down into life and not caring a damn.'

Wodehouse married in 1914 and took American citizenship in 1955. He was created a Knight of the British Empire in the 1975 New Year's Honours List. In a BBC interview he said that he had no ambitions left now that he had been knighted and there was a waxwork of him in Madame Tussaud's. He died on St Valentine's Day, 1975, at the age of ninety-three.

P. G. Wodehouse in Penguin

P. G. Wodehouse
Carry On, Jeeves

P.G. Wodehouse

Carry on, Jeeves

PENGUIN BOOKS

PENGUIN BOOKS

Published by the Penguin Group
Penguin Books Ltd, 80 Strand, London WC2R 0RL, England
Penguin Putnam Inc., 375 Hudson Street, New York, New York 10014, USA
Penguin Books Australia Ltd, 250 Camberwell Road, Camberwell, Victoria 3124, Australia
Penguin Books Canada Ltd, 10 Alcorn Avenue, Toronto, Ontario, Canada M4V 3B2
Penguin Books India (P) Ltd, 11 Community Centre, Panchsheel Park, New Delhi – 110 017, India
Penguin Books (NZ) Ltd, Cnr Rosedale and Airborne Roads, Albany, Auckland, New Zealand
Penguin Books (South Africa) (Pty) Ltd, 24 Sturdee Avenue, Rosebank 2196, South Africa

Penguin Books Ltd, Registered Offices: 80 Strand, London WC2R 0RL, England

www.penguin.com

First published in Great Britain by Hebert Jenkins Ltd 1925
Published in Penguin Books 1957
This edition published 1999

28

Set in 9/11pt Monotype Trump
Typeset by Rowland Phototypesetting Ltd,
Bury St Edmunds, Suffolk
Printed in England by Clays Ltd, St Ives plc

ISBN-13: 978-0-140-28408-9
ISBN-10: 0-140-28408-7

TO BERNARD LE STRANGE

Contents

1 — Jeeves Takes Charge

Now, touching this business of old Jeeves – my man, you know – how do we stand? Lots of people think I'm much too dependent on him. My Aunt Agatha, in fact, has even gone so far as to call him my keeper. Well, what I say is: Why not? The man's a genius. From the collar upward he stands alone, I gave up trying to run my own affairs within a week of his coming to me. That was about half a dozen years ago, directly after the rather rummy business of Florence Craye, my Uncle Willoughby's book, and Edwin, the Boy Scout.

The thing really began when I got back to Easeby, my uncle's place in Shropshire. I was spending a week or so there, as I generally did in the summer; and I had had to break my visit to come back to London to get a new valet. I had found Meadowes, the fellow I had taken to Easeby with me, sneaking my silk socks, a thing no bloke of spirit could stick at any price. It transpiring, moreover, that he had looted a lot of other things here and there about the place, I was reluctantly compelled to hand the misguided blighter the mitten and go to London to ask the registry office to dig up another specimen for my approval. They sent me Jeeves.

I shall always remember the morning he came. It so happened that the night before I had been present at a rather cheery little supper, and I was feeling pretty rocky. On top of this I was trying to read a book Florence Craye had given me. She had been one of the house-party at Easeby, and two or three days before I left we had got engaged. I was due back at the end of the week, and I knew she would expect me to have finished the book by then. You see, she was particularly keen on boosting me up a bit nearer her own plane of intellect. She was a girl with a wonderful profile, but steeped to the gills in serious purpose. I can't give you a better idea of the way things stood than by telling you that the book she'd given me to read was called *Types of Ethical Theory*, and that when I opened it at random I struck a page beginning:

> The postulate or common understanding involved in speech is certainly co-extensive, in the obligation it carries, with the social organism of which language is the instrument, and the ends of which it is an effort to subserve.

All perfectly true, no doubt; but not the sort of thing to spring on a lad with a morning head.

I was doing my best to skim through this bright little volume when the bell rang. I crawled off the sofa and opened the door. A kind of darkish sort of respectful Johnnie stood without.

'I was sent by the agency, sir,' he said. 'I was given to understand that you required a valet.'

I'd have preferred an undertaker; but I told him to stagger in, and he floated noiselessly through the doorway like a healing zephyr. That impressed me from the start. Meadowes had had flat feet and used to clump. This fellow didn't seem to have any feet at all. He just streamed in. He had a grave, sympathetic face, as if he, too, knew what it was to sup with the lads.

'Excuse me, sir,' he said gently.

Then he seemed to flicker, and wasn't there any longer. I heard him moving about in the kitchen, and presently he came back with a glass on a tray.

'If you would drink this, sir,' he said, with a kind of bedside manner, rather like the royal doctor shooting the bracer into the sick prince. 'It is a little preparation of my own invention. It is the Worcester Sauce that gives it its colour. The raw egg makes it nutritious. The red pepper gives it its bite. Gentlemen have told me they have found it extremely invigorating after a late evening.'

I would have clutched at anything that looked like a lifeline that morning. I swallowed the stuff. For a moment I felt as if somebody had touched off a bomb inside the old bean and was strolling down my throat with a lighted torch, and then everything seemed suddenly to get all right. The sun shone in through the window; birds twittered in the tree-tops; and, generally speaking, hope dawned once more.

'You're engaged!' I said, as soon as I could say anything.

I perceived clearly that this cove was one of the world's workers, the sort no home should be without.

'Thank you, sir. My name is Jeeves.'

'You can start in at once?'

'Immediately, sir.'

'Because I'm due down at Easeby, in Shropshire, the day after tomorrow.'

'Very good, sir.' He looked past me at the mantelpiece. 'That is an excellent likeness of Lady Florence Craye, sir. It is two years since I saw her ladyship. I was at one time in Lord Worplesdon's employment. I tendered my resignation because I could not see eye to eye with his lordship in his desire to dine in dress trousers, a flannel shirt, and a shooting coat.'

He couldn't tell me anything I didn't know about the old boy's eccentricity. This Lord Worplesdon was Florence's father. He was the old buster who, a few years later, came down to breakfast one morning, lifted the first cover he saw, said 'Eggs! Eggs! Eggs! Damn all eggs!' in an overwrought sort of voice, and instantly legged it for France, never to return to the bosom of his family. This, mind you, being a bit of luck for the bosom of the family, for old Worplesdon had the worst temper in the county.

I had known the family ever since I was a kid, and from boyhood up this old boy had put the fear of death into me. Time, the great healer, could never remove from my memory the occasion when he found me – then a stripling of fifteen – smoking one of his special cigars in the stables. He got after me with a hunting-crop just at the moment when I was beginning to realize that what I wanted most on earth was solitude and repose, and chased me more than a mile across difficult country. If there was a flaw, so to speak, in the pure joy of being engaged to Florence, it was the fact that she rather took after her father, and one was never certain when she might erupt. She had a wonderful profile, though.

'Lady Florence and I are engaged, Jeeves,' I said.

'Indeed, sir?'

You know, there was a kind of rummy something about his manner. Perfectly all right and all that, but not what you'd call chirpy. It somehow gave me the impression that he wasn't keen on Florence. Well, of course, it wasn't my business. I supposed that while he had been valeting old Worplesdon she must have trodden on his toes in some way. Florence was a dear girl, and, seen sideways, most awfully good-looking; but if she had a fault it was a tendency to be a bit imperious with the domestic staff.

At this point in the proceedings there was another ring at the front door. Jeeves shimmered out and came back with a telegram. I opened it. It ran:

Return immediately. Extremely urgent. Catch first train. Florence.

'Rum!' I said.

'Sir?'

'Oh, nothing!'

It shows how little I knew Jeeves in those days that I didn't go a bit deeper into the matter with him. Nowadays I would never dream of reading a rummy communication without asking him what he thought of it. And this one was devilish odd. What I mean is, Florence knew I was going back to Easeby the day after tomorrow, anyway; so why the hurry call? Something must have happened, of course; but I couldn't see what on earth it could be.

'Jeeves,' I said, 'we shall be going down to Easeby this afternoon. Can you manage it?'

'Certainly, sir.'

'You can get your packing done and all that?'

'Without any difficulty, sir. Which suit will you wear for the journey?'

'This one.'

I had on a rather sprightly young check that morning, to which I was a good deal attached; I fancied it, in fact, more than a little. It was perhaps rather sudden till you got used to it, but, nevertheless, an extremely sound effort, which many lads at the club and elsewhere had admired unrestrainedly.

'Very good, sir.'

Again there was that kind of rummy something in his manner. It was the way he said it, don't you know. He didn't like the suit. I pulled myself together to assert myself. Something seemed to tell me that, unless I was jolly careful and nipped this lad in the bud, he would be starting to boss me. He had the aspect of a distinctly resolute blighter.

Well, I wasn't going to have any of that sort of thing, by Jove! I'd seen so many cases of fellows who had become perfect slaves to their valets. I remember poor old Aubrey Fothergill telling me – with absolute tears in his eyes, poor chap! – one night at the club, that he had been compelled to give up a favourite pair of brown shoes simply because Meekyn, his man, disapproved of them. You have to keep these fellows in their place, don't you know. You have to work the good old iron-hand-in-the-velvet-glove wheeze. If you give them a what's-its-name, they take a thingummy.

'Don't you like this suit, Jeeves?' I said coldly.

'Oh, yes, sir.'

'Well, what don't you like about it?'

'It is a very nice suit, sir.'

'Well, what's wrong with it? Out with it, dash it!'

'If I might make the suggestion, sir, a simple brown or blue, with a hint of some quiet twill –'

'What absolute rot!'

'Very good, sir.'

'Perfectly blithering, my dear man!'

'As you say, sir.'

I felt as if I had stepped on the place where the last stair ought to have been, but wasn't. I felt defiant, if you know what I mean, and there didn't seem anything to defy.

'All right, then,' I said.

'Yes, sir.'

And then he went away to collect his kit, while I started in again on *Types of Ethical Theory* and took a stab at a chapter headed 'Idiopsychological Ethics'.

Most of the way down in the train that afternoon, I was wondering what could be up at the other end. I simply couldn't see what could have happened. Easeby wasn't one of those country houses you read about in the society novels, where young girls are lured on to play baccarat and then skinned to the bone of their jewellery, and so on. The house-party I had left had consisted entirely of law-abiding birds like myself.

Besides, my uncle wouldn't have let anything of that kind go on in his house. He was a rather stiff, precise sort of old boy, who liked a quiet life. He was just finishing a history of the family or something, which he had been working on for the last year, and didn't stir much from the library. He was rather a good instance of what they say about its being a good scheme for a fellow to sow his wild oats. I'd been told that in his youth Uncle Willoughby had been a bit of a rounder. You would never have thought it to look at him now.

When I got to the house, Oakshott, the butler, told me that Florence was in her room, watching her maid pack. Apparently there was a dance on at a house about twenty miles away that night, and she was motoring over with some of the Easeby lot and would be away some nights. Oakshott said she had told him to tell her the moment I arrived; so I trickled into the smoking-room and waited, and presently in she came. A glance showed me that she was perturbed, and even peeved. Her eyes had a goggly look, and altogether she appeared considerably pipped.

'Darling!' I said, and attempted the good old embrace; but she side-stepped like a bantam-weight.

'Dont'!'

'What's the matter?'

'Everything's the matter! Bertie, you remember asking me, when you left, to make myself pleasant to your uncle?'

'Yes.'

The idea being, of course, that as at that time I was more or less dependent on Uncle Willoughby I couldn't very well marry without his approval. And though I knew he wouldn't have any objection to Florence, having known her father since they were at Oxford together, I hadn't wanted to take any chances; so I had told her to make an effort to fascinate the old boy.

'You told me it would please him particularly if I asked him to read me some of his history of the family.'

'Wasn't he pleased?'

'He was delighted. He finished writing the thing yesterday afternoon, and read me nearly all of it last night. I have never had such a shock in my life. The book is an outrage. It is impossible. It is horrible!'

'But, dash it, the family weren't so bad as all that.'

'It is not a history of the family at all. Your uncle has written his reminiscences! He calls them "Recollections of a Long Life"!'

I began to understand. As I say, Uncle Willoughby had been somewhat on the tabasco side as a young man, and it began to look as if he might have turned out something pretty fruity if he had started recollecting his long life.

'If half of what he has written is true,' said Florence, 'your uncle's youth must have been perfectly appalling. The moment we began to read he plunged straight into a most scandalous story of how he and my father were thrown out of a music-hall in 1887!'

'Why?'

'I decline to tell you why.'

It must have been something pretty bad. It took a lot to make them chuck people out of music-halls in 1887.

'Your uncle specifically states that father had drunk a quart and a half of champagne before beginning the evening,' she went on. 'The book is full of stories like that. There is a dreadful one about Lord Emsworth.'

'Lord Emsworth? Not the one we know? Not the one at Blandings?'

A most respectable old Johnnie, don't you know. Doesn't do a thing nowadays but dig in the garden with a spud.

'The very same. That is what makes the book so unspeakable. It is full of stories about people one knows who are the essence of propriety today, but who seem to have behaved, when they were in London in the eighties, in a manner that would not have been tolerated in the fo'c'sle of a whaler. Your uncle seems to remember everything disgraceful that happened to anybody when he was in his early twenties. There is a story about Sir Stanley Gervase-Gervase at Rosherville Gardens which

is ghastly in its perfection of detail. It seems that Sir
Stanley – but I can't tell you!'

'Have a dash!'

'No!'

'Oh, well, I shouldn't worry. No publisher will print
the book if it's as bad as all that.'

'On the contrary, your uncle told me that all
negotiations are settled with Riggs and Ballinger, and
he's sending off the manuscript tomorrow for immediate
publication. They make a special thing of that sort of
book. They published Lady Carnaby's *Memories of
Eighty Interesting Years*.'

'I read 'em!'

'Well, then, when I tell you that Lady Carnaby's
Memories are simply not to be compared with your
uncle's Recollections, you will understand my state of
mind. And father appears in nearly every story in the
book! I am horrified at the things he did when he was a
young man!'

'What's to be done?'

'The manuscript must be intercepted before it reaches
Riggs and Ballinger, and destroyed!'

I sat up.

This sounded rather sporting.

'How are you going to do it?' I inquired.

'How can I do it? Didn't I tell you the parcel goes off
tomorrow? I am going to the Murgatroyds' dance tonight
and shall not be back till Monday. You must do it. That
is why I telegraphed to you.'

'What!'

She gave me a look.

'Do you mean to say you refuse to help me, Bertie?'

'No; but – I say!'

'It's quite simple.'

'But even if I – What I mean is – Of course, anything I
can do – but – if you know what I mean –'

'You say you want to marry me, Bertie?'

'Yes, of course; but still –'

For a moment she looked exactly like her old father.

'I will never marry you if those Recollections are published.'

'But, Florence, old thing!'

'I mean it. You may look on it as a test, Bertie. If you have the resource and courage to carry this thing through, I will take it as evidence that you are not the vapid and shiftless person most people think you. If you fail, I shall know that your Aunt Agatha was right when she called you a spineless invertebrate and advised me strongly not to marry you. It will be perfectly simple for you to intercept the manuscript, Bertie. It only requires a little resolution.'

'But suppose Uncle Willoughby catches me at it? He'd cut me off with a bob.'

'If you care more for your uncle's money than for me –'

'No, no! Rather not!'

'Very well, then. The parcel containing the manuscript will, of course, be placed on the hall table tomorrow for Oakshott to take to the village with the letters. All you have to do is to take it away and destroy it. Then your uncle will think it has been lost in the post.'

It sounded thin to me.

'Hasn't he got a copy of it?'

'No; it has not been typed. He is sending the manuscript just as he wrote it.'

'But he could write it over again.'

'As if he would have the energy!'

'But –'

'If you are going to do nothing but make absurd objections, Bertie –'

'I was only pointing things out.'

'Well, don't! Once and for all, will you do me this quite simple act of kindness?'

The way she put it gave me an idea.

'Why not get Edwin to do it? Keep it in the family, kind of, don't you know. Besides, it would be a boon to the kid.'

A jolly bright idea it seemed to me. Edwin was her young brother, who was spending his holidays at Easeby. He was a ferret-faced kid, whom I had disliked since birth. As a matter of fact, talking of Recollections and Memories, it was young blighted Edwin who, nine years before, had led his father to where I was smoking his cigar and caused all the unpleasantness. He was fourteen now and had just joined the Boy Scouts. He was one of those thorough kids, and took his responsibilities pretty seriously. He was always in a sort of fever because he was dropping behind schedule with his daily acts of kindness. However hard he tried, he'd fall behind; and then you would find him prowling about the house, setting such a clip to try and catch up with himself that Easeby was rapidly becoming a perfect hell for man and beast.

The idea didn't seem to strike Florence.

'I shall do nothing of the kind, Bertie. I wonder you can't appreciate the compliment I am paying you – trusting you like this.'

'Oh, I see that all right, but what I mean is, Edwin would do it so much better than I would. These Boy Scouts are up to all sorts of dodges. They spoor, don't you know, and take cover and creep about, and what not.'

'Bertie, will you or will you not do this perfectly trivial thing for me? If not, say so now, and let us end this farce of pretending that you care a snap of the fingers for me.'

'Dear old soul, I love you devotedly!'

'Then will you or will you not –'

'Oh, all right,' I said. 'All right! All right! All right!'

And then I tottered forth to think it over. I met Jeeves in the passage just outside.

'I beg your pardon, sir. I was endeavouring to find you.'

'What's the matter?'

'I felt that I should tell you, sir, that somebody has been putting black polish on our brown walking shoes.'

'What! Who? Why?'

'I could not say, sir.'

'Can anything be done with them?'

'Nothing, sir.'

'Damn!'

'Very good, sir.'

I've often wondered since then how these murderer fellows manage to keep in shape while they're contemplating their next effort. I had a much simpler sort of job on hand, and the thought of it rattled me to such an extent in the night watches that I was a perfect wreck next day. Dark circles under the eyes – I give you my word! I had to call on Jeeves to rally round with one of those life-savers of his.

From breakfast on I felt like a bag-snatcher at a railway station. I had to hang about waiting for the parcel to be put on the hall table, and it wasn't put. Uncle Willoughby was a fixture in the library, adding the finishing touches to the great work, I supposed, and the more I thought the thing over the less I liked it. The chances against my pulling it off seemed about three to two, and the thought of what would happen if I didn't gave me cold shivers down the spine. Uncle Willoughby was a pretty mild sort of old boy, as a rule, but I've known him to cut up rough, and, by Jove, he was scheduled to extend himself if he caught me trying to get away with his life work.

It wasn't till nearly four that he toddled out of the library with the parcel under his arm, put it on the table, and toddled off again. I was hiding a bit to the south-east at the moment, behind a suit of armour. I bounded out and legged it for the table. Then I ripped upstairs to hide the swag. I charged in like a mustang and nearly stubbed my toe on young blighted Edwin, the Boy Scout. He was standing at the chest of drawers, confound him, messing about with my ties.

'Hallo!' he said.

'What are you doing here?'

'I'm tidying your room. It's my last Saturday's act of kindness.'

'Last Saturday's.'

'I'm five days behind. I was six till last night, but I polished your shoes.'

'Was it you –'

'Yes. Did you see them? I just happened to think of it. I was in here, looking round. Mr Berkeley had this room while you were away. He left this morning. I thought perhaps he might have left something in it that I could have sent on. I've often done acts of kindness that way.'

'You must be a comfort to one and all!'

It became more and more apparent to me that this infernal kid must somehow be turned out eftsoons or right speedily. I had hidden the parcel behind my back, and I didn't think he had seen it; but I wanted to get at that chest of drawers quick, before anyone else came along.

'I shouldn't bother about tidying the room,' I said.

'I like tidying it. It's not a bit of trouble – really.'

'But it's quite tidy now.'

'Not so tidy as I shall make it.'

This was getting perfectly rotten. I didn't want to murder the kid, and yet there didn't seem any other way of shifting him. I pressed down the mental accelerator. The old lemon throbbed fiercely. I got an idea.

'There's something much kinder than that which you could do,' I said. 'You see that box of cigars? Take it down to the smoking-room and snip off the ends for me. That would save me no end of trouble. Stagger along, laddie.'

He seemed a bit doubtful, but he staggered. I shoved the parcel into a drawer, locked it, trousered the key, and felt better. I might be a chump, but, dash it, I could out-general a mere kid with a face like a ferret. I went downstairs again. Just as I was passing the smoking-room door out curveted Edwin. It seemed to me that if he wanted to do a real act of kindness he would commit suicide.

'I'm snipping them,' he said.

'Snip on! Snip on!'

'Do you like them snipped much, or only a bit?'

'Medium.'

'All right. I'll be getting on, then.'

'I should.'

And we parted.

Fellows who know all about that sort of thing – detectives, and so on – will tell you that the most difficult thing in the world is to get rid of the body. I remember, as a kid, having to learn by heart a poem about a bird by the name of Eugene Aram, who had the deuce of a job in this respect. All I can recall of the actual poetry is the bit that goes:

> Tum-tum, tum-tum, tum-tumty-tum,
> I slew him, tum-tum tum!

But I recollect that the poor blighter spent much of his valuable time dumping the corpse into ponds and burying it, and what not, only to have it pop out at him again. It was about an hour after I had shoved the parcel into the drawer when I realized that I had let myself in for just the same sort of thing.

Florence had talked in an airy sort of way about

destroying the manuscript; but when one came down to it, how the deuce can a chap destroy a great chunky mass of paper in somebody else's house in the middle of summer? I couldn't ask to have a fire in my bedroom, with the thermometer in the eighties. And if I didn't burn the thing, how else could I get rid of it? Fellows on the battlefield eat dispatches to keep them from falling into the hands of the enemy, but it would have taken me a year to eat Uncle Willoughby's Recollections.

I'm bound to say the problem absolutely baffled me. The only thing seemed to be to leave the parcel in the drawer and hope for the best.

I don't know whether you have ever experienced it, but it's a dashed unpleasant thing having a crime on one's conscience. Towards the end of the day the mere sight of the drawer began to depress me. I found myself getting all on edge; and once when Uncle Willoughby trickled silently into the smoking-room when I was alone there and spoke to me before I knew he was there, I broke the record for the sitting high jump.

I was wondering all the time when Uncle Willoughby would sit up and take notice. I didn't think he would have time to suspect that anything had gone wrong till Saturday morning, when he would be expecting, of course, to get the acknowledgement of the manuscript from the publishers. But early on Friday evening he came out of the library as I was passing and asked me to step in. He was looking considerably rattled.

'Bertie,' he said – he always spoke in a precise sort of pompous kind of way – 'an exceedingly disturbing thing has happened. As you know, I dispatched the manuscript of my book to Messrs Riggs and Ballinger, the publishers, yesterday afternoon. It should have reached them by the first post this morning. Why I should have been uneasy I cannot say, but my mind was not altogether at rest respecting the safety of the parcel. I therefore telephoned to Messrs Riggs and Ballinger a few moments back to make inquiries. To my consternation they informed me that they were not yet in receipt of my manuscript.'

'Very rum!'

'I recollect distinctly placing it myself on the hall table in good time to be taken to the village. But here is a sinister thing. I have spoken to Oakshott, who took the rest of the letters to the post office, and he cannot recall seeing it there. He is, indeed, unswerving in his assertions that when he went to the hall to collect the letters there was no parcel among them.'

'Sounds funny!'

'Bertie, shall I tell you what I suspect?'

'What's that?'

'The suspicion will no doubt sound to you incredible, but it alone seems to fit the facts as we know them. I incline to the belief that the parcel has been stolen.'

'Oh, I say! Surely not!'

'Wait! Hear me out. Though I have said nothing to you before, or to anyone else, concerning the matter, the fact remains that during the past few weeks a number of objects – some valuable, others not – have disappeared in this house. The conclusion to which one is irresistibly impelled is that we have a kleptomaniac in our midst. It is a peculiarity of kleptomania, as you are no doubt aware, that the subject is unable to differentiate between the intrinsic values of objects. He will purloin an old coat as readily as a diamond ring, or a tobacco pipe costing but a few shillings with the same eagerness as a purse of gold. The fact that this manuscript of mine could be of no possible value to any outside person convinces me that – '

'But, uncle, one moment; I know all about those things that were stolen. It was Meadowes, my man, who pinched them. I caught him snaffling my silk socks. Right in the act, by Jove!'

He was tremendously impressed.

16

'You amaze me, Bertie! Send for the man at once and question him.'

'But he isn't here. You see, directly I found that he was a sock-sneaker I gave him the boot. That's why I went to London – to get a new man.'

'Then, if the man Meadowes is no longer in the house it could not be he who purloined my manuscript. The whole thing is inexplicable.'

After which we brooded for a bit. Uncle Willoughby pottered about the room, registering baffledness, while I sat sucking at a cigarette, feeling rather like a chappie I'd once read about in a book, who murdered another cove and hid the body under the dining-room table, and then had to be the life and soul of a dinner party, with it there all the time. My guilty secret oppressed me to such an extent that after a while I couldn't stick it any longer. I lit another cigarette and started for a stroll in the grounds, by way of cooling off.

It was one of those still evenings you get in the summer, when you can hear a snail clear its throat a mile away. The sun was sinking over the hills and the gnats were fooling about all over the place, and everything smelled rather topping – what with the falling dew and so on – and I was just beginning to feel a little soothed by the peace of it all when suddenly I heard my name spoken.

'It's about Bertie.'

It was the loathsome voice of young blighted Edwin! For a moment I couldn't locate it. Then I realized that it came from the library. My stroll had taken me within a few yards of the open window.

I had often wondered how those Johnnies in books did it – I mean the fellows with whom it was the work of a moment to do about a dozen things that ought to have taken them about ten minutes. But, as a matter of fact, it was the work of a moment with me to chuck away my cigarette, swear a bit, leap about ten yards, dive into a bush that stood near the library window, and stand there with my ears flapping. I was as certain as I've ever been of anything that all sorts of rotten things were in the offing.

'About Bertie?' I heard Uncle Willoughby say.

'About Bertie and your parcel. I heard you talking to him just now. I believe he's got it.'

When I tell you that just as I heard these frightful words a fairly substantial beetle of sorts dropped from the bush down the back of my neck, and I couldn't even stir to squash the same, you will understand that I felt pretty rotten. Everything seemed against me.

'What do you mean, boy? I was discussing the disappearance of my manuscript with Bertie only a moment back, and he professed himself as perplexed by the mystery as myself.'

'Well, I was in his room yesterday afternoon, doing him an act of kindness, and he came in with a parcel. I could see it, though he tried to keep it behind his back. And then he asked me to go to the smoking-room and snip some cigars for him; and about two minutes afterwards he came down – and he wasn't carrying anything. So it must be in his room.'

I understand they deliberately teach these dashed Boy Scouts to cultivate their powers of observation and deduction and what not. Devilish thoughtless and inconsiderate of them, I call it. Look at the trouble it causes.

'It sounds incredible,' said Uncle Willoughby, thereby bucking me up a trifle.

'Shall I go and look in his room?' asked young blighted Edwin. 'I'm sure the parcel's there.'

'But what could be his motive for perpetrating this extraordinary theft?'

'Perhaps he's a – what you said just now.'

'A kleptomaniac? Impossible!'

'It might have been Bertie who took all those things

from the very start,' suggested the little brute hopefully.
'He may be like Raffles.'

'Raffles?'

'He's a chap in a book who went about pinching
things.'

'I cannot believe that Bertie would – ah – go about
pinching things.'

'Well, I'm sure he's got the parcel. I'll tell you
what you might do. You might say that Mr Berkeley
wired that he had left something here. He had Bertie's
room, you know. You might say you wanted to look
for it.'

'That would be possible. I – '

I didn't wait to hear any more. Things were getting
too hot. I sneaked softly out of my bush and raced for
the front door. I sprinted up to my room and made for
the drawer where I had put the parcel. And then I found I
hadn't the key. It wasn't for the deuce of a time that I
recollected I had shifted it to my evening trousers the
night before and must have forgotten to take it out
again.

Where the dickens were my evening things? I had
looked all over the place before I remembered that Jeeves
must have taken them away to brush. To leap at the bell
and ring it was, with me, the work of a moment. I had
just rung it when there was a footstep outside, and in
came Uncle Willoughby.

'Oh, Bertie,' he said, without a blush, 'I have – ah –
received a telegram from Berkeley, who occupied this
room in your absence, asking me to forward him his – er
– his cigarette-case, which, it would appear, he
inadvertently omitted to take with him when he left the
house. I cannot find it downstairs; and it has, therefore,
occurred to me that he may have left it in this room. I
will – er – just take a look round.'

It was one of the most disgusting spectacles I've ever
seen – this white-haired old man, who should have been

thinking of the hereafter, standing there lying like an actor.

'I haven't seen it anywhere,' I said.

'Nevertheless, I will search. I must – ah – spare no effort.'

'I should have seen it if it had been here – what?'

'It may have escaped your notice. It is – er – possibly in one of the drawers.'

He began to nose about. He pulled out drawer after drawer, pottering round like an old bloodhound, and babbling from time to time about Berkeley and his cigarette-case in a way that struck me as perfectly ghastly. I just stood there, losing weight every moment.

Then he came to the drawer where the parcel was.

'This appears to be locked,' he said, rattling the handle.

'Yes; I shouldn't bother about that one. It – it's – er – locked, and all that sort of thing.'

'You have not the key?'

A soft, respectful voice spoke behind me.

'I fancy, sir, that this must be the key you require. It was in the pocket of your evening trousers.'

It was Jeeves. He had shimmered in, carrying my evening things, and was standing there holding out the key. I could have massacred the man.

'Thank you,' said my uncle.

'Not at all, sir.'

The next moment Uncle Willoughby had opened the drawer. I shut my eyes.

'No,' said Uncle Willoughby, 'there is nothing here. The drawer is empty. Thank you, Bertie. I hope I have not disturbed you. I fancy – er – Berkeley must have taken his case with him after all.'

When he had gone I shut the door carefully. Then I turned to Jeeves. The man was putting my evening things out on a chair.

'Er – Jeeves!'

'Sir?'

'Oh, nothing.'

It was deuced difficult to know how to begin.

'Er – Jeeves!'

'Sir?'

'Did you – Was there – Have you by chance –'

'I removed the parcel this morning, sir.'

'Oh – ah – why?'

'I considered it more prudent, sir.'

I mused for a while.

'Of course, I suppose all this seems tolerably rummy to you, Jeeves?'

'Not at all, sir. I chanced to overhear you and Lady Florence speaking of the matter the other evening, sir.'

'Did you, by Jove?'

'Yes, sir.'

'Well – er – Jeeves, I think that, on the whole, if you were to – as it were – freeze on to that parcel until we get back to London –'

'Exactly, sir.'

'And then we might – er – so to speak – chuck it away somewhere – what?'

'Precisely, sir.'

'I'll leave it in your hands.'

'Entirely, sir.'

'You know, Jeeves, you're by way of being rather a topper.'

'I endeavour to give satisfaction, sir.'

'One in a million, by Jove!'

'It is very kind of you to say so, sir.'

'Well, that's about all, then, I think.'

'Very good, sir.'

Florence came back on Monday. I didn't see her till we were all having tea in the hall. It wasn't till the crowd had cleared away a bit that we got a chance of having a word together.

'Well, Bertie?' she said.

'It's all right.'

'You have destroyed the manuscript?'

'Not exactly; but –'

'What do you mean?'

I mean I haven't absolutely –'

'Bertie, your manner is furtive!'

'It's all right. It's this way –'

And I was just going to explain how things stood when out of the library came leaping Uncle Willoughby, looking as braced as a two-year-old. The old boy was a changed man.

'A most remarkable thing, Bertie! I have just been speaking with Mr Riggs on the telephone, and he tells me he received my manuscript by the first post this morning. I cannot imagine what can have caused the delay. Our postal facilities are extremely inadequate in the rural districts. I shall write to headquarters about it. It is insufferable if valuable parcels are to be delayed in this fashion.'

I happened to be looking at Florence's profile at the moment, and at this juncture she swung round and gave me a look that went right through me like a knife. Uncle Willoughby meandered back to the library, and there was a silence that you could have dug bits out of with a spoon.

'I can't understand it,' I said at last. 'I can't understand it, by Jove!'

'I can. I can understand it perfectly, Bertie. Your heart failed you. Rather than risk offending your uncle you –'

'No, no! Absolutely!'

'You preferred to lose me rather than risk losing the money. Perhaps you did not think I meant what I said. I meant every word. Our engagement is ended.'

'But – I say!'

'Not another word!'

'But, Florence, old thing!'

'I do not wish to hear any more. I see now that your
Aunt Agatha was perfectly right. I consider that I have
had a very lucky escape. There was a time when I
thought that, with patience, you might be moulded into
something worth while. I see now that you are
impossible!'

And she popped off, leaving me to pick up the pieces.
When I had collected the debris to some extent I went to
my room and rang for Jeeves. He came in looking as if
nothing had happened or was ever going to happen. He
was the calmest thing in captivity.

'Jeeves!' I yelled. 'Jeeves, that parcel has arrived in
London!'

'Yes, sir?'

'Did you send it?'

'Yes, sir. I acted for the best, sir. I think that both you
and Lady Florence overestimated the danger of people
being offended at being mentioned in Sir Willoughby's
Recollections. It has been my experience, sir, that the
normal person enjoys seeing his or her name in print,
irrespective of what is said about them. I have an aunt,
sir, who a few years ago was a martyr to swollen limbs.
She tried Walkinshaw's Supreme Ointment and obtained
considerable relief – so much so that she sent them an
unsolicited testimonial. Her pride at seeing her
photograph in the daily papers in connexion with
descriptions of her lower limbs before taking, which
were nothing less than revolting, was so intense that it
led me to believe that publicity, of whatever sort, is
what nearly everybody desires. Moreover, if you have
ever studied psychology, sir, you will know that
respectable old gentlemen are by no means averse to
having it advertised that they were extremely wild in
their youth. I have an uncle –'

I cursed his aunts and his uncles and him and all the
rest of the family.

'Do you know that Lady Florence has broken off her engagement with me?'

'Indeed, sir?'

Not a bit of sympathy! I might have been telling him it was a fine day.

'You're sacked!'

'Very good, sir.'

He coughed gently.

'As I am no longer in your employment, sir, I can speak freely without appearing to take a liberty. In my opinion you and Lady Florence were quite unsuitably matched. Her ladyship is of a highly determined and arbitrary temperament, quite opposed to your own. I was in Lord Worplesdon's service for nearly a year, during which time I had ample opportunities of studying her ladyship. The opinion of the servants' hall was far from favourable to her. Her ladyship's temper caused a good deal of adverse comment among us. It was at times quite impossible. You would not have been happy, sir!'

'Get out!'

'I think you would also have found her educational methods a little trying, sir. I have glanced at the book her ladyship gave you – it has been lying on your table since our arrival – and it is, in my opinion, quite unsuitable. You would not have enjoyed it. And I have it from her ladyship's own maid, who happened to overhear a conversation between her ladyship and one of the gentlemen staying here – Mr Maxwell, who is employed in an editorial capacity by one of the reviews – that it was her intention to start you almost immediately upon Nietzsche. You would not enjoy Nietzsche, sir. He is fundamentally unsound.'

'Get out!'

'Very good, sir.'

It's rummy how sleeping on a thing often makes you feel quite different about it. It's happened to me over and over again. Somehow or other, when I woke next morning the old heart didn't feel half so broken as it had done. It was a perfectly topping day, and there was something about the way the sun came in at the window and the row the birds were kicking up in the ivy that made me half wonder whether Jeeves wasn't right. After all, though she had a wonderful profile, was it such a catch being engaged to Florence Craye as the casual observer might imagine? Wasn't there something in what Jeeves had said about her character? I began to realize that my ideal wife was something quite different, something a lot more clinging and drooping and prattling, and what not.

I had got as far as this in thinking the thing out when that *Types of Ethical Theory* caught my eye. I opened it, and I give you my honest word this was what hit me:

Of the two antithetic terms in the Greek philosophy one only was real and self-subsisting; and that one was Ideal Thought as opposed to that which it has to penetrate and mould. The other, corresponding to our Nature, was in itself phenomenal, unreal, without any permanent footing, having no predicates that held true for two moments together; in short, redeemed from negation only by including indwelling realities appearing through.

Well – I mean to say – what? And Nietzsche, from all accounts, a lot worse than that!

'Jeeves,' I said, when he came in with my morning tea, 'I've been thinking it over. You're engaged again.'

'Thank you, sir.'

I sucked down a cheerful mouthful. A great respect for this bloke's judgement began to soak through me.

'Oh, Jeeves,' I said; 'about that check suit.'

'Yes, sir?'

'Is it really a frost?'

'A trifle too bizarre, sir, in my opinion.'

'But lots of fellows have asked me who my tailor is.'

'Doubtless in order to avoid him, sir.'

'He's supposed to be one of the best men in London.'

'I am saying nothing against his moral character, sir.'

I hesitated a bit. I had a feeling that I was passing into this chappie's clutches, and that if I gave in now I should become just like poor old Aubrey Fothergill, unable to call my soul my own. On the other hand, this was obviously a cove of rare intelligence, and it would be a comfort in a lot of ways to have him doing the thinking for me. I made up my mind.

'All right, Jeeves,' I said. 'You know! Give the bally thing away to somebody!'

He looked down at me like a father gazing tenderly at the wayward child.

'Thank you, sir. I gave it to the under-gardener last night. A little more tea, sir?'

2 — The Artistic Career of Corky

You will notice, as you flit through these reminiscences of mine, that from time to time the scene of action is laid in and around the city of New York; and it is just possible that this may occasion the puzzled look and the start of surprise. 'What,' it is possible that you may ask yourselves, 'is Bertram doing so far from his beloved native land?'

Well, it's a fairly longish story; but, reefing it down a bit and turning it for the nonce into a two-reeler, what happened was that my Aunt Agatha on one occasion sent me over to America to try to stop young Gussie, my cousin, marrying a girl on the vaudeville stage, and I got the whole thing so mixed up that I decided it would be a sound scheme to stop on in New York for a bit instead of going back and having long, cosy chats with her about the affair.

So I sent Jeeves out to find a decent flat, and settled down for a spell of exile.

I'm bound to say New York's a most sprightly place to be exiled in. Everybody was awfully good to me, and there seemed to be plenty of things going on so, take it for all in all, I didn't undergo any frightful hardships. Blokes introduced me to other blokes, and so on and so forth, and it wasn't long before I knew squads of the right sort, some who rolled in the stuff in houses up by the Park, and others who lived with the gas turned down mostly around Washington Square – artists and writers and so forth. Brainy coves.

Corky, the bird I am about to treat of, was one of the artists. A portrait-painter, he called himself, but as a matter of fact his score up to date had been nil. You see, the catch about portrait-painting – I've looked into the thing a bit – is that you can't start painting portraits till people come along and ask you to, and they won't come and ask you to until you've painted a lot first. This makes it kind of difficult, not to say tough, for the ambitious youngster.

Corky managed to get along by drawing an occasional picture for the comic papers – he had rather a gift for funny stuff when he got a good idea – and doing bedsteads and chairs and things for the advertisements. His principal source of income, however, was derived from biting the ear of a rich uncle – one Alexander Worple, who was in the jute business. I'm a bit foggy as to what jute is, but it's apparently something the populace is pretty keen on, for Mr Worple had made quite an indecently large stack out of it.

Now, a great many fellows think that having a rich uncle is a pretty soft snap; but, according to Corky, such is not the case. Corky's uncle was a robust sort of cove, who looked like living for ever. He was fifty-one, and it seemed as if he might go to par. It was not this, however, that distressed poor Corky, for he was not bigoted and had no objection to the man going on living. What Corky kicked at was the way the above Worple used to harry him.

Corky's uncle, you see, didn't want him to be an artist. He didn't think he had any talent in that direction. He was always urging him to chuck Art and go into the jute business and start at the bottom and work his way up. And what Corky said was that, while he didn't know what they did at the bottom of a jute business, instinct told him that it was something too beastly for words. Corky, moreover, believed in his future as an artist. Some day, he said, he was going to make a hit. Meanwhile, by using the utmost tact and persuasiveness, he was inducing his uncle to cough up very grudgingly a small quarterly allowance.

He wouldn't have got this if his uncle hadn't had a hobby. Mr Worple was peculiar in this respect. As a rule, from what I've observed, the American captain of industry doesn't do anything out of business hours. When he has put the cat out and locked up the office for the night, he just relapses into a state of coma from which he emerges only to start being a captain of industry again. But Mr Worple in his spare time was what is known as an ornithologist. He had written a book called *American Birds*, and was writing another, to be called *More American Birds*. When he had finished that, the presumption was that he would begin a third, and keep on till the supply of American birds gave out. Corky used to go to him about once every three months and let him talk about American birds. Apparently you could do what you liked with old Worple if you gave him his head first on his pet subject, so these little chats used to make Corky's allowance all right for the time being. But it was pretty rotten for the poor chap. There was the frightful suspense, you see, and, apart from that, birds, except when broiled and in the society of a cold bottle, bored him stiff.

To complete the character-study of Mr Worple, he was a man of extremely uncertain temper, and his general tendency was to think that Corky was a poor chump and that whatever step he took in any direction on his own account was just another proof of his innate idiocy. I should imagine Jeeves feels very much the same about me.

So when Corky trickled into my apartment one afternoon, shooing a girl in front of him, and said, 'Bertie, I want you to meet my fiancée, Miss Singer,' the aspect of the matter which hit me first was precisely the one which he had come to consult me about. The very first words I spoke were, 'Corky, how about your uncle?'

The poor chap gave one of those mirthless laughs. He was looking anxious and worried, like a man who has done the murder all right but can't think what the deuce to do with the body.

'We're so scared, Mr Wooster,' said the girl. 'We were hoping that you might suggest a way of breaking it to him.'

Muriel Singer was one of those very quiet, appealing girls who have a way of looking at you with their big eyes as if they thought you were the greatest thing on earth and wondered that you hadn't got on to it yet yourself. She sat there in a sort of shrinking way, looking at me as if she were saying to herself, 'Oh, I do hope this great strong man isn't going to hurt me.' She gave a fellow a protective kind of feeling, made him want to stroke her hand and say, 'There, there, little one!' or words to that effect. She made me feel that there was nothing I wouldn't do for her. She was rather like one of those innocent-tasting American drinks which creep imperceptibly into your system so that, before you know what you're doing, you're starting out to reform the world by force if necessary and pausing on your way to tell the large man in the corner that, if he looks at you like that, you will knock his head off. What I mean is, she made me feel alert and dashing, like a knight-errant or something of that kind. I felt that I was with her in this thing to the limit.

'I don't see why your uncle shouldn't be most awfully bucked,' I said to Corky. 'He will think Miss Singer the ideal wife for you.'

Corky declined to cheer up.

'You don't know him. Even if he did like Muriel, he wouldn't admit it. That's the sort of pig-headed ass he is. It would be a matter of principle with him to kick. All he would consider would be that I had gone and taken an important step without asking his advice, and he would raise Cain automatically. He's always done it.'

I strained the old bean to meet this emergency.

'You want to work it so that he makes Miss Singer's acquaintance without knowing that you know her. Then you come along –'

'But how can I work it that way?'

I saw his point. That was the catch.

'There's only one thing to do,' I said.

'What's that?'

'Leave it to Jeeves.'

And I rang the bell.

'Sir?' said Jeeves, kind of manifesting himself. One of the rummy things about Jeeves is that, unless you watch like a hawk, you very seldom see him come into a room. He's like one of those weird birds in India who dissolve themselves into thin air and nip through space in a sort of disembodied way and assemble the parts again just where they want them. I've got a cousin who's what they call a Theosophist, and he says he's often nearly worked the thing himself, but couldn't quite bring it off, probably owing to having fed in his boyhood on the flesh of animals slain in anger and pie.

The moment I saw the man standing there, registering respectful attention, a weight seemed to roll off my mind. I felt like a lost child who spots his father in the offing.

'Jeeves,' I said, 'we want your advice.'

'Very good, sir.'

I boiled down Corky's painful case into a few well-chosen words.

'So you see what it amounts to, Jeeves. We want you to suggest some way by which Mr Worple can make Miss Singer's acquaintance without getting on to the fact that Mr Corcoran already knows her. Understand?'

'Perfectly, sir.'

'Well, try to think of something.'

'I have thought of something already, sir.'

'You have!'

'The scheme I would suggest cannot fail of success, but it has what may seem to you a drawback, sir, in that it requires a certain financial outlay.'

'He means,' I translated to Corky, 'that he has got a pippin of an idea, but it's going to cost a bit.'

Naturally the poor chap's face dropped, for this seemed to dish the whole thing. But I was still under the influence of the girl's melting gaze, and I saw that this was where I started in as the knight-errant.

'You can count on me for all that sort of thing, Corky,' I said. 'Only too glad. Carry on, Jeeves.'

'I would suggest, sir, that Mr Corcoran take advantage of Mr Worple's attachment to ornithology.'

'How on earth did you know that he was fond of birds?'

'It is the way these New York apartments are constructed, sir. Quite unlike our London houses. The partitions between the rooms are of the flimsiest nature. With no wish to overhear, I have sometimes heard Mr Corcoran expressing himself with a generous strength on the subject I have mentioned.'

'Oh! Well?'

'Why should not the young lady write a small volume, to be entitled – let us say – *The Children's Book of American Birds* and dedicate it to Mr Worple? A limited edition could be published at your expense, sir, and a great deal of the book would, of course, be given over to eulogistic remarks concerning Mr Worple's own larger treatise on the same subject. I should recommend the dispatching of a presentation copy to Mr Worple, immediately on publication, accompanied by a letter in which the young lady asks to be allowed to make the acquaintance of one to whom she owes so much. This would, I fancy, produce the desired result, but as I say, the expense involved would be considerable.'

I felt like the proprietor of a performing dog on the vaudeville stage when the tyke has just pulled off his trick without a hitch. I had betted on Jeeves all along, and I had known that he wouldn't let me down. It beats me sometimes why a man with his genius is satisfied to hang around pressing my clothes and what not. If I had half Jeeves's brain I should have a stab at being Prime Minister or something.

'Jeeves,' I said, 'that is absolutely ripping! One of your very best efforts.'

'Thank you, sir.'

The girl made an objection.

'But I'm sure I couldn't write a book about anything. I can't even write good letters.'

'Muriel's talents,' said Corky, with a little cough, 'lie more in the direction of the drama, Bertie. I didn't mention it before, but one of our reasons for being a trifle nervous as to how Uncle Alexander will receive the news is that Muriel is in the chorus of that show *Choose your Exit* at the Manhattan. It's absurdly unreasonable, but we both feel that that fact might increase Uncle Alexander's natural tendency to kick like a steer.'

I saw what he meant. I don't know why it is – one of these psychology sharps could explain it, I suppose – but uncles and aunts, as a class, are always dead against the drama, legitimate or otherwise. They don't seem able to stick it at any price.

But Jeeves had a solution, of course.

'I fancy it would be a simple matter, sir, to find some impecunious author who would be glad to do the actual composition of the volume for a small fee. It is only necessary that the young lady's name should appear on the title page.'

'That's true,' said Corky. 'Sam Patterson would do it for a hundred dollars. He writes a novelette, three short stories, and ten thousand words of a serial for one of the all-fiction magazines under different names every month. A little thing like this would be nothing to him. I'll get after him right away.'

'Fine!'

'Will that be all, sir?' said Jeeves. 'Very good, sir. Thank you, sir.'

I always used to think that publishers had to be devilish intelligent fellows, loaded down with the grey matter; but I've got their number now. All a publisher has to do is to write cheques at intervals, while a lot of deserving and industrious chappies rally round and do the real work. I know, because I've been one myself. I simply sat tight in the old flat with a fountain-pen, and in due season a topping, shiny book came along.

I happened to be down at Corky's place when the first copies of *The Children's Book of American Birds* bobbed up. Muriel Singer was there, and we were talking of things in general when there was a bang at the door and the parcel was delivered.

It was certainly some book. It had a red cover with a fowl of some species on it, and underneath the girl's name in gold letters. I opened a copy at random.

'Often of a spring morning,' it said at the top of page twenty-one, 'as you wander through the fields, you will hear the sweet-toned, carelessly flowing warble of the purple finch linnet. When you are older you must read all about him in Mr Alexander Worple's wonderful book, *American Birds*.'

You see. A boost for the uncle right away. And only a few pages later there he was in the limelight again in connexion with the yellow-billed cuckoo. It was great stuff. The more I read, the more I admired the chap who had written it and Jeeves's genius in putting us on to the wheeze. I didn't see how the uncle could fail to drop. You can't call a chap the world's greatest authority on the yellow-billed cuckoo without rousing a certain disposition towards chumminess in him.

'It's a cert!' I said.

'An absolute cinch!' said Corky.

And a day or two later he meandered up the Avenue to my flat to tell me that all was well. The uncle had written Muriel a letter so dripping with the milk of human kindness that if he hadn't known Mr Worple's handwriting Corky would have refused to believe him the author of it. Any time it suited Miss Singer to call, said the uncle, he would be delighted to make her acquaintance.

Shortly after this I had to go out of town. Divers sound sportsmen had invited me to pay visits to their country places, and it wasn't for several months that I settled down in the city again. I had been wondering a lot, of course, about Corky, whether it all turned out right, and so forth, and my first evening in New York, happening to pop into a quiet sort of little restaurant which I go to when I don't feel inclined for the bright lights, I found Muriel Singer there, sitting by herself at a table near the door. Corky, I took it, was out telephoning. I went up and passed the time of day.

'Well, well, well, what?' I said.

'Why, Mr Wooster! How do you do?'

'Corky around?'

'I beg your pardon?'

'You're waiting for Corky, aren't you?'

'Oh, I didn't understand. No, I'm not waiting for him.'

It seemed to me that there was a sort of something in her voice, a kind of thingummy, you know.

'I say, you haven't had a row with Corky, have you?'

'A row?'

'A spat, don't you know – little misunderstanding – faults on both sides – er – and all that sort of thing.'

'Why, whatever makes you think that?'

'Oh, well, as it were, what? What I mean is – I thought

you usually dined with him before you went to the
theatre.'

'I've left the stage now.'

Suddenly the whole thing dawned on me. I had
forgotten what a long time I had been away.

'Why, of course, I see now! You're married!'

'Yes.'

'How perfectly topping! I wish you all kinds of
happiness.'

'Thank you so much. Oh, Alexander,' she said,
looking past me, 'this is a friend of mine – Mr Wooster.'

I spun round. A bloke with a lot of stiff grey hair and
a red sort of healthy face was standing there. Rather a
formidable Johnnie, he looked, though peaceful at the
moment.

'I want you to meet my husband, Mr Wooster. Mr
Wooster is a friend of Bruce's, Alexander.'

The old boy grasped my hand warmly, and that was
all that kept me from hitting the floor in a heap. The
place was rocking. Absolutely.

'So you know my nephew, Mr Wooster?' I heard him
say. 'I wish you would try to knock a little sense into
him and make him quit this playing at painting. But I
have an idea that he is steadying down. I noticed it first
that night he came to dinner with us, my dear, to be
introduced to you. He seemed altogether quieter and
more serious. Something seemed to have sobered him.
Perhaps you will give us the pleasure of your company at
dinner tonight, Mr Wooster? Or have you dined?'

I said I had. What I needed then was air, not dinner. I
felt that I wanted to get into the open and think this
thing out.

When I reached my flat I heard Jeeves moving about
in his lair. I called him.

'Jeeves,' I said, 'now is the time for all good men to
come to the aid of the party. A stiff b-and-s first of all,
and then I've a bit of news for you.'

He came back with a tray and a long glass.

'Better have one yourself, Jeeves. You'll need it.'

'Later on, perhaps, thank you, sir.'

'All right. Please yourself. But you're going to get a shock. You remember my friend, Mr Corcoran?'

'Yes, sir.'

'And the girl who was to slide gracefully into his uncle's esteem by writing the book on birds?'

'Perfectly, sir.'

'Well, she's slid. She's married the uncle.'

He took it without blinking. You can't rattle Jeeves.

'That was always a development to be feared, sir.'

'You don't mean to tell me that you were expecting it?'

'It crossed my mind as a possibility.'

'Did it, by Jove! Well, I think you might have warned us!'

'I hardly liked to take the liberty, sir.'

Of course, as I saw after I had had a bite to eat and was in a calmer frame of mind, what had happened wasn't my fault, if you came down to it. I couldn't be expected to foresee that the scheme, in itself a cracker-jack, would skid into the ditch as it had done; but all the same I'm bound to admit that I didn't relish the idea of meeting Corky again until time, the great healer, had been able to get in a bit of soothing work. I cut Washington Square out absolutely for the next few months. I gave it the complete miss-in-baulk. And then, just when I was beginning to think I might safely pop down in that direction and gather up the dropped threads, so to speak, time, instead of working the healing wheeze, went and pulled the most awful bone and put the lid on it. Opening the paper one morning, I read that Mrs Alexander Worple had presented her husband with a son and heir.

I was so dashed sorry for poor old Corky that I hadn't

the heart to touch my breakfast. I was bowled over. Absolutely. It was the limit.

I hardly knew what to do. I wanted, of course, to rush down to Washington Square and grip the poor blighter silently by the hand; and then, thinking it over, I hadn't the nerve. Absent treatment seemed the touch. I gave it him in waves.

But after a month or so I began to hesitate again. It struck me that it was playing it a bit low-down on the poor chap, avoiding him like this just when he probably wanted his pals to surge round him most. I pictured him sitting in his lonely studio with no company but his bitter thoughts, and the pathos of it got me to such an extent that I bounded straight into a taxi and told the driver to go all out for the studio.

I rushed in, and there was Corky, hunched up at the easel, painting away, while on the model throne sat a severe-looking female of middle age, holding a baby.

A fellow has to be ready for that sort of thing.

'Oh, ah!' I said, and started to back out.

Corky looked over his shoulder.

'Hallo, Bertie. Don't go. We're just finishing for the day. That will be all this afternoon,' he said to the nurse, who got up with the baby and decanted it into a perambulator which was standing in the fairway.

'At the same hour tomorrow, Mr Corcoran?'

'Yes, please.'

'Good afternoon.'

'Good afternoon.'

Corky stood there, looking at the door, and then he turned to me and began to get it off his chest. Fortunately, he seemed to take it for granted that I knew all about what had happened, so it wasn't as awkward as it might have been.

'It's my uncle's idea,' he said. 'Muriel doesn't know about it yet. The portrait's to be a surprise for her on her birthday. The nurse takes the kid out ostensibly to get a breather, and they beat it down here. If you want an instance of the irony of fate, Bertie, get acquainted with this. Here's the first commission I have ever had to paint a portrait, and the sitter is that human poached egg that has butted in and bounced me out of my inheritance. Can you beat it! I call it rubbing the thing in to expect me to spend my afternoons gazing into the ugly face of a little brat who to all intents and purposes has hit me behind the ear with a black-jack and swiped all I possess. I can't refuse to paint the portrait, because if I did my uncle would stop my allowance; yet every time I look up and catch that kid's vacant eye, I suffer agonies. I tell you, Bertie, sometimes when he gives me a patronizing glance and then turns away and is sick, as if it revolted him to look at me, I come within an ace of occupying the entire front page of the evening papers as the latest murder sensation. There are moments when I can almost see the headlines: "Promising Young Artist Beans Baby With Axe."'

I patted his shoulder silently. My sympathy for the poor old scout was too deep for words.

I kept away from the studio for some time after that, because it didn't seem right to me to intrude on the poor chappie's sorrow. Besides, I'm bound to say that nurse intimidated me. She reminded me so infernally of Aunt Agatha. She was the same gimlet-eyed type.

But one afternoon Corky called me on the phone.

'Bertie!'

'Hallo?'

'Are you doing anything this afternoon?'

'Nothing special.'

'You couldn't come down here, could you?'

'What's the trouble? Anything up?'

'I've finished the portrait.'

'Good boy! Stout work!'

'Yes.' His voice sounded rather doubtful. 'The fact is, Bertie, it doesn't look quite right to me. There's something about it – My uncle's coming in half an hour to inspect it, and – I don't know why it is, but I kind of feel I'd like your moral support!'

I began to see that I was letting myself in for something. The sympathetic cooperation of Jeeves seemed to me to be indicated.

'You think he'll cut up rough?'

'He may.'

I threw my mind back to the red-faced chappie I had met at the restaurant, and tried to picture him cutting up rough. It was only too easy. I spoke to Corky firmly on the telephone.

'I'll come,' I said.

'Good!'

'But only if I may bring Jeeves.'

'Why Jeeves? What's Jeeves got to do with it? Who wants Jeeves? Jeeves is the fool who suggested the scheme that has led –'

'Listen, Corky, old top! If you think I am going to face that uncle of yours without Jeeves's support, you're mistaken. I'd sooner go into a den of wild beasts and bite a lion on the back of the neck.'

'Oh, all right,' said Corky. Not cordially, but he said it; so I rang for Jeeves, and explained the situation.

'Very good, sir,' said Jeeves.

We found Corky near the door, looking at the picture with one hand up in a defensive sort of way, as if he thought it might swing on him.

'Stand right where you are, Bertie,' he said, without moving. 'Now, tell me honestly, how does it strike you?'

The light from the big window fell right on the picture. I took a good look at it. Then I shifted a bit nearer and took another look. Then I went back to where I had been at first, because it hadn't seemed quite so bad from there.

'Well?' said Corky anxiously.

I hesitated a bit.

'Of course, old man, I only saw the kid once, and then only for a moment, but – but it *was* an ugly sort of kid, wasn't it, if I remember rightly?'

'As ugly as that?'

I looked again, and honesty compelled me to be frank.

'I don't see how it could have been, old chap.'

Poor old Corky ran his fingers through his hair in a temperamental sort of way. He groaned.

'You're quite right, Bertie. Something's gone wrong with the darned thing. My private impression is that, without knowing it, I've worked that stunt that Sargent used to pull – painting the soul of the sitter. I've got through the mere outward appearance, and have put the child's soul on canvas.'

'But could a child of that age have a soul like that? I don't see how he could have managed it in the time. What do you think, Jeeves?'

'I doubt it, sir.'

'It – it sort of leers at you, doesn't it?'

'You've noticed that, too?' said Corky.

'I don't see how one could help noticing.'

'All I tried to do was to give the little brute a cheerful expression. But, as it has worked out, he looks positively dissipated.'

'Just what I was going to suggest, old man. He looks as if he were in the middle of a colossal spree, and enjoying every minute of it. Don't you think so, Jeeves?'

'He has a decidedly inebriated air, sir.'

Corky was starting to say something, when the door opened and the uncle came in.

For about three seconds all was joy, jollity and goodwill. The old boy shook hands with me, slapped Corky on the back, said he didn't think he had ever seen such a fine day, and whacked his leg with his stick. Jeeves had projected himself into the background, and he didn't notice him.

'Well, Bruce, my boy; so the portrait is really finished, is it – really finished? Well, bring it out. Let's have a look at it. This will be a wonderful surprise for your aunt. Where is it? Let's –'

And then he got it – suddenly, when he wasn't set for the punch; and he rocked back on his heels.

'Oosh!' he exclaimed. And for perhaps a minute there was one of the scaliest silences I've ever run up against.

'Is this a practical joke?' he said at last, in a way that set about sixteen draughts cutting through the room at once.

I thought it was up to me to rally round old Corky.

'You want to stand a bit farther away from it,' I said.

'You're perfectly right!' he snorted. 'I do! I want to stand so far away from it that I can't see the thing with a telescope!' He turned on Corky like an untamed tiger of the jungle who has just located a chunk of meat. 'And this – this – is what you have been wasting your time and my money for all these years! A painter! I wouldn't let you paint a house of mine. I gave you this commission, thinking that you were a competent worker, and this – this – this extract from a comic supplement is the result!' He swung towards the door, lashing his tail and growling to himself. 'This ends it. If you wish to continue this foolery of pretending to be an artist because you want an excuse for idleness, please yourself. But let me tell you this. Unless you report at my office on Monday morning, prepared to abandon all this idiocy and start in at the bottom of the business to work your way up, as you should have done half a dozen years ago, not another cent – not another cent – not another – Boosh!'

Then the door closed and he was no longer with us. And I crawled out of the bomb-proof shelter.

'Corky, old top!' I whispered faintly.

Corky was standing staring at the picture. His face was set. There was a hunted look in his eye.

'Well, that finishes it!' he muttered brokenly.

'What are you going to do?'

'Do? What can I do? I can't stick on here if he cuts off supplies. You heard what he said. I shall have to go to the office on Monday.'

I couldn't think of a thing to say. I knew exactly how he felt about the office. I don't know when I've been so infernally uncomfortable. It was like hanging round trying to make conversation to a pal who's just been sentenced to twenty years in quod.

And then a soothing voice broke the silence.

'If I might make a suggestion, sir!'

It was Jeeves. He had slid from the shadows and was gazing gravely at the picture. Upon my word, I can't give you a better idea of the shattering effect of Corky's Uncle Alexander when in action than by saying that he had absolutely made me forget for the moment that Jeeves was there.

'I wonder if I have ever happened to mention to you, sir, a Mr Digby Thistleton, with whom I was once in service? Perhaps you have met him? He was a financier. He is now Lord Bridgworth. It was a favourite saying of his that there is always a way. The first time I heard him use the expression was after the failure of a patent depilatory which he promoted.'

'Jeeves,' I said, 'what on earth are you talking about?'

'I mentioned Mr Thistleton, sir, because his was in some respects a parallel case to the present one. His depilatory failed, but he did not despair. He put it on the market again under the name of Hair-o, guaranteed to produce a full crop of hair in a few months. It was advertised, if you remember, sir, by a humorous picture of a billiard ball, before and after taking, and made such a substantial fortune that Mr Thistleton was soon afterwards elevated to the peerage for services to his Party. It seems to me that, if Mr Corcoran looks into the matter, he will find, like Mr Thistleton, that there is always a way. Mr Worple himself suggested the solution of the difficulty. In the heat of the moment he compared the portrait to an extract from a coloured comic supplement. I consider the suggestion a very valuable one, sir. Mr Corcoran's portrait may not have pleased Mr Worple as a likeness of his only child, but I have no doubt that editors would gladly consider it as a foundation for a series of humorous drawings. If Mr Corcoran will allow me to make the suggestion, his talent has always been for the humorous. There is something about this picture – something bold and vigorous, which arrests the attention. I feel sure it would be highly popular.'

Corky was glaring at the picture, and making a sort of dry, sucking noise with his mouth. He seemed completely overwrought.

And then suddenly he began to laugh in a wild way.

'Corky, old man!' I said, massaging him tenderly. I feared the poor blighter was hysterical.

He began to stagger about all over the floor.

'He's right! The man's absolutely right! Jeeves, you're a life-saver. You've hit on the greatest idea of the age. Report at the office on Monday! Start at the bottom of the business! I'll buy the business if I feel like it. I know the man who runs the comic section of the *Sunday Star*. He'll eat this thing. He was telling me only the other day how hard it was to get a good new series. He'll give me anything I ask for a real winner like this. I've got a gold mine. Where's my hat? I've got an income for life! Where's that confounded hat? Lend me a five, Bertie. I want to take a taxi down to Park Row!'

Jeeves smiled paternally. Or, rather, he had a kind of paternal muscular spasm about the mouth, which is the nearest he ever gets to smiling.

'If I might make the suggestion, Mr Corcoran – for a title of the series which you have in mind – "The Adventures of Baby Blobbs".'

Corky and I looked at the picture, then at each other in an awed way. Jeeves was right. There could be no other title.

'Jeeves,' I said. It was a few weeks later, and I had just finished looking at the comic section of the *Sunday Star*. 'I'm an optimist. I always have been. The older I get, the more I agree with Shakespeare and those poet Johnnies about it always being darkest before the dawn and there's a silver lining and what you lose on the swings you make up on the roundabouts. Look at Mr Corcoran, for instance. There was a fellow, one would have said, clear up to the eyebrows in the soup. To all appearances he had got it right in the neck. Yet look at him now. Have you seen these pictures?'

'I took the liberty of glancing at them before bringing them to you, sir. Extremely diverting.'

'They have made a big hit, you know.'

'I anticipated it, sir.'

I leaned back against the pillows.

'You know, Jeeves, you're a genius. You ought to be drawing a commission on these things.'

'I have nothing to complain of in that respect, sir. Mr Corcoran has been most generous. I am putting out the brown suit, sir.'

'No, I think I'll wear the blue with the faint red stripe.'

'Not the blue with the faint red stripe, sir.'

'But I rather fancy myself in it.'

'Not the blue with the faint red stripe, sir.'

'Oh, all right, have it your own way.'

'Very good, sir. Thank you, sir.'

3 — Jeeves and the Unbidden Guest

I'm not absolutely certain of my facts, but I rather fancy it's Shakespeare – or, if not, it's some equally brainy bird – who says that it's always just when a fellow is feeling particularly braced with things in general that Fate sneaks up behind him with the bit of lead piping. And what I'm driving at is that the man is perfectly right. Take, for instance, the business of Lady Malvern and her son Wilmot. That was one of the scaliest affairs I was ever mixed up with, and a moment before they came into my life I was just thinking how thoroughly all right everything was.

I was still in New York when the thing started, and it was about the time of year when New York is at its best. It was one of those topping mornings, and I had just climbed out from under the cold shower, feeling like a million dollars. As a matter of fact, what was bucking me up more than anything was the fact that the day before I had asserted myself with Jeeves – absolutely asserted myself, don't you know. You see, the way things had been going on I was rapidly becoming a dashed serf. The man had jolly well oppressed me. I didn't so much mind when he made me give up one of my new suits, because Jeeves's judgement about suits is sound and can generally be relied upon.

But I as near as a toucher rebelled when he wouldn't let me wear a pair of cloth-topped boots which I loved like a couple of brothers. And, finally, when he tried to tread on me like a worm in the matter of a hat, I put the Wooster foot down and showed him in no uncertain manner who was who.

It's a long story, and I haven't time to tell you now, but the nub of the thing was that he wanted me to wear the White House Wonder – as worn by President Coolidge – when I had set my heart on the Broadway Special, much patronized by the Younger Set; and the end of the matter was that, after a rather painful scene, I bought the Broadway Special. So that's how things were on this particular morning, and I was feeling pretty manly and independent.

Well, I was in the bathroom, wondering what there was going to be for breakfast while I massaged the spine with a rough towel and sang slightly, when there was a tap at the door. I stopped singing and opened the door an inch.

'What ho, without there!' I said.

'Lady Malvern has called, sir.'

'Eh?'

'Lady Malvern, sir. She is waiting in the sitting-room.'

'Pull yourself together, Jeeves, my man,' I said rather severely, for I bar practical jokes before breakfast. 'You know perfectly well there's no one waiting for me in the sitting-room. How could there be when it's barely ten o'clock yet?'

'I gathered from her ladyship, sir, that she had landed from an ocean liner at an early hour this morning.'

This made the thing a bit more plausible. I remembered that when I had arrived in America about a year before, the proceedings had begun at some ghastly hour like six, and that I had been shot out on to a foreign shore considerably before eight.

'Who the deuce is Lady Malvern, Jeeves?'

'Her ladyship did not confide in me, sir.'

'Is she alone?'

'Her ladyship is accompanied by a Lord Pershore, sir. I fancy that his lordship would be her ladyship's son.'

'Oh, well, put out rich raiment of sorts, and I'll be dressing.'

'Our heather-mixture lounge is in readiness, sir.'

'Then lead me to it.'

While I was dressing I kept trying to think who on earth Lady Malvern could be. It wasn't till I had climbed through the top of my shirt and was reaching out for the studs that I remembered.

'I've placed her, Jeeves. She's a pal of my Aunt Agatha.'

'Indeed, sir?'

'Yes. I met her at lunch one Sunday before I left London. A very vicious specimen. Writes books. She wrote a book on social conditions in India when she came back from the Durbar.'

'Yes, sir? Pardon me, sir, but not that tie.'

'Eh?'

'Not that tie with the heather-mixture lounge, sir.'

It was a shock to me. I thought I had quelled the fellow. It was rather a solemn moment. What I mean is, if I weakened now, all my good work the night before would be thrown away. I braced myself.

'What's wrong with this tie? I've seen you give it a nasty look before. Speak out like a man! What's the matter with it?'

'Too ornate, sir.'

'Nonsense! A cheerful pink. Nothing more.'

'Unsuitable, sir.'

'Jeeves, this is the tie I wear!'

'Very good, sir.'

Dashed unpleasant. I could see that the man was wounded. But I was firm. I tied the tie, got into the coat and waistcoat, and went into the sitting-room.

'Hullo-ullo-ullo!' I said. 'What?'

'Ah! How do you do, Mr Wooster? You have never met my son Wilmot, I think? Motty, darling, this is Mr Wooster.'

Lady Malvern was a hearty, happy, healthy, overpowering sort of dashed female, not so very tall but

48

making up for it by measuring about six feet from the
O. P. to the Prompt Side. She fitted into my biggest
arm-chair as if it had been built round her by someone
who knew they were wearing arm-chairs tight about the
hips that season. She had bright, bulging eyes and a lot
of yellow hair, and when she spoke she showed about
fifty-seven front teeth. She was one of those women who
kind of numb a fellow's faculties. She made me feel as if
I were ten years old and had been brought into the
drawing-room in my Sunday clothes to say
how-d'you-do. Altogether by no means the sort of thing
a chappie would wish to find in his sitting-room before
breakfast.

Motty, the son, was about twenty-three, tall and thin
and meek-looking. He had the same yellow hair as his
mother, but he wore it plastered down and parted in the
middle. His eyes bulged, too, but they weren't bright.
They were a dull grey with pink rims. His chin gave up
the struggle about half-way down, and he didn't appear
to have any eyelashes. A mild, furtive, sheepish sort of
blighter, in short.

'Awfully glad to see you,' I said, though this was far
from the case, for already I was beginning to have a sort
of feeling that dirty work was threatening in the offing.
'So you've popped over, eh? Making a long stay in
America?'

'About a month. Your aunt gave me your address and
told me to be sure to call on you.'

I was glad to hear this, for it seemed to indicate that
Aunt Agatha was beginning to come round a bit. As I
believe I told you before, there had been some slight
unpleasantness between us, arising from the occasion
when she had sent me over to New York to disentangle
my cousin Gussie from the clutches of a girl on the
music-hall stage. When I tell you that by the time I had
finished my operations Gussie had not only married the
girl but had gone on the Halls himself and was doing

well, you'll understand that relations were a trifle strained between aunt and nephew.

I simply hadn't dared go back and face her, and it was a relief to find that time had healed the wound enough to make her tell her pals to call on me. What I mean is, much as I liked America, I didn't want to have England barred to me for the rest of my natural; and, believe me, England is a jolly sight too small for anyone to live in with Aunt Agatha, if she's really on the war-path. So I was braced at hearing these words and smiled genially on the assemblage.

'Your aunt said that you would do anything that was in your power to be of assistance to us.'

'Rather! Oh, rather. Absolutely.'

'Thank you so much. I want you to put dear Motty up for a little while.'

I didn't get this for a moment.

'Put him up? For my clubs?'

'No, no! Darling Motty is essentially a home bird. Aren't you, Motty, darling?'

Motty, who was sucking the knob of his stick, uncorked himself.

'Yes, mother,' he said, and corked himself up again.

'I should not like him to belong to clubs. I mean put him up here. Have him to live with you while I am away.'

These frightful words trickled out of her like honey. The woman simply didn't seem to understand the ghastly nature of her proposal. I gave Motty the swift east-to-west. He was sitting with his mouth nuzzling the stick, blinking at the wall. The thought of having this planted on me for an indefinite period appalled me. Absolutely appalled me, don't you know. I was just starting to say that the shot wasn't on the board at any price, and that the first sign Motty gave of trying to nestle into my little home I would yell for the police, when she went on, rolling placidly over me, as it were.

There was something about this woman that sapped one's will-power.

'I am leaving New York by the midday train, as I have to pay a visit to Sing-Sing prison. I am extremely interested in prison conditions in America. After that I work my way gradually across to the coast, visiting the points of interest on the journey. You see, Mr Wooster, I am in America principally on business. No doubt you read my book, *India and the Indians*? My publishers are anxious for me to write a companion volume on the United States. I shall not be able to spend more than a month in the country, as I have to get back for the season, but a month should be ample. I was less than a month in India, and my dear friend Sir Roger Cremorne wrote his *America from Within* after a stay of only two weeks. I should love to take dear Motty with me, but the poor boy gets so sick when he travels by train. I shall have to pick him up on my return.'

From where I sat I could see Jeeves in the dining-room, laying the breakfast table. I wished I could have had a minute with him alone. I felt certain that he would have been able to think of some way of putting a stop to this woman.

'It will be such a relief to know that Motty is safe with you, Mr Wooster. I know what the temptations of a great city are. Hitherto dear Motty has been sheltered from them. He has lived quietly with me in the country. I know that you will look after him carefully, Mr Wooster. He will give very little trouble.' She talked about the poor blighter as if he wasn't there. Not that Motty seemed to mind. He had stopped chewing his walking-stick and was sitting there with his mouth open. 'He is a vegetarian and a teetotaller and is devoted to reading. Give him a nice book and he will be quite contented.' She got up. 'Thank you so much, Mr Wooster. I don't know what I should have done without your help. Come, Motty. We have just time to see a few of the sights before my train goes. But I shall have to rely on you for most of my information about New York, darling. Be sure to keep your eyes open and take notes of your impressions. It will be such a help. Goodbye, Mr Wooster. I will send Motty back early in the afternoon.'

They went out, and I howled for Jeeves.

'Jeeves!'

'Sir?'

'What's to be done? You heard it all, didn't you? You were in the dining-room most of the time. That pill is coming to stay here.'

'Pill, sir?'

'The excrescence.'

'I beg your pardon, sir?'

I looked at Jeeves sharply. This sort of thing wasn't like him. Then I understood. The man was really upset about that tie. He was trying to get his own back.

'Lord Pershore will be staying here from tonight, Jeeves,' I said coldly.

'Very good, sir. Breakfast is ready, sir.'

I could have sobbed into the bacon and eggs. That there wasn't any sympathy to be got out of Jeeves was what put the lid on it. For a moment I almost weakened and told him to destroy the hat and tie if he didn't like them, but I pulled myself together again. I was dashed if I was going to let Jeeves treat me like a bally one-man chain-gang.

But, what with brooding on Jeeves and brooding on Motty, I was in a pretty reduced sort of state. The more I examined the situation, the more blighted it became. There was nothing I could do. If I slung Motty out, he would report to his mother, and she would pass it on to Aunt Agatha, and I didn't like to think what would happen then. Sooner or later I should be wanting to go back to England, and I didn't want to get there and find Aunt Agatha waiting on the quay for me with a stuffed eelskin. There was absolutely nothing for it but to put the fellow up and make the best of it.

About midday Motty's luggage arrived, and soon afterwards a large parcel of what I took to be nice books. I brightened up a little when I saw it. It was one of those massive parcels and looked as if it had enough in it to keep him busy for a year. I felt a trifle more cheerful, and I got my Broadway Special and stuck it on my head, and gave the pink tie a twist, and reeled out to take a bite of lunch with one or two of the lads at a neighbouring hostelry; and what with excellent browsing and sluicing and cheery conversation and what-not, the afternoon passed quite happily. By dinner time I had almost forgotten Motty's existence.

I dined at the club and looked in at a show afterwards, and it wasn't till fairly late that I got back to the flat. There were no signs of Motty, and I took it that he had gone to bed.

It seemed rummy to me, though, that the parcel of nice books was still there with the string and paper on it. It looked as if Motty, after seeing mother off at the station, had decided to call it a day.

Jeeves came in with the nightly whisky and soda. I could tell by the chappie's manner that he was still upset.

'Lord Pershore gone to bed, Jeeves?' I asked, with reserved hauteur and what-not.

'No sir. His lordship has not yet returned.'

'Not returned? What do you mean?'

'His lordship came in shortly after six-thirty, and, having dressed, went out again.'

At this moment there was a noise outside the front door, a sort of scrabbling noise, as if somebody were trying to paw his way through the woodwork. Then a sort of thud.

'Better go and see what that is, Jeeves.'

'Very good, sir.'

He went out and came back again.

'If you would not mind stepping this way sir, I think we might be able to carry him in.'

'Carry him in?'

'His lordship is lying on the mat, sir.'

I went to the front door. The man was right. There was Motty huddled up outside on the floor. He was moaning a bit.

'He's had some sort of dashed fit,' I said. I took another look. 'Jeeves! Someone's been feeding him meat!'

'Sir?'

'He's a vegetarian, you know. He must have been digging into a steak or something. Call up a doctor!'

'I hardly think it will be necessary, sir. If you would take his lordship's legs, while I –'

'Great Scott, Jeeves! You don't think – he can't be –'

'I am inclined to think so, sir.'

And, by Jove, he was right! Once on the right track, you couldn't mistake it. Motty was under the surface. Completely sozzled.

It was the deuce of a shock.

'You never can tell, Jeeves!'

'Very seldom, sir.'

'Remove the eye of authority and where are you?'

'Precisely, sir.'

'Where is my wandering boy tonight and all that sort of thing, what?'

'It would seem so, sir.'

'Well, we had better bring him in, eh?'

'Yes, sir.'

So we lugged him in, and Jeeves put him to bed, and I lit a cigarette and sat down to think the thing over. I had a kind of foreboding. It seemed to me that I had let myself in for something pretty rocky.

Next morning, after I had sucked down a thoughtful cup of tea, I went into Motty's room to investigate. I expected to find the fellow a wreck, but there he was, sitting up in bed, quite chirpy, reading *Gingery Stories*.

'What ho!' I said.

'What ho!' said Motty.

'What ho! What ho!'

'What ho! What ho! What ho!'

After that it seemed rather difficult to go on with the conversation.

'How are you feeling this morning?' I asked.

'Topping!' replied Motty, blithely and with abandon. 'I say, you know, that fellow of yours – Jeeves, you know – is a corker. I had a most frightful headache when I woke up, and he brought me a sort of rummy dark drink, and it put me right again at once. Said it was his own invention. I must see more of that lad. He seems to me distinctly one of the ones.'

I couldn't believe that this was the same blighter who had sat and sucked his stick the day before.

'You ate something that disagreed with you last night, didn't you?' I said, by way of giving him a chance to slide out of it if he wanted to. But he wouldn't have it at any price.

'No!' he replied firmly. 'I didn't do anything of the kind. I drank too much. Much too much. Lots and lots too much. And, what's more, I'm going to do it again. I'm going to do it every night. If ever you see me sober, old top,' he said, with a kind of holy exaltation, 'tap me on the shoulder and say, "Tut! Tut!" and I'll apologize and remedy the defect.'

'But I say, you know, what about me?'

'What about you?'

'Well, I'm, so to speak, as it were, kind of responsible for you. What I mean to say is, if you go doing this sort of thing I'm apt to get in the soup somewhat.'

'I can't help your troubles,' said Motty firmly. 'Listen to me, old thing: this is the first time in my life that I've had a real chance to yield to the temptations of a great city. What's the use of a great city having temptations if fellows don't yield to them? Makes it so bally discouraging for the great city. Besides, mother told me to keep my eyes open and collect impressions.'

I sat on the edge of the bed. I felt dizzy.

'I know just how you feel, old dear,' said Motty consolingly. 'And, if my principles would permit it, I would simmer down for your sake. But duty first! This is the first time I've been let out alone, and I mean to make the most of it. We're only young once. Why interfere with life's morning? Young man, rejoice in thy youth! Tra-la! What ho!'

Put like that, it did seem reasonable.

'All my bally life, dear boy,' Motty went on, 'I've been cooped up in the ancestral home at Much Middlefold, in Shropshire, and till you've been cooped up in Much Middlefold you don't know what cooping is. The only time we get any excitement is when one of the choir-boys is caught sucking chocolate during the sermon. When that happens, we talk about it for days. I've got about a month of New York, and I mean to store up a few happy memories for the long winter evenings. This is my only chance to collect a past, and I'm going to do it. Now tell me, old sport, as man to man, how does one get in touch with that very decent bird Jeeves? Does one ring a bell or shout a bit? I should like to discuss the subject of a good stiff b-and-s with him.'

I had had a sort of vague idea, don't you know, that if I stuck close to Motty and went about the place with him, I might act as a bit of a damper on the gaiety. What I mean is, I thought that if, when he was being the life and soul of the party, he were to catch my reproving eye he might ease up a trifle on the revelry. So the next night I took him along to supper with me. It was the last time. I'm a quiet, peaceful sort of bloke who has lived all his life in London, and I can't stand the pace these swift sportsmen from the rural districts set. What I mean to say is, I'm all for rational enjoyment and so forth, but I think a chappie makes himself conspicuous when he throws soft-boiled eggs at the electric fan. And decent mirth and all that sort of thing are all right, but I do bar dancing on tables and having to dash all over the place dodging waiters, managers, and chuckers-out, just when you want to sit still and digest.

Directly I managed to tear myself away that night and get home, I made up my mind that this was jolly well the last time that I went about with Motty. The only time I met him late at night after that was once when I passed the door of a fairly low-down sort of restaurant and had to step aside to dodge him as he sailed through the air *en route* for the opposite pavement, with a muscular sort of looking fellow peering out after him with a kind of gloomy satisfaction.

In a way, I couldn't help sympathizing with the chap. He had about four weeks to have the good time that ought to have been spread over about ten years, and I didn't wonder at his wanting to be pretty busy. I should have been just the same in his place. Still, there was no denying that it was a bit thick. If it hadn't been for the thought of Lady Malvern and Aunt Agatha in the background, I should have regarded Motty's rapid work with an indulgent smile. But I couldn't get rid of the feeling that, sooner or later, I was the lad who was scheduled to get it behind the ear. And what with brooding on this prospect, and sitting up in the old flat waiting for the familiar footstep, and putting it to bed when it got there, and stealing into the sick-chamber next morning to contemplate the wreckage, I was beginning to lose weight. Absolutely becoming the good old shadow, I give you my honest word. Starting at sudden noises and what-not.

And no sympathy from Jeeves. That was what cut me to the quick. The man was still thoroughly pipped about the hat and tie, and simply wouldn't rally round. One morning I wanted comforting so much that I sank the pride of the Woosters and appealed to the fellow direct.

'Jeeves,' I said, 'this is getting a bit thick!'

'Sir?'

'You know what I mean. This lad seems to have chucked all the principles of a well-spent boyhood. He has got it up his nose!'

'Yes, sir.'

'Well, I shall get blamed, don't you know. You know what my Aunt Agatha is.'

'Yes, sir.'

'Very well, then.'

I waited a moment, but he wouldn't unbend.

'Jeeves,' I said, 'haven't you any scheme up your sleeve for coping with this blighter?'

'No, sir.'

And he shimmered off to his lair. Obstinate devil! So dashed absurd, don't you know. It wasn't as if there was anything wrong with that Broadway Special hat. It was a remarkably priceless effort, and much admired by the lads. But, just because he preferred the White House Wonder, he left me flat.

It was shortly after this that young Motty got the idea of bringing pals back in the small hours to continue the gay revels in the home. This was where I began to crack under the strain. You see, the part of town where I was living wasn't the right place for that sort of thing. I knew lots of chappies down Washington Square way who started the evening at about two a.m. – artists and writers and so forth who frolicked considerably till checked by the arrival of the morning milk. That was all right. They like that sort of thing down there. The neighbours can't get to sleep unless there's someone dancing Hawaiian dances over their heads. But on Fifty-seventh Street the atmosphere wasn't right, and when Motty turned up at three in the morning with a

collection of hearty lads, who only stopped singing their
college song when they started singing 'The Old Oaken
Bucket', there was a marked peevishness among the old
settlers in the flats. The management was extremely
terse over the telephone at breakfast-time, and took a lot
of soothing.

The next night I came home early, after a lonely
dinner at a place which I'd chosen because there didn't
seem any chance of meeting Motty there. The
sitting-room was quite dark, and I was just moving to
switch on the light, when there was a sort of explosion
and something collared hold of my trouser-leg. Living
with Motty had reduced me to such an extent that I was
simply unable to cope with this thing. I jumped
backward with a loud yell of anguish, and tumbled out
into the hall just as Jeeves came out of his den to see
what the matter was.

'Did you call, sir?'

'Jeeves! There's something in there that grabs you by
the leg!'

'That would be Rollo, sir.'

'Eh?'

'I would have warned you of his presence, but I did
not hear you come in. His temper is a little uncertain at
present, as he has not yet settled down.'

'Who the deuce is Rollo?'

'His lordship's bull-terrier, sir. His lordship won him
in a raffle, and tied him to the leg of the table. If you will
allow me, sir, I will go in and switch on the light.'

There really is nobody like Jeeves. He walked straight
into the sitting-room, the biggest feat since Daniel and
the lions' den, without a quiver. What's more, his
magnetism or whatever they call it was such that the
dashed animal, instead of pinning him by the leg,
calmed down as if he had had a bromide, and rolled over
on his back with all his paws in the air. If Jeeves had
been his rich uncle he couldn't have been more

chummy. Yet directly he caught sight of me again, he got all worked up and seemed to have only one idea in life – to start chewing me where he had left off.

'Rollo is not used to you yet, sir,' said Jeeves, regarding the bally quadruped in an admiring sort of way. 'He is an excellent watch-dog.'

'I don't want a watch-dog to keep me out of my rooms.'

'No, sir.'

'Well, what am I to do?'

'No doubt in time the animal will learn to discriminate, sir. He will learn to distinguish your peculiar scent.'

'What do you mean – my peculiar scent? Correct the impression that I intend to hang about in the hall while life slips by, in the hope that one of these days that dashed animal will decide that I smell all right.' I thought for a bit. 'Jeeves!'

'Sir?'

'I'm going away – tomorrow morning by the first train. I shall go and stop with Mr Todd in the country.'

'Do you wish me to accompany you, sir?'

'No.'

'Very good, sir.'

'I don't know when I shall be back. Forward my letters.'

'Yes, sir.'

As a matter of fact, I was back within the week. Rocky Todd, the pal I went to stay with, is a rummy sort of a chap who lives all alone in the wilds of Long Island, and likes it; but a little of that sort of thing goes a long way with me. Dear old Rocky is one of the best, but after a few days in his cottage in the woods, miles away from anywhere, New York, even with Motty on the premises, began to look pretty good to me. The days down on Long Island have forty-eight hours in them; you can't get to

sleep at night because of the bellowing of the crickets;
and you have to walk two miles for a drink and six for
an evening paper. I thanked Rocky for his kind
hospitality, and caught the only train they have down in
those parts. It landed me in New York about
dinner-time. I went straight to the old flat. Jeeves came
out of his lair. I looked round cautiously for Rollo.

'Where's that dog, Jeeves? Have you got him tied
up?'

'The animal is no longer here, sir. His lordship gave
him to the porter, who sold him. His lordship took a
prejudice against the animal on account of being bitten
by him in the calf of the leg.'

I don't think I've ever been so bucked by a bit of
news. I felt I had misjudged Rollo. Evidently, when you
got to know him better, he had a lot of good in him.

'Fine!' I said. 'Is Lord Pershore in, Jeeves?'

'No, sir.'

'Do you expect him back to dinner?'

'No, sir.'

'Where is he?'

'In prison, sir.'

'In prison!'

'Yes, sir.'

'You don't mean – in prison?'

'Yes, sir.'

I lowered myself into a chair.

'Why?' I said.

'He assaulted a constable, sir.'

'Lord Pershore assaulted a constable!'

'Yes, sir.'

I digested this.

'But, Jeeves, I say! This is frightful!'

'Sir?'

'What will Lady Malvern say when she finds out?'

'I do not fancy that her ladyship will find out, sir.'

'But she'll come back and want to know where he is.'

'I rather fancy, sir, that his lordship's bit of time will have run out by then.'

'But supposing it hasn't?'

'In that event, sir, it may be judicious to prevaricate a little.'

'How?'

'If I might make the suggestion, sir, I should inform her ladyship that his lordship has left for a short visit to Boston.'

'Why Boston?'

'Very interesting and respectable centre, sir.'

'Jeeves, I believe you've hit it.'

'I fancy so, sir.'

'Why, this is really the best thing that could have happened. If this hadn't turned up to prevent him, young Motty would have been in a sanatorium by the time Lady Malvern got back.'

'Exactly, sir.'

The more I looked at it in that way, the sounder this prison wheeze seemed to me. There was no doubt in the world that prison was just what the doctor ordered for Motty. It was the only thing that could have pulled him up. I was sorry for the poor blighter, but after all, I reflected, a fellow who had lived all his life with Lady Malvern, in a small village in the interior of Shropshire, wouldn't have much to kick at in a prison. Altogether, I began to feel absolutely braced again. Life became like what the poet Johnnie says – one grand, sweet song. Things went on so comfortably and peacefully for a couple of weeks that I give you my word that I'd almost forgotten such a person as Motty existed. The only flaw in the scheme of things was that Jeeves was still pained and distant. It wasn't anything he said, or did, mind you, but there was a rummy something about him all the time. Once when I was tying the pink tie I caught sight of him in the looking-glass. There was a kind of grieved look in his eye.

And then Lady Malvern came back, a good bit ahead of schedule. I hadn't been expecting her for days. I'd forgotten how time had been slipping along. She turned up one morning while I was still in bed sipping tea and thinking of this and that. Jeeves flowed in with the announcement that he had just loosed her into the sitting-room. I draped a few garments round me and went in.

There she was, sitting in the same arm-chair, looking as massive as ever. The only difference was that she didn't uncover the teeth as she had done the first time.

'Good morning,' I said. 'So you've got back, what?'

'I have got back.'

There was something sort of bleak about her tone, rather as if she had swallowed an east wind. This I took to be due to the fact that she probably hadn't breakfasted. It's only after a bit of breakfast that I'm able to regard the world with that sunny cheeriness which makes a fellow the universal favourite. I'm never much of a lad till I've engulfed an egg or two and a beaker of coffee.

'I suppose you haven't breakfasted?'

'I have not yet breakfasted.'

'Won't you have an egg or something? Or a sausage or something? Or something?'

'No, thank you.'

She spoke as if she belonged to an anti-sausage society or a league for the suppression of eggs. There was a bit of a silence.

'I called on you last night,' she said, 'but you were out.'

'Awfully sorry. Had a pleasant trip?'

'Extremely, thank you.'

'See everything? Niagara Falls, Yellowstone Park, and the jolly old Grand Canyon, and what not?'

'I saw a great deal.'

There was another slightly *frappé* silence. Jeeves

floated silently into the dining-room and began to lay the breakfast-table.

'I hope Wilmot was not in your way, Mr Wooster?'

I had been wondering when she was going to mention Motty.

'Rather not! Great pals. Hit it off splendidly.'

'You were his constant companion, then?'

'Absolutely. We were always together. Saw all the sights, don't you know. We'd take in the Museum of Art in the morning, and have a bit of lunch at some good vegetarian place, and then toddle along to a sacred concert in the afternoon, and home to an early dinner. We usually played dominoes after dinner. And then the early bed and the refreshing sleep. We had a great time. I was awfully sorry when he went away to Boston.'

'Oh! Wilmot is in Boston?'

'Yes. I ought to have let you know, but of course we didn't know where you were. You were dodging all over the place like a snipe – I mean, don't you know, dodging all over the place, and we couldn't get at you. Yes, Motty went off to Boston.'

'You're sure he went to Boston?'

'Oh, absolutely.' I called out to Jeeves, who was now messing about in the next room with forks and so forth: 'Jeeves, Lord Pershore didn't change his mind about going to Boston, did he?'

'No, sir.'

'I thought I was right. Yes, Motty went to Boston.'

'Then how do you account, Mr Wooster, for the fact that when I went yesterday afternoon to Blackwell's Island prison, to secure material for my book, I saw poor, dear Wilmot there, dressed in a striped suit, seated beside a pile of stones with a hammer in his hands?'

I tried to think of something to say, but nothing came. A fellow has to be a lot broader about the forehead than I am to handle a jolt like this. I strained the old bean till it creaked, but between the collar and the hair parting nothing stirred. I was dumb. Which was lucky, because I wouldn't have had a chance to get any persiflage out of my system. Lady Malvern collared the conversation. She had been bottling it up, and now it came out with a rush.

'So this is how you have looked after my poor, dear boy, Mr Wooster! So this is how you have abused my trust! I left him in your charge, thinking that I could rely on you to shield him from evil. He came to you innocent, unversed in the ways of the world, confiding, unused to the temptations of a large city, and you led him astray!'

I hadn't any remarks to make. All I could think of was the picture of Aunt Agatha drinking all this in and reaching out to sharpen the hatchet against my return.

'You deliberately – '

Far away in the misty distance a soft voice spoke:

'If I might explain, your ladyship.'

Jeeves had projected himself in from the dining-room and materialized on the rug. Lady Malvern tried to freeze him with a look, but you can't do that sort of thing to Jeeves. He is look-proof.

'I fancy, your ladyship, that you may have misunderstood Mr Wooster, and that he may have given you the impression that he was in New York when his lordship was – removed. When Mr Wooster informed your ladyship that his lordship had gone to Boston, he was relying on the version I had given him of his lordship's movements. Mr Wooster was away, visiting a friend in the country, at the time, and knew nothing of the matter till your ladyship informed him.'

Lady Malvern gave a kind of grunt. It didn't rattle Jeeves.

'I feared Mr Wooster might be disturbed if he knew the truth, as he is so attached to his lordship and has taken such pains to look after him, so I took the liberty of telling him that his lordship had gone away for a visit.

It might have been hard for Mr Wooster to believe that his lordship had gone to prison voluntarily and from the best motives, but your ladyship, knowing him better, will readily understand.'

'What!' Lady Malvern goggled at him. 'Did you say that Lord Pershore went to prison voluntarily?'

'If I might explain, your ladyship. I think that your ladyship's parting words made a deep impression on his lordship. I have frequently heard him speak to Mr Wooster of his desire to do something to follow your ladyship's instructions and collect material for your ladyship's book on America. Mr Wooster will bear me out when I say that his lordship was frequently extremely depressed at the thought that he was doing so little to help.'

'Absolutely, by Jove! Quite pipped about it!' I said.

'The idea of making a personal examination into the prison system of the country – from within – occurred to his lordship very suddenly one night. He embraced it eagerly. There was no restraining him.'

Lady Malvern looked at Jeeves, then at me, then at Jeeves again. I could see her struggling with the thing.

'Surely, your ladyship,' said Jeeves, 'it is more reasonable to suppose that a gentleman of his lordship's character went to prison of his own volition than that he committed some breach of the law which necessitated his arrest?'

Lady Malvern blinked. Then she got up.

'Mr Wooster,' she said, 'I apologize. I have done you an injustice. I should have known Wilmot better. I should have had more faith in his pure, fine spirit.'

'Absolutely!' I said.

'Your breakfast is ready, sir,' said Jeeves.

I sat down and dallied in a dazed sort of way with a poached egg.

'Jeeves,' I said, 'you are certainly a life-saver.'

'Thank you, sir.'

'Nothing would have convinced my Aunt Agatha, that I hadn't lured that blighter into riotous living.'

'I fancy you are right, sir.'

I champed my egg for a bit. I was most awfully moved, don't you know, by the way Jeeves had rallied round. Something seemed to tell me that this was an occasion that called for rich rewards. For a moment I hesitated. Then I made up my mind.

'Jeeves!'

'Sir?'

'That pink tie.'

'Yes, sir?'

'Burn it.'

'Thank you, sir.'

'And, Jeeves.'

'Yes, sir?'

'Take a taxi and get me that White House Wonder hat, as worn by President Coolidge.'

'Thank you very much, sir.'

I felt most awfully braced. I felt as if the clouds had rolled away and all was as it used to be. I felt like one of those chappies in the novels who calls off the fight with his wife in the last chapter and decides to forget and forgive. I felt I wanted to do all sorts of other things to show Jeeves that I appreciated him.

'Jeeves,' I said, 'it isn't enough. Is there anything else you would like?'

'Yes, sir. If I may make the suggestion – fifty dollars.'

'Fifty dollars?'

'It will enable me to pay a debt of honour, sir. I owe it to his lordship.'

'You owe Lord Pershore fifty dollars?'

'Yes, sir. I happened to meet him in the street the night his lordship was arrested. I had been thinking a good deal about the most suitable method of inducing him to abandon his mode of living, sir. His lordship was a little over-excited at the time, and I fancy that he mistook me for a friend of his. At any rate, when I took the liberty of wagering him fifty dollars that he would not punch a passing policeman in the eye, he accepted the bet very cordially and won it.'

I produced my pocket-book and counted out a hundred.

'Take this, Jeeves,' I said; 'fifty isn't enough. Do you know, Jeeves, you're – well, you absolutely stand alone!'

'I endeavour to give satisfaction, sir,' said Jeeves.

4 — Jeeves and the Hard-Boiled Egg

Sometimes of a morning, as I've sat in bed sucking down the early cup of tea and watched Jeeves flitting about the room and putting out the raiment for the day, I've wondered what the deuce I should do if the fellow ever took it into his head to leave me. It's not so bad when I'm in New York, but in London the anxiety is frightful. There used to be all sorts of attempts on the part of low blighters to sneak him away from me. Young Reggie Foljambe to my certain knowledge offered him double what I was giving him, and Alistair Bingham-Reeves, who's got a valet who had been known to press his trousers sideways, used to look at him, when he came to see me, with a kind of glittering, hungry eye which disturbed me deucedly. Bally pirates!

The thing, you see, is that Jeeves is so dashed competent. You can spot it even in the way he shoves studs into a shirt.

I rely on him absolutely in every crisis, and he never lets me down. And, what's more, he can always be counted on to extend himself on behalf of any pal of mine who happens to be to all appearances knee-deep in the bouillon. Take the rather rummy case, for instance, of dear old Bicky and his uncle, the hard-boiled egg.

It happened after I had been in America for a few months. I got back to the flat latish one night, and when Jeeves brought me the final drink he said:

'Mr Bickersteth called to see you this evening, sir, while you were out.'

'Oh?' I said.

'Twice, sir. He appeared a trifle agitated.'

'What, pipped?'

'He gave that impression, sir.'

I sipped the whisky. I was sorry if Bicky was in trouble, but, as a matter of fact, I was rather glad to have something I could discuss freely with Jeeves just then, because things had been a bit strained between us for some time, and it had been rather difficult to hit on anything to talk about that wasn't apt to take a personal turn. You see, I had decided – rightly or wrongly – to grow a moustache, and this had cut Jeeves to the quick. He couldn't stick the thing at any price, and I had been living ever since in an atmosphere of bally disapproval till I was getting jolly well fed up with it. What I mean is, while there's no doubt that in certain matters of dress Jeeves's judgement is absolutely sound and should be followed, it seemed to me that it was getting a bit too thick if he was going to edit my face as well as my costume. No one can call me an unreasonable chappie, and many's the time I've given in like a lamb when Jeeves has voted against one of my pet suits or ties; but when it comes to a valet's staking out a claim on your upper lip you've simply got to have a bit of the good old bulldog pluck and defy the blighter.

'He said that he would call again later, sir.'

'Something must be up, Jeeves.'

'Yes, sir.'

I gave the moustache a thoughtful twirl. It seemed to hurt Jeeves a good deal, so I chucked it.

'I see by the paper, sir, that Mr Bickersteth's uncle is arriving on the *Carmantic*.'

'Yes?'

'His Grace the Duke of Chiswick, sir.'

This was news to me, that Bicky's uncle was a duke. Rum, how little one knows about one's pals. I had met Bicky for the first time at a species of beano or jamboree down in Washington Square, not long after my arrival in

New York. I suppose I was a bit homesick at the time, and I rather took to Bicky when I found that he was an Englishman and had, in fact, been up at Oxford with me. Besides, he was a frightful chump, so we naturally drifted together; and while we were taking a quiet snort in a corner that wasn't all cluttered up with artists and sculptors, he furthermore endeared himself to me by a most extraordinarily gifted imitation of a bull-terrier chasing a cat up a tree. But, though we had subsequently become extremely pally, all I really knew about him was that he was generally hard up, and had an uncle who relieved the strain a bit from time to time by sending him monthly remittances.

'If the Duke of Chiswick is his uncle,' I said, 'why hasn't he a title? Why isn't he Lord What-Not?'

'Mr Bickersteth is the son of His Grace's late sister, sir, who married Captain Rollo Bickersteth of the Coldstream Guards.'

Jeeves knows everything.

'Is Mr Bickersteth's father dead too?'

'Yes, sir.'

'Leave any money?'

'No, sir.'

I began to understand why poor old Bicky was always more or less on the rocks. To the casual and irreflective observer it may sound a pretty good wheeze having a duke for an uncle, but the trouble about old Chiswick was that, though an extremely wealthy old buster, owning half London and about five counties up north, he was notoriously the most prudent spender in England. He was what Americans call a hard-boiled egg. If Bicky's people hadn't left him anything and he depended on what he could prise out of the old duke, he was in a pretty bad way. Not that that explained why he was hunting me like this, because he was a chap who never borrowed money. He said he wanted to keep his pals, so never bit anyone's ear on principle.

At this juncture the door-bell rang. Jeeves floated out to answer it.

'Yes, sir. Mr Wooster has just returned,' I heard him say. And Bicky came beetling in, looking pretty sorry for himself.

'Hallo, Bicky,' I said. 'Jeeves told me you had been trying to get me. What's the trouble, Bicky?'

'I'm in a hole, Bertie. I want your advice.'

'Say on, old lad.'

'My uncle's turning up tomorrow, Bertie.'

'So Jeeves told me.'

'The Duke of Chiswick, you know.'

'So Jeeves told me.'

Bicky seemed a bit surprised.

'Jeeves seems to know everything.'

'Rather rummily, that's exactly what I was thinking just now myself.'

'Well, I wish,' said Bicky, gloomily, 'that he knew a way to get me out of the hole I'm in.'

'Mr Bickersteth is in a hole, Jeeves,' I said, 'and wants you to rally round.'

'Very good, sir.'

Bicky looked a bit doubtful.

'Well, of course, you know, Bertie, this thing is by way of being a bit private and all that.'

'I shouldn't worry about that, old top. I bet Jeeves knows all about it already. Don't you, Jeeves?'

'Yes, sir.'

'Eh?' said Bicky, rattled.

'I am open to correction, sir, but is not your dilemma due to the fact that you are at a loss to explain to His Grace why you are in New York instead of in Colorado?'

Bicky rocked like a jelly in a high wind.

'How the deuce do you know anything about it?'

'I chanced to meet His Grace's butler before we left England. He informed me that he happened to overhear

His Grace speaking to you on the matter, sir, as he passed the library door.'

Bicky gave a hollow sort of laugh.

'Well, as everybody seems to know all about it, there's no need to try to keep it dark. The old boy turfed me out, Bertie, because he said I was a brainless nincompoop. The idea was that he would give me a remittance on condition that I dashed out to some blighted locality of the name of Colorado and learned farming or ranching, or whatever they call it, at some bally ranch or farm, or whatever it's called. I didn't fancy the idea a bit. I should have had to ride horses and pursue cows, and so forth. At the same time, don't you know, I had to have that remittance.'

'I get you absolutely, old thing.'

'Well, when I got to New York it looked a decent sort of place to me, so I thought it would be a pretty sound notion to stop here. So I cabled to my uncle telling him that I had dropped into a good business wheeze in the city and wanted to chuck the ranch idea. He wrote back that it was all right, and here I've been ever since. He thinks I'm doing well at something or other over here. I never dreamed, don't you know, that he would ever come out here. What on earth am I to do?'

'Jeeves,' I said, 'what on earth is Mr Bickersteth to do?'

'You see,' said Bicky, 'I had a wireless from him to say that he was coming to stay with me – to save hotel bills, I suppose. I've always given him the impression that I was living in pretty good style. I can't have him to stay at my boarding-house.'

'Thought of anything, Jeeves?' I said.

'To what extent, sir, if the question is not a delicate one, are you prepared to assist Mr Bickersteth?'

'I'll do anything I can for you, of course, Bicky, old man.'

'Then, if I might make the suggestion, sir, you might lend Mr Bickersteth –'

'No, by Jove!' said Bicky firmly. 'I never have touched you, Bertie, and I'm not going to start now. I may be a chump, but it's my boast that I don't owe a penny to a single soul – not counting tradesmen, of course.'

'I was about to suggest, sir, that you might lend Mr Bickersteth this flat. Mr Bickersteth could give His Grace the impression that he was the owner of it. With your permission I could convey the notion that I was in Mr Bickersteth's employment and not in yours. You would be residing here temporarily as Mr Bickersteth's guest. His Grace would occupy the second spare bedroom. I fancy that you would find this answer satisfactory, sir.'

Bicky had stopped rocking himself and was staring at Jeeves in an awed sort of way.

'I would advocate the dispatching of a wireless message to His Grace on board the vessel, notifying him of the change of address. Mr Bickersteth could meet His Grace at the dock and proceed directly here. Will that meet the situation, sir?'

'Absolutely.'

'Thank you, sir.'

Bicky followed him with his eye till the door closed.

'How does he do it, Bertie?' he said. 'I'll tell you what I think it is. I believe it's something to do with the shape of his head. Have you ever noticed his head, Bertie, old man? It sort of sticks out at the back!'

I hopped out of bed pretty early next morning, so as to be among those present when the old boy should arrive. I knew from experience that these ocean liners fetch up at the dock at a deucedly ungodly hour. It wasn't much after nine by the time I'd dressed and had my morning tea and was leaning out of the window, watching the street for Bicky and his uncle. It was one of those jolly,

peaceful mornings that make a chappie wish he'd got a
soul or something, and I was just brooding on life in
general when I became aware of the dickens of a spat in
progress down below. A taxi had driven up, and an old
boy in a top hat had got out and was kicking up a
frightful row about the fare. As far as I could make out,
he was trying to get the cabby to switch from New York
to London prices, and the cabby had apparently never
heard of London before, and didn't seem to think a lot of
it now. The old boy said that in London the trip would
have set him back a shilling, and the cabby said he
should worry. I called to Jeeves.

'The duke has arrived, Jeeves.'

'Yes, sir?'

'That'll be him at the door now.'

Jeeves made a long arm and opened the front door,
and the old boy crawled in.

'How do you do, sir?' I said, bustling up and being the
ray of sunshine. 'Your nephew went down to the dock to
meet you, but you must have missed him. My name's
Wooster, don't you know. Great pal of Bicky's, and all
that sort of thing. I'm staying with him, you know.
Would you like a cup of tea? Jeeves, bring a cup of tea.'

Old Chiswick had sunk into an arm-chair and was
looking about the room.

'Does this luxurious flat belong to my nephew
Francis?'

'Absolutely.'

'It must be terribly expensive.'

'Pretty well, of course. Everything costs a lot over
here, you know.'

He moaned. Jeeves filtered in with the tea. Old
Chiswick took a stab at it to restore his tissues, and
nodded.

'A terrible country, Mr Wooster! A terrible country.
Nearly eight shillings for a short cab-drive. Iniquitous!'
He took another look round the room. It seemed to

fascinate him. 'Have you any idea how much my nephew pays for this flat, Mr Wooster?'

'About two hundred dollars a month, I believe.'

'What! Forty pounds a month!'

I began to see that, unless I made the thing a bit more plausible, the scheme might turn out a frost. I could guess what the old boy was thinking. He was trying to square all this prosperity with what he knew of poor old Bicky. And one had to admit that it took a lot of squaring, for dear old Bicky, though a stout fellow and absolutely unrivalled as an imitator of bull-terriers and cats, was in many ways one of the most pronounced fatheads that ever pulled on a suit of gents' underwear.

'I suppose it seems rummy to you,' I said, 'but the fact is New York often bucks fellows up and makes them show a flash of speed that you wouldn't have imagined them capable of. It sort of develops them. Something in the air, don't you know. I imagine that Bicky in the past, when you knew him, may have been something of a chump, but it's quite different now. Devilish efficient sort of bird, and looked on in commercial circles as quite the nib!'

'I am amazed! What is the nature of my nephew's business, Mr Wooster?'

'Oh, just business, don't you know. The same sort of thing Rockefeller and all these coves do, you know.' I slid for the door. 'Awfully sorry to leave you, but I've got to meet some of the lads elsewhere.'

Coming out of the lift I met Bicky bustling in from the street.

'Hallo, Bertie. I missed him. Has he turned up?'

'He's upstairs now, having some tea.'

'What does he think of it all?'

'He's absolutely rattled.'

'Ripping! I'll be toddling up, then. Toodle-oo, Bertie, old man. See you later.'

'Pip-pip, Bicky, dear boy.'

He trotted off, full of merriment and good cheer, and I went off to the club to sit in the window and watch the traffic coming up one way and going down the other.

It was latish in the evening when I looked in at the flat to dress for dinner.

'Where's everybody, Jeeves?' I said, finding no little feet pattering about the place. 'Gone out?'

'His Grace desired to see some of the sights of the city, sir. Mr Bickersteth is acting as his escort. I fancy their immediate objective was Grant's Tomb.'

'I suppose Mr Bickersteth is a bit bucked at the way things are going – what?'

'Sir?'

'I say, I take it that Mr Bickersteth is tolerably full of beans.'

'Not altogether, sir.'

'What's his trouble now?'

'The scheme which I took the liberty of suggesting to Mr Bickersteth and yourself has, unfortunately, not answered entirely satisfactorily, sir.'

'Surely the duke believes that Mr Bickersteth is doing well in business, and all that sort of thing?'

'Exactly, sir. With the result that he has decided to cancel Mr Bickersteth's monthly allowance, on the ground that, as Mr Bickersteth is doing so well on his own account, he no longer requires pecuniary assistance.'

'Great Scott, Jeeves! This is awful!'

'Somewhat disturbing, sir.'

'I never expected anything like this!'

'I confess I scarcely anticipated the contingency myself, sir.'

'I suppose it bowled the poor blighter over absolutely?'

'Mr Bickersteth appeared somewhat taken aback, sir.'

My heart bled for Bicky.

'We must do something, Jeeves.'

'Yes, sir.'

'Can you think of anything?'

'Not at the moment, sir.'

'There must be something we can do.'

'It was a maxim of one of my former employers, sir – as I believe I mentioned to you once before – the present Lord Bridgworth, that there is always a way. No doubt we shall be able to discover some solution of Mr Bickersteth's difficulty, sir.'

'Well, have a stab at it, Jeeves.'

'I will spare no pains, sir.'

I went and dressed sadly. It will show you pretty well how pipped I was when I tell you that I as near as a toucher put on a white tie with a dinner-jacket. I sallied out for a bit of food more to pass the time than because I wanted it. It seemed brutal to be wading into the bill of fare with poor old Bicky headed for the bread-line.

When I got back old Chiswick had gone to bed, but Bicky was there, hunched up in an arm-chair, brooding pretty tensely, with a cigarette hanging out of the corner of his mouth and a more or less glassy stare in his eyes.

'This is a bit thick, old thing – what!' I said.

He picked up his glass and drained it feverishly, overlooking the fact that it hadn't anything in it.

'I'm done, Bertie!' he said.

He had another go at the glass. It didn't seem to do him any good.

'If only this had happened a week later, Bertie! My next month's money was due to roll in on Saturday. I could have worked a wheeze I've been reading about in the magazine advertisements. It seems that you can make a dashed amount of money if you can only collect a few dollars and start a chicken-farm. Jolly life, too, keeping hens!' He had begun to get quite worked up at the thought of it, but he slopped back in his chair at this juncture with a good deal of gloom. 'But, of course, it's no good,' he said, 'because I haven't the cash.'

'You've only to say the word, you know, Bicky, old top.'

'Thanks awfully, Bertie, but I'm not going to sponge on you.'

That's always the way in this world. The chappies you'd like to lend money to won't let you, whereas the chappies you don't want to lend it to will do everything except actually stand you on your head and lift the specie out of your pockets. As a lad who has always rolled tolerably freely in the right stuff, I've had lots of experience of the second class. Many's the time, back in London, I've hurried along Piccadilly and felt the hot breath of the toucher on the back of my neck and heard his sharp, excited yapping as he closed in on me. I've simply spent my life scattering largesse to blighters I didn't care a hang for; yet here was I now, dripping doubloons and pieces of eight and longing to hand them over, and Bicky, poor fish, absolutely on his uppers, not taking any at any price.

'Well, there's only one hope then.'

'What's that?'

'Jeeves.'

'Sir?'

There was Jeeves, standing behind me, full of zeal. In this matter of shimmering into rooms the man is rummy to a degree. You're sitting in the old arm-chair, thinking of this and that, and then suddenly you look up, and there he is. He moves from point to point with as little uproar as a jelly-fish. The thing startled poor old Bicky considerably. He rose from his seat like a rocketing pheasant. I'm used to Jeeves now, but often in the days when he first came to me I've bitten my tongue freely on finding him unexpectedly in my midst.

'Did you call, sir?'

'Oh, there you are, Jeeves!'

'Precisely, sir.'

'Any ideas, Jeeves?'

'Why, yes, sir. Since we had our recent conversation I fancy I have found what may prove a solution. I do not wish to appear to be taking a liberty, sir, but I think that we have overlooked His Grace's potentialities as a source of revenue.'

Bicky laughed what I have sometimes seen described as a hollow, mocking laugh, a sort of bitter cackle from the back of the throat, rather like a gargle.

'I do not allude, sir,' explained Jeeves, 'to the possibility of inducing His Grace to part with money. I am taking the liberty of regarding His Grace in the light of an at present – if I may say so – useless property, which is capable of being developed.'

Bicky looked at me in a helpless kind of way. I'm bound to say I didn't get it myself.

'Couldn't you make it a bit easier, Jeeves?'

'In a nutshell, sir, what I mean is this: His Grace is, in a sense, a prominent personage. The inhabitants of this country, as no doubt you are aware, sir, are peculiarly addicted to shaking hands with prominent personages. It occurred to me that Mr Bickersteth or yourself might know of persons who would be willing to pay a small fee – let us say two dollars or three – for the privilege of an introduction, including handshake, to His Grace.'

Bicky didn't seem to think much of it.

'Do you mean to say that anyone would be mug enough to part with solid cash just to shake hands with my uncle?'

'I have an aunt, sir, who paid five shillings to a young fellow for bringing a moving-picture actor to tea at her house one Sunday. It gave her social standing among the neighbours.'

Bicky wavered.

'If you think it could be done –'

'I feel convinced of it, sir.'

'What do you think, Bertie?'

'I'm for it, old boy, absolutely. A very brainy wheeze.'

'Thank you, sir. Will there be anything further? Good night, sir.'

And he flitted out, leaving us to discuss details.

Until we started this business of floating old Chiswick as a money-making proposition I had never realized what a perfectly foul time those Stock Exchange fellows must have when the public isn't biting freely. Nowadays I read that bit they put in the financial reports about 'The market opened quietly' with a sympathetic eye, for, by Jove, it certainly opened quietly for us. You'd hardly believe how difficult it was to interest the public and make them take a flutter on the old boy. By the end of a week the only name we had on our list was a delicatessen-store keeper down in Bicky's part of the town, and as he wanted us to take it out in sliced ham instead of cash that didn't help much. There was a gleam of light when the brother of Bicky's pawnbroker offered ten dollars, money down, for an introduction to old Chiswick, but the deal fell through, owing to its turning out that the chap was an anarchist and intended to kick the old boy instead of shaking hands with him. At that, it took me the deuce of a time to persuade Bicky not to grab the cash and let things take their course. He seemed to regard the pawnbroker's brother rather as a sportsman and benefactor of his species than otherwise.

The whole thing, I'm inclined to think, would have been off if it hadn't been for Jeeves. There is no doubt that Jeeves is in a class of his own. In the matter of brain and resource I don't think I have ever met a chappie so supremely like mother made. He trickled into my room one morning with the good old cup of tea, and intimated that there was something doing.

'Might I speak to you with regard to that matter of His Grace, sir?'

'It's all off. We've decided to chuck it.'

'Sir?'

'It won't work. We can't get anybody to come.'

'I fancy I can arrange that aspect of the matter, sir.'

'Do you mean to say you've managed to get anybody?'

'Yes, sir. Eighty-seven gentlemen from Birdsburg, sir.'

I sat up in bed and spilt the tea.

'Birdsburg?'

'Birdsburg, Missouri, sir.'

'How did you get them?'

'I happened last night, sir, as you had intimated that you would be absent from home, to attend a theatrical performance, and entered into conversation between the acts with the occupant of the adjoining seat. I had observed that he was wearing a somewhat ornate decoration in his buttonhole, sir – a large blue button with the words "Boost for Birdsburg" upon it in red letters, scarcely a judicious addition to a gentleman's evening costume. To my surprise I noticed that the auditorium was full of persons similarly decorated. I ventured to inquire the explanation, and was informed that these gentlemen, forming a party of eighty-seven, are a convention from a town of the name of Birdsburg in the State of Missouri. Their visit, I gathered, was purely of a social and pleasurable nature, and my informant spoke at some length of the entertainments arranged for their stay in the city. It was when he related with a considerable amount of satisfaction and pride that a deputation of their number had been introduced to and had shaken hands with a well-known prize-fighter that it occurred to me to broach the subject of His Grace. To make a long story short, sir, I have arranged, subject to your approval, that the entire convention shall be presented to His Grace tomorrow afternoon.'

I was amazed.

'Eighty-seven, Jeeves! At how much a head?'

'I was obliged to agree to a reduction for quantity, sir. The terms finally arrived at were one hundred and fifty dollars for the party.'

I thought a bit.

'Payable in advance?'

'No, sir. I endeavoured to obtain payment in advance, but was not successful.'

'Well, anyway, when we get it I'll make it up to five hundred. Bicky'll never know. Do you suppose Mr Bickersteth would suspect anything, Jeeves, if I made it up to five hundred?'

'I fancy not, sir. Mr Bickersteth is an agreeable gentleman, but not bright.'

'All right, then. After breakfast run down to the bank and get me some money.'

'Yes, sir.'

'You know, you're a bit of a marvel, Jeeves.'

'Thank you, sir.'

'Right ho!'

'Very good, sir.'

When I took dear old Bicky aside in the course of the morning and told him what had happened he nearly broke down. He tottered into the sitting-room and buttonholed old Chiswick, who was reading the comic section of the morning paper with a kind of grim resolution.

'Uncle,' he said, 'are you doing anything special tomorrow afternoon? I mean to say, I've asked a few of my pals in to meet you, don't you know.'

The old boy cocked a speculative eye at him.

'There will be no reporters among them?'

'Reporters? Rather not. Why?'

'I refuse to be badgered by reporters. There were a number of adhesive young men who endeavoured to elicit from me my views on America while the boat was approaching the dock. I will not be subjected to this persecution again.'

'That'll be absolutely all right, uncle. There won't be a newspaper man in the place.'

'In that case I shall be glad to make the acquaintance of your friends.'

'You'll shake hands with them, and so forth?'

'I shall naturally order my behaviour according to the accepted rules of civilized intercourse.'

Bicky thanked him heartily and came off to lunch with me at the club, where he babbled freely of hens, incubators, and other rotten things.

After mature consideration we had decided to unleash the Birdsburg contingent on the old boy ten at a time. Jeeves brought his theatre pal round to see us, and we arranged the whole thing with him. A very decent chappie, but rather inclined to collar the conversation and turn it in the direction of his home-town's new water-supply system. We settled that, as an hour was about all he would be likely to stand, each gang should consider itself entitled to seven minutes of the duke's society by Jeeves's stop-watch, and that when their time was up Jeeves should slide into the room and cough meaningly. Then we parted with what I believe are called mutual expressions of goodwill, the Birdsburg chappie extending a cordial invitation to us all to pop out some day and take a look at the new water-supply system, for which we thanked him.

Next day the deputation rolled in. The first shift consisted of the cove we had met and nine others almost exactly like him in every respect. They all looked deuced keen and business-like, as if from youth up they had been working in the office and catching the boss's eye and what not. They shook hands with the old boy with a good deal of apparent satisfaction – all except one chappie, who seemed to be brooding about something – and then they stood off and became chatty.

'What message have you for Birdsburg, duke?' asked our pal.

The old boy seemed a bit rattled.

'I have never been to Birdsburg.'

The chappie seemed pained.

'You should pay it a visit,' he said. 'The most rapidly growing city in the country. Boost for Birdsburg!'

'Boost for Birdsburg!' said the other chappies reverently.

The chappie who had been brooding suddenly gave tongue.

'Say!'

He was a stout sort of well-fed cove with one of those determined chins and a cold eye.

The assemblage looked at him.

'As a matter of business,' said the chappie – 'mind you, I'm not questioning anybody's good faith, but, as a matter of strict business – I think this gentleman here ought to put himself on record before witnesses as stating that he really is a duke.'

'What do you mean, sir?' cried the old boy, getting purple.

'No offence, simply business. I'm not saying anything, mind you, but there's one thing that seems kind of funny to me. This gentleman here says his name's Mr Bickersteth, as I understand it. Well, if you're the Duke of Chiswick, why isn't he Lord Percy Something? I've read English novels, and I know all about it.'

'This is monstrous!'

'Now don't get hot under the collar. I'm only asking. I've a right to know. You're going to take our money, so it's only fair that we should see that we get our money's worth.'

The water-supply cove chipped in:

'You're quite right, Simms. I overlooked that when making the agreement. You see, gentlemen, as business men we've a right to reasonable guarantees of good faith. We are paying Mr Bickersteth here a hundred and fifty dollars for this reception, and we naturally want to know –'

Old Chiswick gave Bicky a searching look; then he turned to the water-supply chappie. He was frightfully calm.

'I can assure you that I know nothing of this,' he said quite politely. 'I should be grateful if you would explain.'

'Well, we arranged with Mr Bickersteth that eighty-seven citizens of Birdsburg should have the privilege of meeting and shaking hands with you for a financial consideration mutually arranged, and what my friend Simms here means – and I'm with him – is that we have only Mr Bickersteth's word for it – and he is a stranger to us – that you are the Duke of Chiswick at all.'

Old Chiswick gulped.

'Allow me to assure you, sir,' he said in a rummy kind of voice, 'that I am the Duke of Chiswick.'

'Then that's all right,' said the chappie heartily. 'That was all we wanted to know. Let the thing go on.'

'I am sorry to say,' said old Chiswick, 'that it cannot go on. I am feeling a little tired. I fear I must ask to be excused.'

'But there are seventy-seven of the boys waiting round the corner at this moment, duke, to be introduced to you.'

'I fear I must disappoint them.'

'But in that case the deal would have to be off.'

'That is a matter for you and my nephew to discuss.'

The chappie seemed troubled.

'You really won't meet the rest of them?'

'No!'

'Well, then, I guess we'll be going.'

They went out, and there was a pretty solid silence. Then old Chiswick turned to Bicky:

'Well?'

Bicky didn't seem to have anything to say.

'Was it true what that man said?'

'Yes, uncle.'

'What do you mean by playing this trick?'

Bicky seemed pretty well knocked out, so I put in a word: 'I think you'd better explain the whole thing, Bicky, old top.'

Bicky's adam's apple jumped about a bit; then he started.

'You see, you had cut off my allowance, uncle, and I wanted a bit of money to start a chicken farm. I mean to say it's an absolute cert if you once get a bit of capital. You buy a hen, and it lays an egg every day of the week, and you sell the egg, say, seven for twenty-five cents. Keep of hen costs nothing. Profit practically –'

'What is all this nonsense about hens? You led me to suppose you were a substantial business man.'

'Old Bicky rather exaggerated, sir,' I said, helping the chappie out. 'The fact is, the poor old lad is absolutely dependent on that remittance of yours, and when you cut it off, don't you know, he was pretty solidly in the soup, and had to think of some way of closing in on a bit of the ready pretty quick. That's why we thought of this hand-shaking scheme.'

Old Chiswick foamed at the mouth.

'So you have lied to me! You have deliberately deceived me as to your financial status!'

'Poor old Bicky didn't want to go to that ranch,' I explained. 'He doesn't like cows and horses, but he rather thinks he would be hot stuff among the hens. All he wants is a bit of capital. Don't you think it would be rather a wheeze if you were to –'

'After what has happened? After this – this deceit and foolery? Not a penny!'

'But –'

'Not a penny!'

There was a respectful cough in the background.

'If I might make a suggestion, sir?'

Jeeves was standing on the horizon, looking devilish brainy.

'Go ahead, Jeeves!' I said.

'I would merely suggest, sir, that if Mr Bickersteth is in need of a little ready money, and is at a loss to obtain it elsewhere he might secure the sum he requires by describing the occurrences of this afternoon for the Sunday issue of one of the more spirited and enterprising newspapers.'

'By Jove!' I said.

'By George!' said Bicky.

'Great heavens!' said old Chiswick.

'Very good, sir,' said Jeeves.

Bicky turned to old Chiswick with a gleaming eye.

'Jeeves is right! I'll do it! The *Chronicle* would jump at it. They eat that sort of stuff.'

Old Chiswick gave a kind of moaning howl.

'I absolutely forbid you, Francis, to do this thing!'

'That's all very well,' said Bicky, wonderfully braced, 'but if I can't get the money any other way –'

'Wait! Er – wait, my boy! You are so impetuous! We might arrange something.'

'I won't go to that bally ranch.'

'No, no! No, no, my boy! I would not suggest it. I would not for a moment suggest it. I – I think –' He seemed to have a bit of a struggle with himself. 'I – I think that, on the whole it would be best if you returned with me to England. I – I might – in fact, I think I see my way to doing – to – I might be able to utilize your services in some secretarial position.'

'I shouldn't mind that.'

'I should not be able to offer you a salary, but, as you know, in English political life the unpaid secretary is a recognized figure –'

'The only figure I'll recognize,' said Bicky firmly, 'is five hundred quid a year, paid quarterly.'

'My dear boy!'

'Absolutely!'

'But your recompense, my dear Francis, would consist

88

in the unrivalled opportunities you would have, as my secretary, to gain experience, to accustom yourself to the intricacies of political life, to – in fact, you would be in an exceedingly advantageous position.'

'Five hundred a year!' said Bicky, rolling it round his tongue. 'Why, that would be nothing to what I could make if I started a chicken farm. It stands to reason. Suppose you have a dozen hens. Each of the hens has a dozen chickens. After a bit the chickens grow up and have a dozen chickens each themselves, and then they all start laying eggs! There's a fortune in it. You can get anything you like for eggs in America. Fellows keep them on ice for years and years, and don't sell them till they fetch about a dollar a whirl. You don't think I'm going to chuck a future like this for anything under five hundred o' goblins a year – what?'

A look of anguish passed over old Chiswick's face, then he seemed to be resigned to it. 'Very well, my boy,' he said.

'What ho!' said Bicky. 'All right, then.'

'Jeeves,' I said. Bicky had taken the old boy off to dinner to celebrate, and we were alone. 'Jeeves, this has been one of your best efforts.'

'Thank you, sir.'

'It beats me how you do it.'

'Yes, sir?'

'The only trouble is you haven't got much out of it yourself.'

'I fancy Mr Bickersteth intends – I judge from his remarks – to signify his appreciation of anything I have been fortunate enough to do to assist him, at some later date when he is in a more favourable position to do so.'

'It isn't enough, Jeeves!'

'Sir?'

It was a wrench, but I felt it was the only possible thing to be done.

'Bring my shaving things.'

A gleam of hope shone in the man's eye, mixed with doubt.

'You mean, sir?'

'And shave off my moustache.'

There was a moment's silence. I could see the fellow was deeply moved.

'Thank you very much indeed, sir,' he said, in a low voice.

5 — The Aunt and the Sluggard

Now that it's all over, I may as well admit that there
was a time during the affair of Rockmetteller Todd when
I thought that Jeeves was going to let me down. Silly of
me, of course, knowing him as I do, but that is what I
thought. It seemed to me that the man had the
appearance of being baffled.

The Rocky Todd business broke loose early one
morning in spring. I was in bed, restoring the physique
with my usual nine hours of the dreamless, when the
door flew open and somebody prodded me in the lower
ribs and began to shake the bedclothes in an unpleasant
manner. And after blinking a bit and generally pulling
myself together, I located Rocky, and my first
impression was that it must be some horrid dream.

Rocky, you see, lived down on Long Island
somewhere, miles away from New York; and not only
that, but he had told me himself more than once that he
never got up before twelve, and seldom earlier than one.
Constitutionally the laziest young devil in America, he
had hit on a walk in life which enabled him to go the
limit in that direction. He was a poet. At least, he wrote
poems when he did anything; but most of his time, as far
as I could make out, he spent in a sort of trance. He told
me once that he could sit on a fence, watching a worm
and wondering what on earth it was up to for hours at a
stretch.

He had his scheme of life worked out to a fine point.
About once a month he would take three days writing a
few poems; the other three hundred and twenty-nine
days of the year he rested. I didn't know there was

enough money in poetry to support a chappie, even in
the way in which Rocky lived; but it seems that, if you
stick to exhortations to young men to lead the strenuous
life and don't shove in any rhymes, American editors
fight for the stuff. Rocky showed me one of his things
once. It began:

Be!
Be!
    The past is dead,
    Tomorrow is not born.
    Be today!
Today!
    Be with every nerve,
    With every fibre,
    With every drop of your red blood!
Be!
Be!

There were three more verses, and the thing was
printed opposite the frontispiece of a magazine with a
sort of scroll round it, and a picture in the middle of a
fairly nude chappie with bulging muscles giving the
rising sun the glad eye. Rocky said they gave him a
hundred dollars for it, and he stayed in bed till four in
the afternoon for over a month.

As regarded the future he was pretty solid, owing to
the fact that he had a moneyed aunt tucked away
somewhere in Illinois. It's a curious thing how many of
my pals seem to have aunts and uncles who are their
main source of supply. There is Bicky for one, with his
uncle the Duke of Chiswick; Corky, who, until things
went wrong, looked to Alexander Worple, the bird
specialist, for sustenance. And I shall be telling you a
story shortly of a dear old friend of mine, Oliver
Sipperley, who had an aunt in Yorkshire. These things
cannot be mere coincidence. They must be meant. What

I'm driving at is that Providence seems to look after the chumps of this world; and, personally, I'm all for it. I suppose the fact is that, having been snootered from infancy upwards by my own aunts, I like to see that it is possible for these relatives to have a better and a softer side.

However, this is more or less of a side-track. Coming back to Rocky, what I was saying was that he had this aunt in Illinois; and, as he had been named Rockmetteller after her (which in itself, you might say, entitled him to substantial compensation) and was her only nephew, his position looked pretty sound. He told me that when he did come into the money he meant to do no work at all, except perhaps an occasional poem recommending the young man with life opening out before him with all its splendid possibilities to light a pipe and shove his feet up on the mantelpiece.

And this was the man who was prodding me in the ribs in the grey dawn!

'Read this, Bertie!' babbled old Rocky.

I could just see that he was waving a letter or something equally foul in my face. 'Wake up and read this!'

I can't read before I've had my morning tea and a cigarette. I groped for the bell.

Jeeves came in, looking as fresh as a dewy violet. It's a mystery to me how he does it.

'Tea, Jeeves.'

'Very good, sir.'

I found that Rocky was surging round with his beastly letter again.

'What is it?' I said. 'What on earth's the matter?'

'Read it!'

'I can't. I haven't had my tea.'

'Well, listen then.'

'Who's it from?'

'My aunt.'

At this point I fell asleep again. I woke to hear him saying:

'So what on earth am I to do?'

Jeeves flowed in with the tray, like some silent stream meandering over its mossy bed; and I saw daylight.

'Read it again, Rocky, old top,' I said. 'I want Jeeves to hear it. Mr Todd's aunt has written him a rather rummy letter, Jeeves, and we want your advice.'

'Very good, sir.'

He stood in the middle of the room, registering devotion to the cause, and Rocky started again:

'My dear Rockmetteller,

'I have been thinking things over for a long while, and I have come to the conclusion that I have been very thoughtless to wait so long before doing what I am made up my mind to do now.'

'What do you make of that, Jeeves?'

'It seems a little obscure at present, sir, but no doubt it becomes clearer at a later point in the communication.'

'Proceed, old scout,' I said, champing my bread and butter.

'You know how all my life I have longed to visit New York and see for myself the wonderful gay life of which I have read so much. I fear that now it will be impossible for me to fulfil my dream. I am old and worn out. I seem to have no strength left in me.'

'Sad, Jeeves, what?'

'Extremely, sir.'

'Sad nothing!' said Rocky. 'It's sheer laziness. I went to see her last Christmas and she was bursting with health. Her doctor told me himself that there was nothing wrong with her whatever. But she will insist that she's a hopeless invalid, so he has to agree with her.

She's got a fixed idea that the trip to New York would kill her; so, though it's been her ambition all her life to come here, she stays where she is.'

'Rather like the chappie whose heart, was "in the Highlands a-chasing of the deer", Jeeves?'

'The cases are in some respects parallel, sir.'

'Carry on, Rocky, dear boy.'

'So I have decided that, if I cannot enjoy all the marvels of the city myself, I can at least enjoy them through you. I suddenly thought of this yesterday after reading a beautiful poem in the Sunday paper about a young man who had longed all his life for a certain thing and won it in the end only when he was too old to enjoy it. It was very sad, and it touched me.'

'A thing,' interpolated Rocky bitterly, 'that I've not been able to do in ten years.'

'As you know, you will have my money when I am gone; but until now I have never been able to see my way to giving you an allowance. I have now decided to do so – on one condition. I have written to a firm of lawyers in New York, giving them instructions to pay you quite a substantial sum each month. My one condition is that you live in New York and enjoy yourself as I have always wished to do. I want you to be my representative, to spend this money for me as I should do myself. I want you to plunge into the gay, prismatic life of New York. I want you to be the life and soul of brilliant supper parties.

'Above all, I want you – indeed, I insist on this – to write me letters at least once a week, giving me a full description of all you are doing and all that is going on in the city, so that I may enjoy at second-hand what my wretched health prevents my enjoying for

myself. Remember that I shall expect full details, and
that no detail is too trivial to interest.
Your affectionate Aunt,
Isabel Rockmetteller.'

'What about it?' said Rocky.
'What about it?' I said.
'Yes. What on earth am I going to do?'
It was only then that I really got on to the extremely
rummy attitude of the chappie, in view of the fact that a
quite unexpected mess of good cash had suddenly
descended on him from a blue sky. To my mind it was
an occasion for the beaming smile and the joyous
whoop; yet here the man was, looking and talking as if
Fate had swung on his solar plexus. It amazed me.
'Aren't you bucked?' I said.
'Bucked!'
'If I were in your place I should be frightfully braced. I
consider this pretty soft for you.'
He gave a kind of yelp, stared at me for a moment, and
then began to talk of New York in a way that reminded
me of Jimmy Mundy, the reformer bloke. Jimmy had
just come to New York on a hit-the-trail campaign, and I
had popped in at Madison Square Garden a couple of
days before, for half an hour or so, to hear him. He had
certainly told New York some pretty straight things
about itself, having apparently taken a dislike to the
place, but, by Jove, you know, dear old Rocky made him
look like a publicity agent for the old metrop!
'Pretty soft!' he cried. 'To have to come and live in
New York! To have to leave my little cottage and take a
stuffy, smelly, over-heated hole of an apartment in this
Heaven-forsaken, festering Gehenna. To have to mix
night after night with a mob who think that life is a sort
of St Vitus's dance, and imagine that they're having a
good time because they're making enough noise for six
and drinking too much for ten. I loathe New York,

Bertie. I wouldn't come near the place if I hadn't got to see editors occasionally. There's a blight on it. It's got moral delirium tremens. It's the limit. The very thought of staying more than a day in it makes me sick. And you call this thing pretty soft for me!'

I felt rather like Lot's friends must have done when they dropped in for a quiet chat and their genial host began to criticize the Cities of the Plain. I had no idea old Rocky could be so eloquent.

'It would kill me to have to live in New York,' he went on. 'To have to share the air with six million people! To have to wear stiff collars and decent clothes all the time! To –' He started. 'Good Lord! I suppose I should have to dress for dinner in the evenings. What a ghastly notion!'

I was shocked, absolutely shocked.

'My dear chap!' I said, reproachfully.

'Do you dress for dinner every night, Bertie?'

'Jeeves,' I said coldly. 'How many suits of evening clothes have we?'

'We have three suits of full evening dress, sir; two dinner jackets –'

'Three.'

'For practical purposes two only, sir. If you remember, we cannot wear the third. We have also seven white waistcoats,'

'And shirts?'

'Four dozen, sir.'

'And white ties?'

'The first two shallow shelves in the chest of drawers are completely filled with our white ties, sir.'

I turned to Rocky.

'You see?'

The chappie writhed like an electric fan.

'I won't do it! I can't do it! I'll be hanged if I'll do it! How on earth can I dress up like that? Do you realize that most days I don't get out of my pyjamas till five in the afternoon, and then I just put on an old sweater?'

I saw Jeeves wince, poor chap. This sort of revelation shocked his finest feelings.

'Then, what are you going to do about it?' I said.

'That's what I want to know.'

'You might write and explain to your aunt.'

'I might – if I wanted her to get round to her lawyer's in two rapid leaps and cut me out of her will.'

I saw his point.

'What do you suggest, Jeeves?' I said.

Jeeves cleared his throat respectfully.

'The crux of the matter would appear to be, sir, that Mr Todd is obliged by the conditions under which the money is delivered into his possession to write Miss Rockmetteller long and detailed letters relating to his movements, and the only method by which this can be accomplished, if Mr Todd adheres to his expressed intention of remaining in the country, is for Mr Todd to induce some second party to gather the actual experiences which Miss Rockmetteller wishes reported to her, and to convey these to him in the shape of a careful report, on which it would be possible for him, with the aid of his imagination, to base the suggested correspondence.'

Having got which off the old diaphragm, Jeeves was silent. Rocky looked at me in a helpless sort of way. He hasn't been brought up on Jeeves as I have, and he isn't on to his curves.

'Could he put it a little clearer, Bertie?' he said. 'I thought at the start it was going to make sense, but it kind of flickered. What's the idea?'

'My dear old man, perfectly simple. I knew we could stand on Jeeves. All you've got to do is to get somebody to go round the town for you and take a few notes, and then you work the notes up into letters. That's it, isn't it, Jeeves?'

'Precisely, sir.'

The light of hope gleamed in Rocky's eyes. He looked

at Jeeves in a startled way, dazed by the man's vast intellect.

'But who would do it?' he said. 'It would have to be a pretty smart sort of man, a man who would notice things.'

'Jeeves!' I said. 'Let Jeeves do it.'

'But would he?'

'You would do it, wouldn't you, Jeeves?'

For the first time in our long connexion I observed Jeeves almost smile. The corner of his mouth curved quite a quarter of an inch, and for a moment his eye ceased to look like a meditative fish's.

'I should be delighted to oblige, sir. As a matter of fact, I have already visited some of New York's places of interest on my evening out, and it would be most enjoyable to make a practice of the pursuit.'

'Fine! I know exactly what your aunt wants to hear about, Rocky. She wants an earful of cabaret stuff. The place you ought to go to first, Jeeves, is Reigelheimer's. It's on Forty-second Street. Anybody will show you the way.'

Jeeves shook his head.

'Pardon me, sir. People are no longer going to Reigel-heimer's. The place at the moment is Frolics on the Roof.'

'You see?' I said to Rocky. 'Leave it to Jeeves. He knows.'

It isn't often that you find an entire group of your fellow-humans happy in this world; but our little circle was certainly an example of the fact that it can be done. We were all full of beans. Everything went absolutely right from the start.

Jeeves was happy, partly because he loves to exercise his giant brain, and partly because he was having a corking time among the bright lights. I saw him one night at the Midnight Revels. He was sitting at a table on the edge of the dancing floor, doing himself remarkably well with a fat cigar. His face wore an expression of austere benevolence, and he was making notes in a small book.

As for the rest of us, I was feeling pretty good, because I was fond of old Rocky and glad to be able to do him a good turn. Rocky was perfectly contented, because he was still able to sit on fences in his pyjamas and watch worms. And, as for the aunt, she seemed tickled to death. She was getting Broadway at pretty long range, but it seemed to be hitting her just right. I read one of her letters to Rocky, and it was full of life.

But then Rocky's letters, based on Jeeves's notes, were enough to buck anybody up. It was rummy when you came to think of it. There was I, loving the life, while the mere mention of it gave Rocky a tired feeling; yet here is a letter I wrote home to a pal of mine in London:

Dear Freddie,
    Well, here I am in New York. It's not a bad place. I'm not having a bad time. Everything's not bad. The cabarets aren't bad. Don't know when I shall be back. How's everybody? Cheerio!
Yours,
Bertie.
P.S. – Seen old Ted lately?

Not that I cared about old Ted; but if I hadn't dragged him in I couldn't have got the confounded thing on to the second page.

Now here's old Rocky on exactly the same subject:

Dearest Aunt Isabel,
    How can I ever thank you enough for giving me the opportunity to live in this astounding city! New York seems more wonderful every day.
    Fifth Avenue is at its best, of course, just now. The dresses are magnificent!

Wads of stuff about the dresses. I didn't know Jeeves was such an authority.

I was out with some of the crowd at the Midnight Revels the other night. We took in a show first, after a little dinner at a new place on Forty-third Street. We were quite a gay party. Georgie Cohan looked in about midnight and got off a good story about Willie Collier. Fred Stone could only stay a minute, but Doug. Fairbanks did all sorts of stunts and made us roar. Ed Wynn was there, and Laurette Taylor showed up with a party. The show at the Revels is quite good. I am enclosing a programme.

Last night a few of us went round to Frolics on the Roof –

And so on and so forth, yards of it. I suppose it's the artistic temperament or something. What I mean is, it's easier for a chappie who's used to writing poems and that sort of tosh to put a bit of a punch into a letter than it is for a fellow like me. Anyway, there's no doubt that Rocky's correspondence was hot stuff. I called Jeeves in and congratulated him.

'Jeeves, you're a wonder!'

'Thank you, sir.'

'How you notice everything at these places beats me. I couldn't tell you a thing about them, except that I've had a good time.'

'It's just a knack, sir.'

'Well, Mr Todd's letters ought to brace Miss Rockmetteller all right, what?'

'Undoubtedly, sir,' agreed Jeeves.

And, by Jove, they did! They certainly did, by George! What I mean to say is, I was sitting in the apartment one afternoon, about a month after the thing had started, smoking a cigarette and resting the old bean, when the door opened and the voice of Jeeves burst the silence like a bomb.

It wasn't that he spoke loud. He has one of those soft, soothing voices that slide through the atmosphere like the note of a far-off sheep. It was what he said that made me leap like a young gazelle.

'Miss Rockmetteller!'

And in came a large, solid female.

The situation floored me. I'm not denying it. Hamlet must have felt much as I did when his father's ghost bobbed up in the fairway. I'd come to look on Rocky's aunt as such a permanency at her own home that it didn't seem possible that she could really be here in New York. I stared at her. Then I looked at Jeeves. He was standing there in an attitude of dignified detachment, the chump, when, if ever he should have been rallying round the young master, it was now.

Rocky's aunt looked less like an invalid than anyone I've ever seen, except my Aunt Agatha. She had a good deal of Aunt Agatha about her, as a matter of fact. She looked as if she might be deucedly dangerous if put upon; and something seemed to tell me that she would certainly regard herself as put upon if she ever found out the game which poor old Rocky had been pulling on her.

'Good afternoon,' I managed to say.

'How do you do?' she said. 'Mr Cohan?'

'Er-no.'

'Mr Fred Stone?'

'Not absolutely. As a matter of fact, my name's Wooster – Bertie Wooster.'

She seemed disappointed. The fine old name of Wooster appeared to mean nothing in her life.

'Isn't Rockmetteller home?' she said. 'Where is he?'

She had me with the first shot. I couldn't think of anything to say. I couldn't tell her that Rocky was down in the country, watching worms.

There was the faintest flutter of sound in the

background. It was the respectful cough with which Jeeves announces that he is about to speak without having been spoken to.

'If you remember, sir, Mr Todd went out in the automobile with a party earlier in the afternoon.'

'So he did, Jeeves; so he did,' I said, looking at my watch. 'Did he say when he would be back?'

'He gave me to understand, sir, that he would be somewhat late in returning.'

He vanished; and the aunt took the chair which I'd forgotten to offer her. She looked at me in rather a rummy way. It was a nasty look. It made me feel as if I were something the dog had brought in and intended to bury later on, when he had time. My own Aunt Agatha, back in England, has looked at me in exactly the same way many a time, and it never fails to make my spine curl.

'You seem very much at home here, young man. Are you a great friend of Rockmetteller's?'

'Oh, yes, rather!'

She frowned as if she had expected better things of old Rocky.

'Well, you need to be,' she said, 'the way you treat his flat as your own!'

I give you my word, this quite unforeseen slam simply robbed me of the power of speech. I'd been looking on myself in the light of the dashing host, and suddenly to be treated as an intruder jarred me. It wasn't, mark you, as if she had spoken in a way to suggest that she considered my presence in the place as an ordinary social call. She obviously looked on me as a cross between a burglar and the plumber's man come to fix the leak in the bathroom. It hurt her – my being there.

At this juncture, with the conversation showing every sign of being about to die in awful agonies, an idea came to me. Tea – the good old stand-by.

'Would you care for a cup of tea?' I said.

'Tea?'

She spoke as if she had never heard of the stuff.

'Nothing like a cup after a journey,' I said. 'Bucks you up! Puts a bit of zip into you. What I mean is, restores you, and so on, don't you know. I'll go and tell Jeeves.'

I tottered down the passage to Jeeves's lair. The man was reading the evening paper as if he hadn't a care in the world.

'Jeeves,' I said, 'we want some tea.'

'Very good, sir.'

'I say, Jeeves, this is a bit thick, what?'

I wanted sympathy, don't you know – sympathy and kindness. The old nerve centres had had the deuce of a shock.

'She's got the idea this place belongs to Mr Todd. What on earth put that into her head?'

Jeeves filled the kettle with a restrained dignity.

'No doubt because of Mr Todd's letters, sir,' he said. 'It was my suggestion, sir, if you remember, that they should be addressed from this apartment in order that Mr Todd should appear to possess a good central residence in the city.'

I remembered. We had thought it a brainy scheme at the time.

'Well, it's dashed awkward, you know, Jeeves. She looks on me as an intruder. By Jove! I suppose she thinks I'm someone who hangs about here, touching Mr Todd for free meals and borrowing his shirts.'

'Extremely probable, sir.'

'It's pretty rotten you know.'

'Most disturbing, sir.'

'And there's another thing: What are we to do about Mr Todd? We've got to get him up here as soon as ever we can. When you have brought the tea you had better go out and send him a telegram, telling him to come up by the next train.'

'I have already done so, sir. I took the liberty of writing the message and dispatching it by the lift attendant.'

'By Jove, you think of everything, Jeeves!'

'Thank you, sir. A little buttered toast with the tea? Just so, sir. Thank you.'

I went back to the sitting-room. She hadn't moved an inch. She was still bolt upright on the edge of her chair, gripping her umbrella like a hammer-thrower. She gave me another of those looks as I came in. There was no doubt about it; for some reason she had taken a dislike to me. I suppose because I wasn't George M. Cohan. It was a bit hard on a chap.

'This is a surprise, what?' I said, after about five minutes' restful silence, trying to crank the conversation up again.

'What is a surprise?'

'Your coming here, don't you know, and so on.'

She raised her eyebrows and drank me in a bit more through her glasses.

'Why is it surprising that I should visit my only nephew?' she said.

'Oh, rather,' I said. 'Of course! Certainly. What I mean is –'

Jeeves projected himself into the room with the tea. I was jolly glad to see him. There's nothing like having a bit of business arranged for one when one isn't certain of one's lines. With the teapot to fool about with I felt happier.

'Tea, tea, tea – what! What!' I said.

It wasn't what I had meant to say. My idea had been to be a good deal more formal, and so on. Still, it covered the situation. I poured her out a cup. She sipped it and put the cup down with a shudder.

'Do you mean to say, young man,' she said, frostily, 'that you expect me to drink this stuff?'

'Rather! Bucks you up, you know.'

'What do you mean by the expression "Bucks you up"?'

'Well, makes you full of beans, you know. Makes you fizz.'

'I don't understand a word you say. You're English, aren't you?'

I admitted it. She didn't say a word. And she did it in a way that made it worse than if she had spoken for hours. Somehow it was brought home to me that she didn't like Englishmen, and that if she had had to meet an Englishman I was the one she'd have chosen last.

Conversation languished once more after that.

Then I tried again. I was becoming more convinced every moment that you can't make a real lively *salon* with a couple of people, especially if one of them lets it go a word at a time.

'Are you comfortable at your hotel?' I said.

'At which hotel?'

'The hotel you're staying at.'

'I am not staying at an hotel.'

'Stopping with friends – what?'

'I am naturally stopping with my nephew.'

I didn't get it for the moment; then it hit me.

'What! Here?' I gurgled.

'Certainly! Where else should I go?'

The full horror of the situation rolled over me like a wave. I couldn't see what on earth I was to do. I couldn't explain that this wasn't Rocky's flat without giving the poor old chap away hopelessly, because she would then ask me where he did live, and then he would be right in the soup. I was trying to recover from the shock when she spoke again.

'Will you kindly tell my nephew's manservant to prepare my room? I wish to lie down.'

'Your nephew's manservant?'

'The man you call Jeeves. If Rockmetteller has gone for an automobile ride there is no need for you to wait for him. He will naturally wish to be alone with me when he returns.'

I found myself tottering out of the room. The thing was too much for me. I crept into Jeeves's den.

'Jeeves!' I whispered.

'Sir?'

'Mix me a b-and-s, Jeeves. I feel weak.'

'Very good, sir.'

'This is getting thicker every minute, Jeeves.'

'Sir?'

'She thinks you're Mr Todd's man. She thinks the whole place is his, and everything in it. I don't see what you're to do, except stay on and keep it up. We can't say anything or she'll get on to the whole thing, and I don't want to let Mr Todd down. By the way, Jeeves, she wants you to prepare her bed.'

He looked wounded.

'It is hardly my place, sir –'

'I know – I know. But do it as a personal favour to me. If you come to that, it's hardly my place to be flung out of the flat like this and have to go to an hotel, what?'

'Is it your intention to go to an hotel, sir? What will you do for clothes?'

'Good Lord! I hadn't thought of that. Can you put a few things in a bag when she isn't looking, and sneak them down to me at the St Aurea?'

'I will endeavour to do so, sir.'

'Well, I don't think there's anything more, is there? Tell Mr Todd where I am when he gets here.'

'Very good, sir.'

I looked round the place. The moment of parting had come. I felt sad. The whole thing reminded me of one of those melodramas where they drive chappies out of the old homestead into the snow.

'Good-bye, Jeeves,' I said.

'Good-bye, sir.'

And I staggered out.

You know, I rather think I agree with those poet-and-philosopher Johnnies who insist that a fellow ought to be devilish pleased if he has a bit of trouble. All that stuff about being refined by suffering, you know. Suffering does give a chap a sort of broader and more sympathetic outlook. It helps you to understand other people's misfortunes if you've been through the same thing yourself.

As I stood in my lonely bedroom at the hotel, trying to tie my white tie myself, it struck me for the first time that there must be whole squads of chappies in the world who had to get along without a man to look after them. I'd always thought of Jeeves as a kind of natural phenomenon; but, by Jove! of course, when you come to think of it, there must be quite a lot of fellows who have to press their own clothes themselves, and haven't got anybody to bring them tea in the morning, and so on. It was rather a solemn thought, don't you know. I mean to say, ever since then I've been able to appreciate the frightful privations the poor have to stick.

I got dressed somehow. Jeeves hadn't forgotten a thing in his packing. Everything was there, down to the final stud. I'm not sure this didn't make me feel worse. It kind of deepened the pathos. It was like what somebody or other wrote about the touch of a vanished hand.

I had a bit of dinner somewhere and went to a show of some kind; but nothing seemed to make any difference. I simply hadn't the heart to go on to supper anywhere. I just went straight up to bed. I don't know when I've felt so rotten. Somehow I found myself moving about the room softly, as if there had been a death in the family. If I had had anybody to talk to I should have talked in a whisper; in fact, when the telephone-bell rang I answered in such a sad, hushed voice that the fellow at the other end of the wire said 'Hallo!' five times, thinking he hadn't got me.

It was Rocky. The poor old scout was deeply agitated.

'Bertie! Is that you, Bertie? Oh, gosh! I'm having a time!'

'Where are you speaking from?'

'The Midnight Revels. We've been here an hour, and I think we're a fixture for the night. I've told Aunt Isabel I've gone out to call up a friend to join us. She's glued to a chair, with this-is-the-life written all over her, taking it in through the pores. She loves it, and I'm nearly crazy.'

'Tell me all, old top,' I said.

'A little more of this,' he said, 'and I shall sneak quietly off to the river and end it all. Do you mean to say you go through this sort of thing every night, Bertie, and enjoy it? It's simply infernal! I was just snatching a wink of sleep behind the bill of fare just now when about a million yelling girls swooped down, with toy balloons. There are two orchestras here, each trying to see if it can't play louder than the other. I'm a mental and physical wreck. When your telegram arrived I was just lying down for a quiet pipe, with a sense of absolute peace stealing over me. I had to get dressed and sprint two miles to catch the train. It nearly gave me heart-failure; and on top of that I almost got brain fever inventing lies to tell Aunt Isabel. And then I had to cram myself into these confounded evening clothes of yours.'

I gave a sharp wail of agony. It hadn't struck me till then that Rocky was depending on my wardrobe to see him through.

'You'll ruin them!'

'I hope so,' said Rocky in the most unpleasant way. His troubles seemed to have had the worst effect on his character. 'I should like to get back at them somehow; they've given me a bad enough time. They're about three sizes too small, and something's apt to give at any moment. I wish to goodness it would, and give me a chance to breathe. I haven't breathed since half past seven. Thank heaven, Jeeves managed to get out and buy me a collar that fitted, or I should be a strangled corpse by now! It was touch and go till the stud broke. Bertie, this is pure Hades! Aunt Isabel keeps on urging me to dance. How on earth can I dance when I don't know a soul to dance with? And how the deuce could I, even if I knew every girl in the place? It's taking big chances even to move in these trousers. I had to tell her I've hurt my ankle. She keeps asking me when Cohan and Stone are going to turn up; and it's simply a question of time before she discovers that Stone is sitting two tables away. Something's got to be done, Bertie! You've got to think up some way of getting me out of this mess. It was you who got me into it.'

'Me! What do you mean?'

'Well, Jeeves, then. It's all the same. It was you who suggested leaving it to Jeeves. It was those letters I wrote from his notes that did the mischief. I made them too good. My aunt's just been telling me about it. She says she had resigned herself to ending her life where she was, and then my letters began to arrive, describing the joys of New York; and they stimulated her to such an extent that she pulled herself together and made the trip. She seems to think she's had some miraculous kind of faith cure. I tell you I can't stand it, Bertie! It's got to end!'

'Can't Jeeves think of anything?'

'No. He just hangs round, saying: "Most disturbing, sir!" A fat lot of help that is!'

'Well, old lad,' I said, 'after all, it's far worse for me than it is for you. You've got a comfortable home and Jeeves. And you're saving a lot of money.'

'Saving money? What do you mean – saving money?'

'Why, the allowance your aunt was giving you. I suppose she's paying all the expenses now, isn't she?'

'Certainly she is: but she's stopped the allowance. She wrote the lawyers tonight. She says that, now she's in New York, there is no necessity for it to go on, as we shall always be together, and it's simpler for her to look after that end of it. I tell you, Bertie, I've examined the darned cloud with a microscope, and if it's got a silver lining it's some little dissembler!'

'But, Rocky, old top, it's too bally awful! You've no notion of what I'm going through in this beastly hotel, without Jeeves. I must get back to the flat.'

'Don't come near the flat!'

'But it's my own flat.'

'I can't help that. Aunt Isabel doesn't like you. She asked me what you did for a living. And when I told her you didn't do anything she said she thought as much, and that you were a typical specimen of a useless and decaying aristocracy. So if you think you have made a hit, forget it. Now I must be going back, or she'll be coming out here after me. Good-bye.'

Next morning Jeeves came round. It was all so home-like when he floated noiselessly into the room that I nearly broke down.

'Good morning, sir,' he said. 'I have brought a few more of your personal belongings.'

He began to unstrap the suit-case he was carrying.

'Did you have any trouble sneaking them away?'

'It was not easy, sir. I had to watch my chance. Miss Rockmetteller is a remarkably alert lady.'

'You know, Jeeves, say what you like – this *is* a bit thick, isn't it?'

'The situation is certainly one that has never before come under my notice, sir. I have brought the heather-mixture suit, as the climatic conditions are congenial. Tomorrow, if not prevented, I will endeavour to add the brown lounge with the faint green twill.'

'It can't go on – this sort of thing – Jeeves.'

'We must hope for the best, sir.'

'Can't you think of anything to do?'

'I have been giving the matter considerable thought,

sir, but so far without success. I am placing three silk shirts – the dove-coloured, the light blue, and the mauve – in the first long drawer, sir.'

'You don't mean to say you can't think of anything, Jeeves?'

'For the moment, sir, no. You will find a dozen handkerchiefs and the tan socks in the upper drawer on the left.' He strapped the suit-case and put it on a chair. 'A curious lady, Miss Rockmetteller, sir.'

'You understate it, Jeeves.'

He gazed meditatively out of the window.

'In many ways, sir, Miss Rockmetteller reminds me of an aunt of mine who resides in the south-east portion of London. Their temperaments are much alike. My aunt has the same taste for the pleasures of the great city. It is a passion with her to ride in hansom cabs, sir. Whenever the family take their eyes off her she escapes from the house and spends the day riding about in cabs. On several occasions she has broken into the children's savings bank to secure the means to enable her to gratify this desire.'

'I love to have these little chats with you about your female relatives, Jeeves,' I said coldly, for I felt that the man had let me down, and I was fed up with him. 'But I don't see what all this has got to do with my trouble.'

'I beg your pardon, sir. I am leaving a small assortment of our neckties on the mantelpiece, sir, for you to select according to your preference. I should recommend the blue with the red domino pattern, sir.'

Then he streamed imperceptibly towards the door and flowed silently out.

I've often heard that fellows after some great shock or loss have a habit, after they've been on the floor for a while wondering what hit them, of picking themselves up and piecing themselves together, and sort of taking a whirl at beginning a new life. Time, the great healer, and

Nature adjusting itself and so on and so forth. There's a lot in it. I know, because in my own case, after a day or two of what you might call prostration, I began to recover. The frightful loss of Jeeves made any thought of pleasure more or less a mockery, but at least I found that I was able to have a dash at enjoying life again. What I mean is, I braced up to the extent of going round the cabarets once more, so as to try to forget, if only for the moment.

New York's a small place when it comes to the part of it that wakes up just as the rest is going to bed, and it wasn't long before my tracks began to cross old Rocky's. I saw him once at Peale's, and again at Frolics on the Roof. There wasn't anybody with him either time except the aunt, and, though he was trying to look as if he had struck the ideal life, it wasn't difficult for me, knowing the circumstances, to see that beneath the mask the poor chap was suffering. My heart bled for the fellow. At least, what there was of it that wasn't bleeding for myself bled for him. He had the air of one who was about to crack under the strain.

It seemed to me that the aunt was looking slightly upset also. I took it that she was beginning to wonder when the celebrities were going to surge round, and what had suddenly become of all those wild, careless spirits Rocky used to mix with in his letters. I didn't blame her. I had only read a couple of his letters, but they certainly gave the impression that poor old Rocky was by way of being the hub of New York night life, and that, if by any chance he failed to show up at a cabaret, the management said, 'What's the use?' and put up the shutters.

The next two nights I didn't come across them, but the night after that I was sitting by myself at the Maison Pierre when somebody tapped me on the shoulder-blade, and I found Rocky standing beside me, with a sort of mixed expression of wistfulness and apoplexy on his face. How the man had contrived to wear my evening clothes so many times without disaster was a mystery to me. He confided later that early in the proceedings he had slit the waistcoat up the back and that that had helped a lot.

For a moment I had the idea that he had managed to get away from his aunt for the evening; but, looking past him, I saw that she was in again. She was at a table over by the wall, looking at me as if I were something the management ought to be complained to about.

'Bertie, old scout,' said Rocky, in a quiet, sort of crushed voice, 'we've always been pals, haven't we? I mean, you know I'd do you a good turn if you asked me.'

'My dear old lad,' I said. The man had moved me.

'Then, for Heaven's sake, come over and sit at our table for the rest of the evening.'

Well, you know, there are limits to the sacred claims of friendship.

'My dear chap,' I said, 'you know I'd do anything in reason; but –'

'You must come, Bertie. You've got to. Something's got to be done to divert her mind. She's brooding about something. She's been like that for the last two days. I think she's beginning to suspect. She can't understand why we never seem to meet anyone I know at these joints. A few nights ago I happened to run into two newspaper men I used to know fairly well. That kept me going for a while. I introduced them to Aunt Isabel as David Belasco and Jim Corbett, and it went well. But the effect has worn off now, and she's beginning to wonder again. Something's got to be done, or she will find out everything, and if she does I'd take a nickel for my chance of getting a cent from her later on. So, for the love of Mike, come across to our table and help things along.'

I went along. One has to rally round a pal in distress.

Aunt Isabel was sitting bolt upright, as usual. It
certainly did seem as if she had lost a bit of the zest with
which she had started out to explore Broadway. She
looked as if she had been thinking a good deal about
rather unpleasant things.

'You've met Bertie Wooster, Aunt Isabel?' said Rocky.
'I have.'

'Take a seat, Bertie,' said Rocky.

And so the merry party began. It was one of those
jolly, happy, bread-crumbling parties where you cough
twice before you speak, and then decide not to say it
after all. After we had had an hour of this wild
dissipation, Aunt Isabel said she wanted to go home. In
the light of what Rocky had been telling me, this struck
me as sinister. I had gathered that at the beginning of her
visit she had had to be dragged home with ropes.

It must have hit Rocky the same way, for he gave me
a pleading look.

'You'll come along, won't you, Bertie, and have a
drink at the flat?'

I had a feeling that this wasn't in the contract, but
there wasn't anything to be done. It seemed brutal to
leave the poor chap alone with the woman, so I went
along.

Right from the start, from the moment we stepped
into the taxi, the feeling began to grow that something
was about to break loose. A massive silence prevailed in
the corner where the aunt sat, and, though Rocky,
balancing himself on the little seat in front, did his best
to supply dialogue, we weren't a chatty party.

I had a glimpse of Jeeves as we went into the flat,
sitting in his lair, and I wished I could have called to
him to rally round. Something told me that I was about
to need him.

The stuff was on the table in the sitting-room. Rocky
took up the decanter.

'Say when, Bertie.'

'Stop!' barked the aunt, and he dropped it.

I caught Rocky's eye as he stooped to pick up the ruins. It was the eye of one who sees it coming.

'Leave it there, Rockmetteller!' said Aunt Isabel; and Rocky left it there.

'The time has come to speak,' she said. 'I cannot stand idly by and see a young man going to perdition!'

Poor old Rocky gave a sort of gurgle, a kind of sound rather like the whisky had made running out of the decanter on to my carpet.

'Eh?' he said, blinking.

The aunt proceeded.

'The fault,' she said, 'was mine. I had not then seen the light. But now my eyes are open. I see the hideous mistake I have made. I shudder at the thought of the wrong I did you, Rockmetteller, by urging you into contact with this wicked city.'

I saw Rocky grope feebly for the table. His fingers touched it, and a look of relief came into the poor chappie's face. I understood his feelings.

'But when I wrote you that letter, Rockmetteller, instructing you to go to the city and live its life, I had not had the privilege of hearing Mr Mundy speak on the subject of New York.'

'Jimmy Mundy!' I cried.

You know how it is sometimes when everything seems all mixed up and you suddenly get a clue. When she mentioned Jimmy Mundy I began to understand more or less what had happened. I'd seen it happen before. I remember, back in England, the man I had before Jeeves sneaked off to a meeting on his evening out and came back and denounced me in front of a crowd of chappies I was giving a bit of supper to as a useless blot on the fabric of Society.

The aunt gave me a withering up and down.

'Yes, Jimmy Mundy!' she said. 'I am surprised at a man of your stamp having heard of him. There is no

music, there are no drunken, dancing men, no
shameless, flaunting women at his meetings; so for you
they would have no attraction. But for others, less dead
in sin, he has his message. He has come to save New
York from itself; to force it – in his picturesque phrase –
to hit the trail. It was three days ago, Rockmetteller,
that I first heard him. It was an accident that took me to
his meeting. How often in this life a mere accident may
shape our whole future!

'You had been called away by that telephone message
from Mr Belasco; so you could not take me to the
Hippodrome, as we had arranged. I asked your
man-servant, Jeeves, to take me there. The man has very
little intelligence. He seems to have misunderstood me.
I am thankful that he did. He took me to what I
subsequently learned was Madison Square Garden,
where Mr Mundy is holding his meetings. He escorted
me to a seat and then left me. And it was not till the
meeting had begun that I discovered the mistake which
had been made. My seat was in the middle of a row. I
could not leave without inconveniencing a great many
people, so I remained.'

She gulped.

'Rockmetteller, I have never been so thankful for
anything else. Mr Mundy was wonderful! He was like
some prophet of old, scouring the sins of the people. He
leaped about in a frenzy of inspiration till I feared he
would do himself an injury. Sometimes he expressed
himself in a somewhat odd manner, but every word
carried conviction. He showed me New York in its true
colours. He showed me the vanity and wickedness of
sitting in gilded haunts of vice, eating lobster when
decent people should be in bed.

'He said that the tango and the fox-trot were devices
of the devil to drag people down into the Bottomless Pit.
He said that there was more sin in ten minutes with a
negro banjo orchestra than in all the ancient revels of

Nineveh and Babylon. And when he stood on one leg and pointed right at where I was sitting and shouted "This means you!" I could have sunk through the floor. I came away a changed woman. Surely you must have noticed the change in me, Rockmetteller? You must have seen that I was no longer the careless, thoughtless person who had urged you to dance in those places of wickedness?'

Rocky was holding on to the table as if it was his only friend.

'Yes,' he stammered; 'I – I thought something was wrong.'

'Wrong? Something was right! Everything was right! Rockmetteller, it is not too late for you to be saved. You have only sipped of the evil cup. You have not drained it. It will be hard at first, but you will find that you can do it if you fight with a stout heart against the glamour and fascination of this dreadful city. Won't you, for my sake, try, Rockmetteller? Won't you go to the country tomorrow and begin the struggle? Little by little, if you use your will –'

I can't help thinking it must have been that word 'will' that roused dear old Rocky like a trumpet call. It must have brought home to him the realization that a miracle had come off and saved him from being cut out of Aunt Isabel's. At any rate, as she said it he perked up, let go of the table, and faced her with gleaming eyes.

'Do you want me to go to the country, Aunt Isabel?'

'Yes.'

'To live in the country?'

'Yes, Rockmetteller.'

'Stay in the country all the time? Never come to New York?'

'Yes, Rockmetteller; I mean just that. It is the only way. Only there can you be safe from temptation. Will you do it, Rockmetteller? Will you – for my sake?'

Rocky grabbed the table again. He seemed to draw a lot of encouragement from that table.

'I will!' he said.

'Jeeves,' I said. It was next day, and I was back in the old flat, lying in the old armchair, with my feet upon the good old table. I had just come from seeing dear old Rocky off to his country cottage, and an hour before he had seen his aunt off to whatever hamlet it was that she was the curse of; so we were alone at last. 'Jeeves, there's no place like home – what?'

'Very true, sir.'

'The jolly old roof-tree, and all that sort of thing – what?'

'Precisely, sir.'

I lit another cigarette.

'Jeeves.'

'Sir?'

'Do you know, at one point in the business I really thought you were baffled.'

'Indeed, sir?'

'When did you get the idea of taking Miss Rockmetteller to the meeting? It was pure genius!'

'Thank you, sir. It came to me a little suddenly, one morning when I was thinking of my aunt, sir.'

'Your aunt? The hansom cab one?'

'Yes, sir. I recollected that, whenever we observed one of her attacks coming on, we used to send for the clergyman of the parish. We always found that if he talked to her a while of higher things it diverted her mind from hansom cabs. It occurred to me that the same treatment might prove efficacious in the case of Miss Rockmetteller.'

I was stunned by the man's resource.

'It's brain,' I said; 'pure brain! What do you do to get like that, Jeeves? I believe you must eat a lot of fish, or something. Do you eat a lot of fish, Jeeves?'

'No, sir.'

'Oh, well, then, it's just a gift, I take it; and if you aren't born that way there's no use worrying.'

'Precisely, sir,' said Jeeves. 'If I might make the suggestion sir, I should not continue to wear your present tie. The green shade gives you a slightly bilious air. I should strongly advocate the blue with the red domino pattern instead, sir.'

'All right, Jeeves,' I said humbly. 'You know!'

6 — The Rummy Affair of Old Biffy

'Jeeves,' I said, emerging from the old tub, 'rally round.'

'Yes, sir.'

I beamed on the man with no little geniality. I was putting in a week or two in Paris at the moment, and there's something about Paris that always makes me feel fairly full of *espièglerie* and *joie de vivre*.

'Lay out our gent's medium-smart raiment, suitable for Bohemian revels,' I said. 'I am lunching with an artist bloke on the other side of the river.'

'Very good, sir.'

'And if anybody calls for me, Jeeves, say that I shall be back towards the quiet evenfall.'

'Yes, sir. Mr Biffen rang up on the telephone while you were in your bath.'

'Mr Biffen? Good heavens!'

Amazing how one's always running across fellows in foreign cities – coves, I mean, whom you haven't seen for ages and would have betted weren't anywhere in the neighbourhood. Paris was the last place where I should have expected to find old Biffy popping up. There was a time when he and I had been lads about town together, lunching and dining together practically every day; but some eighteen months back his old godmother had died and left him that place in Herefordshire, and he had retired there to wear gaiters and prod cows in the ribs and generally be the country gentleman and landed proprietor. Since then I had hardly seen him.

'Old Biffy in Paris? What's he doing here?'

'He did not confide in me, sir,' said Jeeves – a trifle frostily, I thought. It sounded somehow as if he didn't like Biffy. And yet they had always been matey enough in the old days.

'Where's he staying?'

'At the Hotel Avenida, Rue du Colisée, sir. He informed me that he was about to take a walk and would call this afternoon.'

'Well, if he comes when I'm out, tell him to wait. And now, Jeeves, *mes gants, mon chapeau, et le whangee de monsieur*. I must be popping.'

It was such a corking day and I had so much time in hand that near the Sorbonne I stopped my cab, deciding to walk the rest of the way. And I had hardly gone three steps and a half when there on the pavement before me stood old Biffy in person. If I had completed the last step I should have rammed him.

'Biffy!' I cried. 'Well, well, well!'

He peered at me in a blinking kind of way, rather like one of his Herefordshire cows prodded unexpectedly while lunching.

'Bertie!' he gurgled, in a devout sort of tone. 'Thank God!' He clutched my arm. 'Don't leave me, Bertie. I'm lost.'

'What do you mean, lost?'

'I came out for a walk and suddenly discovered after a mile or two that I didn't know where on earth I was. I've been wandering round in circles for hours.'

'Why didn't you ask the way?'

'I can't speak a word of French.'

'Well, why didn't you call a taxi?'

'I suddenly discovered I'd left all my money at my hotel.'

'You could have taken a cab and paid it when you got to the hotel.'

'Yes, but I suddenly discovered, dash it, that I'd forgotten its name.'

And there in a nutshell you have Charles Edward Biffen. As vague and woollen-headed a blighter as ever bit a sandwich. Goodness knows – and my Aunt Agatha will bear me out in this – I'm no master-mind myself but compared with Biffy I'm one of the great thinkers of all time.

'I'd give a shilling,' said Biffy wistfully, 'to know the name of that hotel.'

'You can owe it me. Hotel Avenida, Rue du Colisée.'

'Bertie! This is uncanny. How the deuce did you know?'

'That was the address you left with Jeeves this morning.'

'So it was. I had forgotten.'

'Well, come along and have a drink and then I'll put you in a cab and send you home. I'm engaged for lunch, but I've plenty of time.'

We drifted to one of the eleven cafés which jostled each other along the street and I ordered restoratives.

'What on earth are you doing in Paris?' I asked.

'Bertie, old man,' said Biffy solemnly, 'I came here to try and forget.'

'Well, you've certainly succeeded.'

'You don't understand. The fact is, Bertie, old lad, my heart is broken. I'll tell you the whole story.'

'No, I say!' I protested. But he was off.

'Last year,' said Biffy, 'I buzzed over to Canada to do a bit of salmon fishing.'

I ordered another. If this was going to be a fish-story, I needed stimulants.

'On the liner going to New York I met a girl.' Biffy made a sort of curious gulping noise not unlike a bulldog trying to swallow half a cutlet in a hurry so as to be ready for the other half. 'Bertie, old man, I can't describe her. I simply can't describe her.'

This was all to the good.

'She was wonderful! We used to walk on the boat-deck after dinner. She was on the stage. At least, sort of.'

'How do you mean, sort of?'

'Well, she had posed for artists and been a mannequin in a big dressmaker's and all that sort of thing, don't you know. Anyway, she had saved up a few pounds and was on her way to see if she could get a job in New York. She told me all about herself. Her father ran a milk-walk in Clapham. Or it may have been Cricklewood. At least, it was either a milk-walk or a boot-shop.'

'Easily confused.'

'What I'm trying to make you understand,' said Biffy, 'is that she came of good, sturdy, respectable middle-class stock. Nothing flashy about her. The sort of wife any man might have been proud of.'

'Well, whose wife was she?'

'Nobody's. That's the whole point of the story. I wanted her to be mine, and I lost her.'

'Had a quarrel, you mean?'

'No, I don't mean we had a quarrel. I mean I literally lost her. The last I ever saw of her was in the Customs sheds at New York. We were behind a pile of trunks, and I had just asked her to be my wife, and she had just said she would and everything was perfectly splendid, when a most offensive blighter in a peaked cap came up to talk about some cigarettes which he had found at the bottom of my trunk and which I had forgotten to declare. It was getting pretty late by then, for we hadn't docked till about ten-thirty, so I told Mabel to go on to her hotel and I would come round next day and take her to lunch. And since then I haven't set eyes on her.'

'You mean she wasn't at the hotel?'

'Probably she was. But –'

'You don't mean you never turned up?'

'Bertie, old man,' said Biffy, in an overwrought kind of way, 'for Heaven's sake don't keep trying to tell me what I mean and what I don't mean! Let me tell this my own way, or I shall get all mixed up and have to go back to the beginning.'

'Tell it your own way,' I said hastily.

'Well, then, to put it in a word, Bertie, I forgot the name of the hotel. By the time I'd done half an hour's heavy explaining about those cigarettes my mind was a blank. I had an idea I had written the name down somewhere, but I couldn't have done, for it wasn't on any of the papers in my pocket. No, it was no good. She was gone.'

'Why didn't you make inquiries?'

'Well, the fact is, Bertie, I had forgotten her name.'

'Oh, no, dash it!' I said. This seemed a bit too thick even for Biffy. 'How could you forget her name? Besides, you told it me a moment ago. Muriel or something.'

'Mabel,' corrected Biffy coldly. 'It was her surname I'd forgotten. So I gave it up and went to Canada.'

'But half a second,' I said. 'You must have told her your name. I mean, if you couldn't trace her, she could trace you.'

'Exactly. That's what makes it all seem so infernally hopeless. She knows my name and where I live and everything, but I haven't heard a word from her. I suppose, when I didn't turn up at the hotel, she took it that that was my way of hinting delicately that I had changed my mind and wanted to call the thing off.'

'I suppose so,' I said. There didn't seem anything else to suppose. 'Well, the only thing to do is to whizz around and try to heal the wound, what? How about dinner tonight, winding up at the Abbaye or one of those places?'

Biffy shook his head.

'It wouldn't be any good. I've tried it. Besides, I'm leaving on the four o'clock train. I have a dinner engagement tomorrow with a man who's nibbling at that house of mine in Herefordshire.'

'Oh, are you trying to sell that place? I thought you liked it.'

'I did. But the idea of going on living in that great, lonely barn of a house after what has happened appals me, Bertie. So when Sir Roderick Glossop came along – '

'Sir Roderick Glossop! You don't mean the loony-doctor?'

'The great nerve specialist, yes. Why, do you know him?'

It was a warm day, but I shivered.

'I was engaged to his daughter for a week or two,' I said, in a hushed voice. The memory of that narrow squeak always made me feel faint.

'Has he a daughter?' said Biffy absently.

'He has. Let me tell you all about – '

'Not just now, old man,' said Biffy, getting up. 'I ought to be going back to my hotel to see about my packing.'

Which, after I had listened to his story, struck me as pretty low-down. However, the longer you live, the more you realize that the good old sporting spirit of give-and-take has practically died out in our midst. So I boosted him into a cab and went off to lunch.

It can't have been more than ten days after this that I received a nasty shock while getting outside my morning tea and toast. The English papers had arrived, and Jeeves was just drifting out of the room after depositing *The Times* by my bedside, when, as I idly turned the pages in search of the sporting section, a paragraph leaped out and hit me squarely in the eyeball.

As follows: –

FORTHCOMING MARRIAGES
MR C. E. BIFFEN AND MISS GLOSSOP

The engagement is announced between Charles Edward, only son of the late Mr E. C. Biffen, and Mrs Biffen, of 11 Penslow Square, Mayfair, and Honoria Jane Louise, only daughter of Sir Roderick and Lady Glossop, of 6b Harley Street, W.

'Great Scott!' I exclaimed.

'Sir?' said Jeeves, turning at the door.

'Jeeves, you remember Miss Glossop?'

'Very vividly, sir.'

'She's engaged to Mr Biffen!'

'Indeed, sir?' said Jeeves. And, with not another word, he slid out. The blighter's calm amazed and shocked me. It seemed to indicate that there must be a horrible streak of callousness in him. I mean to say, it wasn't as if he didn't know Honoria Glossop.

I read the paragraph again. A peculiar feeling it gave me. I don't know if you have ever experienced the sensation of seeing the announcement of the engagement of a pal of yours to a girl whom you were only saved from marrying yourself by the skin of your teeth. It induces a sort of – well, it's difficult to describe it exactly; but I should imagine a fellow would feel much the same if he happened to be strolling through the jungle with a boyhood chum and met a tigress or a jaguar, or what not, and managed to shin up a tree and looked down and saw the friend of his youth vanishing into the undergrowth in the animal's slavering jaws. A sort of profound, prayerful relief, if you know what I mean, blended at the same time with a pang of pity. What I'm driving at is that, thankful as I was that I hadn't had to marry Honoria myself, I was sorry to see a real good chap like old Biffy copping it. I sucked down a spot of tea and began to brood over the business.

Of course, there are probably fellows in the world – tough, hardy blokes with strong chins and glittering eyes – who could get engaged to this Glossop menace and like it, but I knew perfectly well that Biffy was not one of them. Honoria, you see, is one of those robust, dynamic girls with the muscles of a welterweight and a laugh like a squadron of cavalry charging over a tin bridge. A beastly thing to have to face over the breakfast table. Brainy, moreover. The sort of girl who reduces you to pulp with sixteen sets of tennis and a few rounds of golf and then comes down to dinner as fresh as a daisy, expecting you to take an intelligent interest in Freud. If I had been engaged to her another week, her old father would have had one more patient on his books; and Biffy is much the same quiet sort of peaceful, inoffensive bird as me. I was shocked, I tell you, shocked.

And, as I was saying, the thing that shocked me most was Jeeves's frightful lack of proper emotion. The man happening to float in at this juncture, I gave him one more chance to show some human sympathy.

'You got the name correctly, didn't you, Jeeves?' I said. 'Mr Biffen is going to marry Honoria Glossop, the daughter of the old boy with the egg-like head and the eyebrows.'

'Yes, sir. Which suit would you wish me to lay out this morning?'

And this, mark you, from the man who, when I was engaged to the Glossop, strained every fibre in his brain to extricate me. It beat me. I couldn't understand it.

'The blue with the red twill,' I said coldly. My manner was marked, and I meant him to see that he had disappointed me sorely.

About a week later I went back to London, and scarcely had I got settled in the old flat when Biffy blew in. One glance was enough to tell me that the poisoned wound had begun to fester. The man did not look bright. No, there was no getting away from it, not bright. He had that kind of stunned, glassy expression which I used to see on my own face in the shaving-mirror during my brief engagement to the Glossop pestilence. However, if you don't want to be one of the What is Wrong With This Picture brigade, you must observe the conventions, so I shook his hand as warmly as I could.

'Well, well, old man,' I said. 'Congratulations.'

'Thanks,' said Biffy wanly, and there was rather a weighty silence.

'Bertie,' said Biffy, after the silence had lasted about three minutes.

'Hallo?'

'Is it really true – ?'

'What?'

'Oh, nothing,' said Biffy, and conversation languished again. After about a minute and a half he came to the surface once more.

'Bertie.'

'Still here, old thing. What is it?'

'I say, Bertie, is it really true that you were once engaged to Honoria?'

'It is.'

Biffy coughed.

'How did you get out – I mean, what was the nature of the tragedy that prevented the marriage?'

'Jeeves worked it. He thought out the entire scheme.'

'I think, before I go,' said Biffy thoughtfully, 'I'll just step into the kitchen and have a word with Jeeves.'

I felt that the situation called for complete candour.

'Biffy, old egg,' I said, 'as man to man, do you want to oil out of this thing?'

'Bertie, old cork,' said Biffy earnestly, 'as one friend to another, I do.'

'Then why the dickens did you ever get into it?'

'I don't know. Why did you?'

'I – well, it sort of happened.'

'And it sort of happened with me. You know how it is when your heart's broken. A kind of lethargy comes over you. You get absent-minded and cease to exercise proper precautions, and the first thing you know you're for it. I don't know how it happened, old man, but there it is. And what I want you to tell me is, what's the procedure?'

'You mean, how does a fellow edge out?'

Exactly. I don't want to hurt anybody's feelings, Bertie, but I can't go through with this thing. The shot is not on the board. For about a day and a half I thought it might be all right, but now – You remember that laugh of hers?'

'I do.'

'Well, there's that, and then all this business of never letting a fellow alone – improving his mind and so forth –'

'I know. I know.'

'Very well, then. What do you recommend? What did you mean when you said that Jeeves worked a scheme?'

'Well, you see, old Sir Roderick, who's a loony-doctor and nothing but a loony-doctor, however much you may call him a nerve specialist, discovered that there was a modicum of insanity in my family. Nothing serious. Just one of my uncles. Used to keep rabbits in his bedroom. And the old boy came to lunch here to give me the once-over, and Jeeves arranged matters so that he went away firmly convinced that I was off my onion.'

'I see,' said Biffy thoughtfully. 'The trouble is there isn't any insanity in my family.'

'None?'

It seemed to me almost incredible that a fellow could be such a perfect chump as dear old Biffy without a bit of assistance.

'Not a loony on the list,' he said gloomily. 'It's just like my luck. The old boy's coming to lunch with me tomorrow, no doubt to test me as he did you. And I never felt saner in my life.'

I thought for a moment. The idea of meeting Sir Roderick again gave me a cold shivery feeling; but when there is a chance of helping a pal we Woosters have no thought of self.

'Look here, Biffy,' I said, 'I'll tell you what. I'll roll up for that lunch. It may easily happen that when he finds you are a pal of mine he will forbid the banns right away and no more questions asked.'

'Something in that,' said Biffy, brightening. 'Awfully sporting of you, Bertie.'

'Oh, not at all,' I said. 'And meanwhile I'll consult Jeeves. Put the whole thing up to him and ask his advice. He's never failed me yet.'

Biffy pushed off, a good deal braced, and I went into the kitchen.

'Jeeves,' I said, 'I want your help once more. I've just been having a painful interview with Mr Biffen.'

'Indeed, sir?'

'It's like this,' I said, and told him the whole thing.

It was rummy, but I could feel him freezing from the start. As a rule, when I call Jeeves into conference on one of these little problems, he's all sympathy and bright ideas; but not today.

'I fear, sir,' he said, when I had finished, 'it is hardly my place to intervene in a private matter affecting –'

'Oh come!'

'No, sir. It would be taking a liberty.'

'Jeeves,' I said, tackling the blighter squarely, 'what have you got against old Biffy?'

'I, sir?'

'Yes, you.'

'I assure you, sir!'

'Oh, well, if you don't want to chip in and save a fellow-creature, I suppose I can't make you. But let me tell you this. I am now going back to the sitting-room, and I am going to put in some very tense thinking. You'll look pretty silly when I come and tell you that I've got Mr Biffen out of the soup without your assistance. Extremely silly you'll look.'

'Yes, sir. Shall I bring you a whisky-and-soda, sir?'

'No. Coffee! Strong and black. And if anybody wants to see me, tell 'em that I'm busy and can't be disturbed.'

An hour later I rang the bell.

'Jeeves,' I said with hauteur.

'Yes, sir?'

'Kindly ring Mr Biffen up on the phone and say that Mr Wooster presents his compliments and that he has got it.'

I was feeling more than a little pleased with myself next morning as I strolled round to Biffy's. As a rule the bright ideas you get overnight have a trick of not seeming quite so frightfully fruity when you examine them by the light of day; but this one looked as good at breakfast as it had done before dinner. I examined it narrowly from every angle, and I didn't see how it could fail.

A few days before, my Aunt Emily's son Harold had celebrated his sixth birthday; and, being up against the necessity of weighing in with a present of some kind, I had happened to see in a shop in the Strand a rather sprightly little gadget, well calculated in my opinion to amuse the child and endear him to one and all. It was a bunch of flowers in a sort of holder ending in an ingenious bulb attachment which, when pressed, shot about a pint and a half of pure spring water into the face of anyone who was ass enough to sniff at it. It seemed to me just the thing to please the growing mind of a kid of six, and I had rolled round with it.

But when I got to the house I found Harold sitting in the midst of a mass of gifts so luxurious and costly that I simply hadn't the crust to contribute a thing that had set me back a mere elevenpence-ha'penny; so with rare presence of mind – for we Woosters can think quick on occasion – I wrenched my Uncle James's card off a toy aeroplane, substituted my own, and trousered the squirt, which I took away with me. It had been lying around in my flat ever since, and it seemed to me that the time had come to send it into action.

'Well?' said Biffy anxiously, as I curveted into his sitting-room.

The poor old bird was looking pretty green about the

gills. I recognized the symptoms. I had felt much the same myself when waiting for Sir Roderick to turn up and lunch with me. How the deuce people who have anything wrong with their nerves can bring themselves to chat with that man, I can't imagine; and yet he has the largest practice in London. Scarcely a day passes without his having to sit on somebody's head and ring for the attendant to bring the strait-waistcoat; and his outlook on life has become so jaundiced through constant association with coves who are picking straws out of their hair that I was convinced that Biffy had merely got to press the bulb and nature would do the rest.

So I patted him on the shoulder and said: 'It's all right, old man!'

'What does Jeeves suggest?' asked Biffy eagerly.

'Jeeves doesn't suggest anything.'

'But you said it was all right.'

'Jeeves isn't the only thinker in the Wooster home, my lad. I have taken over your little problem, and I can tell you at once that I have the situation well in hand.'

'You?' said Biffy.

His tone was far from flattering. It suggested a lack of faith in my abilities, and my view was that an ounce of demonstration would be worth a ton of explanation. I shoved the bouquet at him.

'Are you fond of flowers, Biffy?' I said.

'Eh?'

'Smell these.'

Biffy extended the old beak in a careworn sort of way, and I pressed the bulb as per printed instructions on the label.

I do like getting my money's-worth. Elevenpence-ha'penny the thing had cost me, and it would have been cheap at double. The advertisement on the outside of the box had said that its effects were 'indescribably ludicrous', and I can testify that it was no overstatement. Poor old Biffy leaped three feet in the air and smashed a small table.

'There!' I said.

The old egg was a trifle incoherent at first, but he found words fairly soon and began to express himself with a good deal of warmth.

'Calm yourself, laddie,' I said, as he paused for breath. 'It was no mere jest to pass an idle hour. It was a demonstration. Take this, Biffy, with an old friend's blessing, refill the bulb, shove it into Sir Roderick's face, press firmly, and leave the rest to him. I'll guarantee that in something under three seconds the idea will have dawned on him that you are not required in his family.'

Biffy stared at me.

'Are you suggesting that I squirt Sir Roderick?'

'Absolutely. Squirt him good. Squirt as you have never squirted before.'

'But –'

He was still yammering at me in a feverish sort of way when there was a ring at the front-door bell.

'Good Lord!' cried Biffy, quivering like a jelly. 'There he is. Talk to him while I go and change my shirt.'

I had just time to refill the bulb and shove it beside Biffy's plate, when the door opened and Sir Roderick came in. I was picking up the fallen table at the moment, and he started talking brightly to my back.

'Good afternoon. I trust I am not – Mr Wooster!'

I'm bound to say I was not feeling entirely at my ease. There is something about the man that is calculated to strike terror into the stoutest heart. If ever there was a bloke at the very mention of whose name it would be excusable for people to tremble like aspens, that bloke is Sir Roderick Glossop. He has an enormous bald head, all the hair which ought to be on it seeming to have run into his eyebrows, and his eyes go through you like a couple of Death Rays.

'How are you, how are you, how are you?' I said,

overcoming a slight desire to leap backwards out of the window. 'Long time since we met, what?'

'Nevertheless, I remember you most distinctly, Mr Wooster.'

'That's fine,' I said. 'Old Biffy asked me to come and join you in mangling a bit of lunch.'

He waggled the eyebrows at me.

'Are you a friend of Charles Biffen?'

'Oh, rather. Been friends for years and years.'

He drew in his breath sharply, and I could see that Biffy's stock had dropped several points. His eye fell on the floor, which was strewn with things that had tumbled off the upset table.

'Have you had an accident?' he said.

'Nothing serious,' I explained. 'Old Biffy had some sort of fit or seizure just now and knocked over the table.'

'A fit!'

'Or seizure.'

'Is he subject to fits?'

I was about to answer, when Biffy hurried in. He had forgotten to brush his hair, which gave him a wild look, and saw the old boy direct a keen glance at him. It seemed to me that what you might call the preliminary spade-work had been most satisfactorily attended to and that the success of the good old bulb could be in no doubt whatever.

Biffy's man came in with the nose-bags and we sat down to lunch.

It looked at first as though the meal was going to be one of those complete frosts which occur from time to time in the career of a constant luncher-out. Biffy, a very C-3 host, contributed nothing to the feast of reason and flow of soul beyond an occasional hiccup, and every time I started to pull a nifty, Sir Roderick swung round on me with such a piercing stare that it stopped me in my tracks. Fortunately, however, the second course consisted of a chicken fricassee of such outstanding excellence that the old boy, after wolfing a plateful, handed up his dinner-pail for a second instalment and became almost genial.

'I am here this afternoon, Charles,' he said, with what practically amounted to bonhomie, 'on what I might describe as a mission. Yes, a mission. This is most excellent chicken.'

'Glad you like it,' mumbled old Biffy.

'Singularly toothsome,' said Sir Roderick, pronging another half ounce. 'Yes, as I was saying, a mission. You young fellows nowadays are, I know, content to live in the centre of the most wonderful metropolis the world has seen, blind and indifferent to its many marvels. I should be prepared – were I a betting man, which I am not – to wager a considerable sum that you have never in your life visited even so historic a spot as Westminster Abbey. Am I right?'

Biffy gurgled something about always having meant to.

'Nor the Tower of London?'

No, nor the Tower of London.

'And there exists at this very moment, not twenty minutes by cab from Hyde Park Corner, the most supremely absorbing and educational collection of objects, both animate and inanimate, gathered from the four corners of the Empire, that has ever been assembled in England's history. I allude to the British Empire Exhibition now situated at Wembley.'

'A fellow told me one about Wembley yesterday,' I said, to help on the cheery flow of conversation. 'Stop me if you've heard it before. Chap goes up to deaf chap outside the exhibition and says, "Is this Wembley?" "Hey?" says deaf chap. "Is this Wembley?" says chap. "Hey?" says deaf chap. "Is this Wembley?" says chap. "No, Thursday," says deaf chap. Ha, ha, I mean, what?'

The merry laughter froze on my lips. Sir Roderick

sort of just waggled an eyebrow in my direction and I saw that it was back to the basket for Bertram. I never met a man who had such a knack of making a fellow feel like a waste-product.

'Have you yet paid a visit to Wembley, Charles?' he asked. 'No? Precisely as I suspected. Well, that is the mission on which I am here this afternoon. Honoria wishes me to take you to Wembley. She says it will broaden your mind, in which view I am at one with her. We will start immediately after luncheon.'

Biffy cast an imploring look at me.

'You'll come too, Bertie?'

There was such agony in his eyes that I only hesitated for a second. A pal is a pal. Besides, I felt that, if only the bulb fulfilled the high expectations I had formed of it, the merry expedition would be cancelled in no uncertain manner.

'Oh, rather,' I said.

'We must not trespass on Mr Wooster's good nature,' said Sir Roderick, looking pretty puff-faced.

'Oh, that's all right,' I said. 'I've been meaning to go to the good old exhibish for a long time. I'll slip home and change my clothes and pick you up here in my car.'

There was a silence. Biffy seemed too relieved at the thought of not having to spend the afternoon alone with Sir Roderick to be capable of speech, and Sir Roderick was registering silent disapproval. And then he caught sight of the bouquet by Biffy's plate.

'Ah, flowers,' he said. 'Sweet peas, if I am not in error. A charming plant, pleasing alike to the eye and the nose.'

I caught Biffy's eye across the table. It was bulging, and a strange light shone in it.

'Are you fond of flowers, Sir Roderick?' he croaked.

'Extremely.'

'Smell these.'

Sir Roderick dipped his head and sniffed. Biffy's

fingers closed slowly over the bulb. I shut my eyes and clutched the table.

'Very pleasant,' I heard Sir Roderick say. 'Very pleasant indeed.'

I opened my eyes, and there was Biffy leaning back in his chair with a ghastly look, and the bouquet on the cloth beside him. I realized what had happened. In that supreme crisis of his life, with his whole happiness depending on a mere pressure of the fingers, Biffy, the poor spineless fish, had lost his nerve. My closely reasoned scheme had gone phut.

Jeeves was fooling about with the geraniums in the sitting-room window-box when I got home.

'They make a very nice display, sir,' he said, cocking a paternal eye at the things.

'Don't talk to me about flowers,' I said. 'Jeeves, I know now how a general feels when he plans out some great scientific movement and his troops let him down at the eleventh hour.'

'Indeed, sir?'

'Yes,' I said, and told him what had happened.

He listened thoughtfully.

'A somewhat vacillating and changeable young gentleman, Mr Biffen,' was his comment when I had finished. 'Would you be requiring me for the remainder of the afternoon, sir?'

'No. I'm going to Wembley. I just came back to change and get the car. Produce some fairly durable garments which can stand getting squashed by the many-headed, Jeeves, and then phone to the garage.'

'Very good, sir. The grey cheviot lounge will, I fancy, be suitable. Would it be too much if I asked you to give me a seat in the car, sir? I had thought of going to Wembley myself this afternoon.'

'Eh? Oh, all right.'

'Thank you very much, sir.'

I got dressed, and we drove round to Biffy's flat. Biffy

and Sir Roderick got in at the back and Jeeves climbed into the front seat next to me. Biffy looked so ill-attuned to an afternoon's pleasure that my heart bled for the blighter and I made one last attempt to appeal to Jeeves's better feelings.

'I must say, Jeeves,' I said, 'I'm dashed disappointed in you.'

'I am sorry to hear that, sir.'

'Well, I am. Dashed disappointed. I do think you might rally round. Did you see Mr Biffen's face?'

'Yes, sir.'

'Well, then.'

'If you will pardon my saying so, sir, Mr Biffen has surely only himself to thank if he has entered upon matrimonial obligations which do not please him.'

'You're talking absolute rot, Jeeves. You know as well as I do that Honoria Glossop is an Act of God. You might just as well blame a fellow for getting run over by a truck.'

'Yes, sir.'

'Absolutely yes. Besides, the poor ass wasn't in a condition to resist. He told me all about it. He had lost the only girl he had ever loved, and you know what a man's like when that happens to him.'

'How was that, sir?'

'Apparently he fell in love with some girl on the boat going over to New York, and they parted at the Customs sheds, arranging to meet next day at her hotel. Well, you know what Biffy's like. He forgets his own name half the time. He never made a note of the address, and it passed clean out of his mind. He went about in a sort of trance, and suddenly woke up to find that he was engaged to Honoria Glossop.'

'I did not know of this, sir.'

'I don't suppose anybody knows of it except me. He told me when I was in Paris.'

'I should have supposed it would have been feasible to make inquiries, sir.'

'That's what I said. But he had forgotten her name.'

'That sounds remarkable, sir.'

'I said that too. But it's a fact. All he remembered was that her Christian name was Mabel. Well, you can't go scouring New York for a girl named Mabel, what?'

'I appreciate the difficulty, sir.'

'Well, there it is, then.'

'I see, sir.'

We had got into a mob of vehicles outside the Exhibition by this time, and, some tricky driving being indicated, I had to suspend the conversation. We parked ourselves eventually and went in. Jeeves drifted away, and Sir Roderick took charge of the expedition. He headed for the Palace of Industry, with Biffy and myself trailing behind.

Well, you know, I have never been much of a lad for exhibitions. The citizenry in the mass always rather puts me off, and after I have been shuffling along with the multitude for a quarter of an hour or so I feel as if I were walking on hot bricks. About this particular binge, too, there seemed to me a lack of what you might call human interest. I mean to say, millions of people, no doubt, are so constituted that they scream with joy and excitement at the spectacle of a stuffed porcupine fish or a glass jar of seeds from Western Australia – but not Bertram. No; if you will take the word of one who would not deceive you, not Bertram. By the time we had tottered out of the Gold Coast village and were working towards the Palace of Machinery, everything pointed to my shortly executing a quiet sneak in the direction of that rather jolly Planters' Bar in the West Indian section. Sir Roderick had whizzed us past this at a high rate of speed, it touching no chord in him; but I had been able to observe that there was a sprightly sportsman behind the counter mixing things out of bottles and stirring them up with a stick in long glasses that seemed to have ice in them, and the urge came upon me to see more of this man. I was about to drop away from the main body and become a straggler, when something pawed at my coat sleeve. It was Biffy, and he had the air of one who has had about sufficient.

There are certain moments in life when words are not needed. I looked at Biffy, Biffy looked at me. A perfect understanding linked our two souls.

'?'

'!'

Three minutes later we had joined the Planters.

I have never been in the West Indies, but I am in a position to state that in certain of the fundamentals of life they are streets ahead of our European civilization. The man behind the counter, as kindly a bloke as I ever wish to meet, seemed to guess our requirements the moment we hove in view. Scarcely had our elbows touched the wood before he was leaping to and fro, bringing down a new bottle with each leap. A planter, apparently, does not consider he has had a drink unless it contains at least seven ingredients, and I'm not saying, mind you, that he isn't right. The man behind the bar told us the things were called Green Swizzles; and, if ever I marry and have a son, Green Swizzle Wooster is the name that will go down on the register, in memory of the day his father's life was saved at Wembley.

After the third, Biffy breathed a contented sigh.

'Where do you think Sir Roderick is?' he said.

'Biffy, old thing,' I replied frankly, 'I'm not worrying.'

'Bertie, old bird,' said Biffy, 'nor am I.'

He sighed again, and broke a long silence by asking the man for a straw.

'Bertie,' he said, 'I've just remembered something rather rummy. You know Jeeves?'

I said I knew Jeeves.

'Well, a rather rummy incident occurred as we were going into this place. Old Jeeves sidled up to me and said something rather rummy. You'll never guess what it was.'

'No. I don't believe I ever shall.'

'Jeeves said,' proceeded Biffy earnestly, 'and I am quoting his very words – Jeeves said, "Mr Biffen" – addressing me, you understand –'

'I understand.'

'"Mr Biffen," he said, "I strongly advise you to visit the –"'

'The what?' I asked as he paused.

'Bertie, old man,' said Biffy, deeply concerned, 'I've absolutely forgotten!'

I stared at the man.

'What I can't understand,' I said, 'is how you manage to run that Herefordshire place of yours for a day. How on earth do you remember to milk the cows and give the pigs their dinner?'

'Oh, that's all right. There are divers blokes about the places – hirelings and menials, you know – who look after all that.'

'Ah!' I said. 'Well, that being so, let us have one more Green Swizzle, and then hey for the Amusement Park.'

When I indulged in those few rather bitter words about exhibitions, it must be distinctly understood that I was not alluding to what you might call the more earthy portion of these curious places. I yield to no man in my approval of those institutions where on payment of a shilling you are permitted to slide down a slippery runway sitting on a mat. I love the Jiggle-Joggle, and I am prepared to take on all and sundry at Skee Ball for money, stamps, or Brazil nuts.

But, joyous reveller as I am on these occasions, I was simply not in it with old Biffy. Whether it was the Green Swizzles or merely the relief of being parted from Sir Roderick, I don't know, but Biffy flung himself into the pastimes of the proletariat with a zest that was almost frightening. I could hardly drag him away from the Whip, and as for the Switchback, he looked like spending the rest of his life on it. I managed to remove him at last, and he was wandering through the crowd at my side with gleaming eyes, hesitating between having his fortune told and taking a whirl at the Wheel of Joy, when he suddenly grabbed my arm and uttered a sharp animal cry.

'Bertie!'

'Now what?'

He was pointing at a large sign over a building.

'Look! Palace of Beauty!'

I tried to choke him off. I was getting a bit weary by this time. Not so young as I was.

'You don't want to go in there,' I said. 'A fellow at the club was telling me about that. It's only a lot of girls. You don't want to see a lot of girls.'

'I do want to see a lot of girls,' said Biffy firmly. 'Dozens of girls, and the more unlike Honoria they are, the better. Besides, I've suddenly remembered that that's the place Jeeves told me to be sure and visit. It all comes back to me. "Mr Biffen," he said, "I strongly advise you to visit the Palace of Beauty." Now, what the man was driving at or what his motive was, I don't know; but I ask you, Bertie, is it wise, is it safe, is it judicious ever to ignore Jeeves's lightest word? We enter by the door on the left.'

I don't know if you know this Palace of Beauty place? It's a sort of aquarium full of the delicately nurtured instead of fishes. You go in, and there is a kind of cage with a female goggling out at you through a sheet of plate glass. She's dressed in some weird kind of costume, and over the cage is written 'Helen of Troy'. You pass on to the next, and there's another one doing jiu-jitsu with a snake. Sub-title, Cleopatra. You get the idea – Famous Women Through the Ages and all that. I can't say it fascinated me to any great extent. I maintain that lovely woman loses a lot of her charm if you have to stare at her in a tank. Moreover, it gave me a rummy sort of feeling of having wandered into the wrong bedroom at a country house, and I was flying past at a fair rate of speed, anxious to get it over, when Biffy suddenly went off his rocker.

At least, it looked like that. He let out a piercing yell, grabbed my arm with a sudden clutch that felt like the bite of a crocodile, and stood there gibbering.

'Wuk!' ejaculated Biffy, or words to that general import.

A large and interested crowd had gathered round. I think they thought the girls were going to be fed or something. But Biffy paid no attention to them. He was pointing in a loony manner at one of the cages. I forget which it was, but the female inside wore a ruff, so it may have been Queen Elizabeth or Boadicea or someone of that period. She was rather a nice-looking girl, and she was staring at Biffy in much the same pop-eyed way as he was staring at her.

'Mabel!' yelled Biffy, going off in my ear like a bomb.

I can't say I was feeling my chirpiest. Drama is all very well, but I hate getting mixed up in it in a public spot; and I had not realized before how dashed public this spot was. The crowd seemed to have doubled itself in the last five seconds, and, while most of them had their eye on Biffy, quite a goodish few were looking at me as if they thought I was an important principal in the scene and might be expected at any moment to give of my best in the way of wholesome entertainment for the masses.

Biffy was jumping about like a lamb in the springtime – and, what is more, a feeble-minded lamb.

'Bertie! It's her! It's she!' He looked about him wildly. 'Where the deuce is the stage-door?' he cried. 'Where's the manager? I want to see the house-manager immediately.'

And then he suddenly bounded forward and began hammering on the glass with his stick.

'I say, old lad!' I began, but he shook me off.

These fellows who live in the country are apt to go in for fairly sizable clubs instead of the light canes which your well-dressed man about town considers suitable for metropolitan use; and down in Herefordshire, apparently, something in the nature of a knobkerrie is *de rigueur*. Biffy's first slosh smashed the glass all to a hash. Three more cleared the way for him to go into the cage without cutting himself. And, before the crowd had time to realize what a wonderful bob's-worth it was getting in exchange for its entrance fee, he was inside, engaging the girl in earnest conversation. And at the same moment two large policemen rolled up.

You can't make policemen take the romantic view. Not a tear did these two blighters stop to brush away. They were inside the cage and out of it and marching Biffy through the crowd before you had time to blink. I hurried after them, to do what I could in the way of soothing Biffy's last moments, and the poor old lad turned a glowing face in my direction.

'Chiswick, 60873,' he bellowed in a voice charged with emotion. 'Write it down, Bertie, or I shall forget it. Chiswick, 60873. Her telephone number.'

And then he disappeared, accompanied by about eleven thousand sightseers, and a voice spoke at my elbow.

'Mr Wooster! What – what – what is the meaning of this?'

Sir Roderick, with bigger eyebrows than ever, was standing at my side.

'It's all right,' I said. 'Poor old Biffy's only gone off his crumpet.'

He tottered.

'What?'

'Had a sort of fit or seizure, you know.'

'Another!' Sir Roderick drew a deep breath. 'And this is the man I was about to allow my daughter to marry!' I heard him mutter.

I tapped him in a kindly spirit on the shoulder. It took some doing, mark you, but I did it.

'If I were you,' I said, 'I should call that off. Scratch the fixture. Wash it out absolutely, is my advice.'

He gave me a nasty look.

'I do not require your advice, Mr Wooster! I had already arrived independently at the decision of which you speak. Mr Wooster, you are a friend of this man – a fact which should in itself have been sufficient warning to me. You will – unlike myself – be seeing him again. Kindly inform him, when you do see him, that he may consider his engagement at an end.'

'Right-ho,' I said, and hurried off after the crowd. It seemed to me that a little bailing-out might be in order.

It was about an hour later that I shoved my way out to where I had parked the car. Jeeves was sitting in the front seat, brooding over the cosmos. He rose courteously as I approached.

'You are leaving, sir?'

'I am.'

'And Sir Roderick, sir?'

'Not coming. I am revealing no secrets, Jeeves, when I inform you that he and I have parted brass rags. Not on speaking terms now.'

'Indeed, sir? And Mr Biffen? Will you wait for him?'

'No. He's in prison.'

'Really, sir?'

'Yes. I tried to bail him out, but they decided on second thoughts to coop him up for the night.'

'What was his offence, sir?'

'You remember that girl of his I was telling you about? He found her in a tank at the Palace of Beauty and went after her by the quickest route, which was via a plate-glass window. He was then scooped up and borne off in irons by the constabulary.' I gazed sideways at him. It is difficult to bring off a penetrating glance out of the corner of your eye, but I managed it. 'Jeeves,' I said, 'there is more in this than the casual observer would suppose. You told Mr Biffen to go to the Palace of Beauty. Did you know the girl would be there?'

'Yes, sir.'

This was most remarkable and rummy to a degree.

'Dash it, do you know everything?'

'Oh, no, sir,' said Jeeves with an indulgent smile. Humouring the young master.

'Well, how did you know that?'

'I happen to be acquainted with the future Mrs Biffen, sir.'

'I see. Then you knew all about that business in New York?'

'Yes, sir. And it was for that reason that I was not altogether favourably disposed towards Mr Biffen when you were first kind enough to suggest that I might be able to offer some slight assistance. I mistakenly supposed that he had been trifling with the girl's affections, sir. But when you told me the true facts of the case I appreciated the injustice I had done to Mr Biffen and endeavoured to make amends.'

'Well, he certainly owes you a lot. He's crazy about her.'

'That is very gratifying, sir.'

'And she ought to be pretty grateful to you, too. Old Biffy's got fifteen thousand a year, not to mention more cows, pigs, hens, and ducks than he knows what to do with. A dashed useful bird to have in any family.'

'Yes, sir.'

'Tell me, Jeeves,' I said, 'how did you happen to know the girl in the first place?'

Jeeves looked dreamily out into the traffic.

'She is my niece, sir. If I might make the suggestion, sir, I should not jerk the steering wheel with quite such suddenness. We very nearly collided with that omnibus.'

7 — Without the Option

The evidence was all in. The machinery of the law had worked without a hitch. And the beak, having adjusted a pair of pince-nez which looked as though they were going to do a nose dive any moment, coughed like a pained sheep and slipped us the bad news. 'The prisoner, Wooster,' he said – and who can paint the shame and agony of Bertram at hearing himself so described? – 'will pay a fine of five pounds.'

'Oh, rather!' I said. 'Absolutely! Like a shot!'

I was dashed glad to get the thing settled at such a reasonable figure. I gazed across what they call the sea of faces till I picked up Jeeves, sitting at the back. Stout fellow, he had come to see the young master through his hour of trial.

'I say, Jeeves,' I sang out, 'have you got a fiver? I'm a bit short.'

'Silence!' bellowed some officious blighter.

'It's all right,' I said; 'just arranging the financial details. Got the stuff, Jeeves?'

'Yes, sir.'

'Good egg!'

'Are you a friend of the prisoner?' asked the beak.

'I am in Mr Wooster's employment, Your Worship, in the capacity of gentleman's personal gentleman.'

'Then pay the fine to the clerk.'

'Very good, Your Worship.'

The beak gave a coldish nod in my direction, as much as to say that they might now strike the fetters from my wrists; and having hitched up the pince-nez once more, proceeded to hand poor old Sippy one of the nastiest looks ever seen in Bosher Street Police Court.

'The case of the prisoner Leon Trotzky – which,' he said, giving Sippy the eye again, 'I am strongly inclined to think an assumed and fictitious name – is more serious. He has been convicted of a wanton and violent assault upon the police. The evidence of the officer has proved that the prisoner struck him in the abdomen, causing severe internal pain, and in other ways interfered with him in the execution of his duties. I am aware that on the night following the annual aquatic contest between the Universities of Oxford and Cambridge a certain licence is traditionally granted by the authorities, but aggravated acts of ruffianly hooliganism like that of the prisoner Trotzky cannot be overlooked or palliated. He will serve a sentence of thirty days in the Second Division without the option of a fine.'

'No, I say – here – hi – dash it all!' protested poor old Sippy.

'Silence!' bellowed the officious blighter.

'Next case,' said the beak. And that was that.

The whole affair was most unfortunate. Memory is a trifle blurred; but as far as I can piece together the facts, what happened was more or less this:

Abstemious cove though I am as a general thing, there is one night in the year when, putting all other engagements aside, I am rather apt to let myself go a bit and renew my lost youth, as it were. The night to which I allude is the one following the annual aquatic contest between the Universities of Oxford and Cambridge; or, putting it another way, Boat-Race Night. Then, if ever, you will see Bertram under the influence. And on this occasion, I freely admit, I had been doing myself rather juicily, with the result that when I ran into old Sippy opposite the Empire I was in quite fairly bonhomous mood. This being so, it cut me to the quick to perceive that Sippy, generally the brightest of revellers, was far from being his usual sunny self. He had the air of a man with a secret sorrow.

'Bertie,' he said as we strolled along towards Piccadilly Circus, 'the heart bowed down by weight of woe to weakest hope will cling.' Sippy is by way of being an author, though mainly dependent for the necessaries of life on subsidies from an old aunt who lives in the country, and his conversation often takes a literary turn. 'But the trouble is that I have no hope to cling to, weak or otherwise. I am up against it, Bertie.'

'In what way, laddie?'

'I've got to go tomorrow and spend three weeks with some absolutely dud – I will go further – some positively scaly friends of my Aunt Vera. She has fixed the thing up, and may a nephew's curse blister every bulb in her garden.'

'Who are these hounds of hell?' I asked.

'Some people named Pringle. I haven't seen them since I was ten, but I remember them at that time striking me as England's premier warts.'

'Tough luck. No wonder you've lost your morale.'

'The world,' said Sippy, 'is very grey. How can I shake off this awful depression?'

It was then that I got one of those bright ideas one does get round about 11.30 on Boat-Race Night.

'What you want, old man,' I said, 'is a policeman's helmet.'

'Do I, Bertie?'

'If I were you, I'd just step straight across the street and get that one over there.'

'But there's a policeman inside it. You can see him distinctly.'

'What does that matter?' I said. I simply couldn't follow his reasoning.

Sippy stood for a moment in thought.

'I believe you're absolutely right,' he said at last.

'Funny I never thought of it before. You really recommend me to get that helmet?'

'I do, indeed.'

'Then I will,' said Sippy, brightening up in the most remarkable manner.

So there you have the posish, and you can see why, as I left the dock a free man, remorse gnawed at my vitals. In his twenty-fifth year, with life opening out before him and all that sort of thing, Oliver Randolph Sipperley had become a jail-bird, and it was all my fault. It was I who had dragged that fine spirit down into the mire, so to speak, and the question now arose, What could I do to atone?

Obviously the first move must be to get in touch with Sippy and see if he had any last messages and what not. I pushed about a bit, making inquiries, and presently found myself in a little dark room with whitewashed walls and a wooden bench. Sippy was sitting on the bench with his head in his hands.

'How are you, old lad?' I asked in a hushed, bedside voice.

'I'm a ruined man,' said Sippy, looking like a poached egg.

'Oh, come,' I said, 'it's not so bad as all that. I mean to say, you had the swift intelligence to give a false name. There won't be anything about you in the papers.'

'I'm not worrying about the papers. What's bothering me is, how can I go and spend three weeks with the Pringles, starting today, when I've got to sit in a prison cell with a ball and chain on my ankle?'

'But you said you didn't want to go.'

'It isn't a question of wanting, fathead. I've got to go. If I don't my aunt will find out where I am. And if she finds out that I am doing thirty days, without the option, in the lowest dungeon beneath the castle moat – well, where shall I get off?'

I saw his point.

'This is not a thing we can settle for ourselves,' I said gravely. 'We must put our trust in a higher power. Jeeves is the man we must consult.'

And having collected a few of the necessary data, I shook his hand, patted him on the back and tooled off home to Jeeves.

'Jeeves,' I said, when I had climbed outside the pick-me-up which he had thoughtfully prepared against my coming, 'I've got something to tell you; something important; something that vitally affects one whom you have always regarded with – one whom you have always looked upon – one whom you have – well, to cut a long story short, as I'm not feeling quite myself – Mr Sipperley.'

'Yes, sir?'

'Jeeves, Mr Souperley is in the sip.'

'Sir?'

'I mean, Mr Sipperley is in the soup.'

'Indeed, sir?'

'And all owing to me. It was I who, in a moment of mistaken kindness, wishing only to cheer him up and give him something to occupy his mind, recommended him to pinch that policeman's helmet.'

'Is that so, sir?'

'Do you mind not intoning the responses, Jeeves?' I said. 'This is a most complicated story for a man with a headache to have to tell, and if you interrupt you'll make me lose the thread. As a favour to me, therefore, don't do it. Just nod every now and then to show that you're following me.'

I closed my eyes and marshalled the facts.

'To start with then, Jeeves, you may or may not know that Mr Sipperley is practically dependent on his Aunt Vera.'

'Would that be Miss Sipperley of the Paddock, Beckley-on-the-Moor, in Yorkshire, sir?'

'Yes. Don't tell me you know her!'

'Not personally, sir. But I have a cousin residing in the village who has some slight acquaintance with Miss Sipperley. He has described her to me as an imperious and quick-tempered old lady . . . But I beg your pardon, sir, I should have nodded.'

'Quite right, you should have nodded. Yes, Jeeves, you should have nodded. But it's too late now.'

I nodded myself. I hadn't had my eight hours the night before, and what you might call a lethargy was showing a tendency to steal over me from time to time.

'Yes, sir?' said Jeeves.

'Oh – ah – yes,' I said, giving myself a bit of a hitch up. 'Where had I got to?'

'You were saying that Mr Sipperley is practically dependent upon Miss Sipperley, sir.'

'Was I?'

'You were, sir.'

'You're perfectly right; so I was. Well, then, you can readily understand, Jeeves, that he has got to take jolly good care to keep in with her. You get that?'

Jeeves nodded.

'Now mark this closely: The other day she wrote to old Sippy, telling him to come down and sing at her village concert. It was equivalent to a royal command, if you see what I mean, so Sippy couldn't refuse in so many words. But he had sung at her village concert once before and had got the bird in no uncertain manner, so he wasn't playing any return dates. You follow so far, Jeeves?'

Jeeves nodded.

'So what did he do, Jeeves? He did what seemed to him at the moment a rather brainy thing. He told her that, though he would have been delighted to sing at her village concert, by a most unfortunate chance an editor had commissioned him to write a series of articles on the colleges of Cambridge and he was obliged to pop down there at once and would be away for quite three weeks. All clear up to now?'

Jeeves inclined the coco-nut.

'Whereupon, Jeeves, Miss Sipperley wrote back, saying that she quite realized that work must come before pleasure – pleasure being her loose way of describing the act of singing songs at the Beckley-on-the-Moor concert and getting the laugh from the local toughs; but that, if he was going to Cambridge, he must certainly stay with her friends, the Pringles, at their house just outside the town. And she dropped them a line telling them to expect him on the twenty-eighth, and they dropped another line saying right-ho, and the thing was settled. And now Mr Sipperley is in the jug, and what will be the ultimate outcome or upshot? Jeeves, it is a problem worthy of your great intellect. I rely on you.'

'I will do my best to justify your confidence, sir.'

'Carry on, then. And meanwhile pull down the blinds and bring a couple more cushions and heave that small chair this way so that I can put my feet up, and then go away and brood and let me hear from you in – say, a couple of hours, or maybe three. And if anybody calls and wants to see me, inform them that I am dead.'

'Dead, sir?'

'Dead. You won't be so far wrong.'

It must have been well towards evening when I woke up with a crick in my neck but otherwise somewhat refreshed. I pressed the bell.

'I looked in twice, sir,' said Jeeves, 'but on each occasion you were asleep and I did not like to disturb you.'

'The right spirit, Jeeves . . . Well?'

'I have been giving close thought to the little problem which you indicated, sir, and I can see only one solution.'

'One is enough. What do you suggest?'

'That you go to Cambridge in Mr Sipperley's place, sir.'

I stared at the man. Certainly I was feeling a good deal better than I had been a few hours before; but I was far from being in a fit condition to have rot like this talked to me.

'Jeeves,' I said sternly, 'pull yourself together. This is mere babble from the sickbed.'

'I fear I can suggest no other plan of action, sir, which will extricate Mr Sipperley from his dilemma.'

'But think! Reflect! Why, even I, in spite of having had a disturbed night and a most painful morning with the minions of the law, can see that the scheme is a loony one. To put the finger on only one leak in the thing, it isn't me these people want to see; it's Mr Sipperley. They don't know me from Adam.'

'So much the better, sir. For what I am suggesting is that you go to Cambridge, affecting actually to be Mr Sipperley.'

This was too much.

'Jeeves,' I said, and I'm not half sure there weren't tears in my eyes, 'surely you can see for yourself that this is pure banana oil. It is not like you to come into the presence of a sick man and gibber.'

'I think the plan I have suggested would be practicable, sir. While you were sleeping, I was able to have a few words with Mr Sipperley, and he informed me that Professor and Mrs Pringle have not set eyes upon him since he was a lad of ten.'

'No, that's true. He told me that. But even so, they would be sure to ask him questions about my aunt – or rather his aunt. Where would I be then?'

'Mr Sipperley was kind enough to give me a few facts respecting Miss Sipperley, sir, which I jotted down. With these, added to what my cousin has told me of the lady's habits, I think you would be in a position to answer any ordinary question.'

There is something dashed insidious about Jeeves. Time and again since we first came together he has stunned me with some apparently drivelling suggestion or scheme or ruse or plan of campaign, and after about five minutes has convinced me that it is not only sound but fruity. It took nearly a quarter of an hour to reason me into this particular one, it being considerably the weirdest to date; but he did it. I was holding out pretty firmly, when he suddenly clinched the thing.

'I would certainly suggest, sir,' he said, 'that you left London as soon as possible and remained hid for some little time in some retreat where you would not be likely to be found.'

'Eh? Why?'

'During the last hours Mrs Spenser has been on the telephone three times, sir, endeavouring to get into communication with you.'

'Aunt Agatha!' I cried, paling beneath my tan.

'Yes, sir. I gathered from her remarks that she had been reading in the evening paper a report of this morning's proceedings in the police court.'

I hopped from the chair like a jack rabbit of the prairie. If Aunt Agatha was out with her hatchet, a move was most certainly indicated.

'Jeeves,' I said, 'this is a time for deeds, not words. Pack – and that right speedily.'

'I have packed, sir.'

'Find out when there is a train for Cambridge.'

'There is one in forty minutes, sir.'

'Call a taxi.'

'A taxi is at the door, sir.'

'Good!' I said. 'Then lead me to it.'

The Maison Pringle was quite a bit of a way out of Cambridge, a mile or two down the Trumpington Road; and when I arrived everybody was dressing for dinner. So it wasn't till I had shoved on the evening raiment and got down to the drawing-room that I met the gang.

'Hullo-ullo!' I said, taking a deep breath and floating in.

I tried to speak in a clear and ringing voice, but I wasn't feeling my chirpiest. It is always a nervous job for a diffident and unassuming bloke to visit a strange house for the first time; and it doesn't make the thing any better when he goes there pretending to be another fellow. I was conscious of a rather pronounced sinking feeling, which the appearance of the Pringles did nothing to allay.

Sippy had described them as England's premier warts, and it looked to me as if he might be about right. Professor Pringle was a thinnish, baldish, dyspeptic-lookingish cove with an eye like a haddock, while Mrs Pringle's aspect was that of one who had had bad news round about the year 1900 and never really got over it. And I was just staggering under the impact of these two when I was introduced to a couple of ancient females with shawls all over them.

'No doubt you remember my mother?' said Professor Pringle mournfully, indicating Exhibit A.

'Oh-ah!' I said, achieving a bit of a beam.

'And my aunt,' sighed the prof, as if things were getting worse and worse.

'Well, well, well!' I said, shooting another beam in the direction of Exhibit B.

'They were saying only this morning that they remembered you,' groaned the prof, abandoning all hope.

There was a pause. The whole strength of the company gazed at me like a family group out of one of Edgar Allan Poe's less cheery yarns, and I felt my *joie de vivre* dying at the roots.

'I remember Oliver,' said Exhibit A. She heaved a sigh. 'He was such a pretty child. What a pity! What a pity!'

Tactful, of course, and calculated to put the guest completely at his ease.

'I remember Oliver,' said Exhibit B, looking at me in much the same way as the Bosher Street beak had looked at Sippy before putting on the black cap. 'Nasty little boy! He teased my cat.'

'Aunt Jane's memory is wonderful, considering that she will be eighty-seven next birthday,' whispered Mrs Pringle with mournful pride.

'What did you say?' asked the Exhibit suspiciously.

'I said your memory was wonderful.'

'Ah!' The dear old creature gave me another glare. I could see that no beautiful friendship was to be looked for by Bertram in this quarter. 'He chased my Tibby all over the garden, shooting arrows at her from a bow.'

At this moment a cat strolled out from under the sofa and made for me with its tail up. Cats always do take to me, which made it all the sadder that I should be saddled with Sippy's criminal record. I stooped to tickle it under the ear, such being my invariable policy, and the Exhibit uttered a piercing cry.

'Stop him! Stop him!'

She leaped forward, moving uncommonly well for one of her years, and having scooped up the cat, stood eyeing me with bitter defiance, as if daring me to start anything. Most unpleasant.

'I like cats,' I said feebly.

It didn't go. The sympathy of the audience was not with me. And conversation was at what you might call a low ebb, when the door opened and a girl came in.

'My daughter Heloise,' said the prof moodily, as if he hated to admit it.

I turned to mitt the female, and stood there with my hand out, gaping. I can't remember when I've had such a nasty shock.

I suppose everybody has had the experience of

suddenly meeting somebody who reminded them frightfully of some fearful person. I mean to say, by way of an example, once when I was golfing in Scotland I saw a woman come into the hotel who was the living image of my Aunt Agatha. Probably a very decent sort, if I had only waited to see, but I didn't wait. I legged it that evening, utterly unable to stand the spectacle. And on another occasion I was driven out of a thoroughly festive night club because the head waiter reminded me of my Uncle Percy.

Well, Heloise Pringle, in the most ghastly way, resembled Honoria Glossop.

I think I may have told you before about this Glossop scourge. She was the daughter of Sir Roderick Glossop, the loony doctor, and I had been engaged to her for about three weeks, much against my wishes, when the old boy most fortunately got the idea that I was off my rocker and put the bee on the proceedings. Since then the mere thought of her had been enough to make me start out of my sleep with a loud cry. And this girl was exactly like her.

'Er – how are you?' I said.

'How do you do?'

Her voice put the lid on it. It might have been Honoria herself talking. Honoria Glossop has a voice like a lion tamer making some authoritative announcement to one of the troupe, and so had this girl. I backed away convulsively and sprang into the air as my foot stubbed itself against something squashy. A sharp yowl rent the air, followed by an indignant cry, and I turned to see Aunt Jane, on all fours, trying to put things right with the cat, which had gone to earth under the sofa. She gave me a look, and I could see that her worst fears had been realized.

At this juncture dinner was announced – not before I was ready for it.

*

'Jeeves,' I said, when I got him alone that night, 'I am no
faint heart, but I am inclined to think that this binge is
going to prove a shade above the odds.'

'You are not enjoying your visit, sir?'

'I am not, Jeeves. Have you seen Miss Pringle?'

'Yes, sir, from a distance.'

'The best way to see her. Did you observe her keenly?'

'Yes, sir.'

'Did she remind you of anybody?'

'She appeared to me to bear a remarkable likeness to
her cousin, Miss Glossop, sir.'

'Her cousin! You don't mean to say she's Honoria
Glossop's cousin!'

'Yes, sir. Mrs Pringle was a Miss Blatherwick – the
younger of two sisters, the elder of whom married Sir
Roderick Glossop.'

'Great Scott! That accounts for the resemblance.'

'Yes, sir.'

'And what a resemblance, Jeeves! She even talks like
Miss Glossop.'

'Indeed, sir? I have not yet heard Miss Pringle speak.'

'You have missed little. And what it amounts to,
Jeeves, is that, though nothing will induce me to let old
Sippy down, I can see that this visit is going to try me
high. At a pinch, I could stand the prof and wife. I could
even make the effort of a lifetime and bear up against
Aunt Jane. But to expect a man to mix daily with the girl
Heloise – and to do it, what is more, on lemonade,
which is all there was to drink at dinner – is to ask too
much of him. What shall I do, Jeeves?'

'I think that you should avoid Miss Pringle's society
as much as possible.'

'The same great thought had occurred to me,' I said.

It is all very well, though, to talk airily about
avoiding a female's society; but when you are living in
the same house with her, and she doesn't want to avoid
you, it takes a bit of doing. It is a peculiar thing in life

that the people you most particularly want to edge away from always seem to cluster round like a poultice. I hadn't been twenty-four hours in the place before I perceived that I was going to see a lot of this pestilence.

She was one of those girls you're always meeting on the stairs and in passages. I couldn't go into a room without seeing her drift in a minute later. And if I walked in the garden she was sure to leap out at me from a laurel bush or the onion bed or something. By about the tenth day I had begun to feel absolutely haunted.

'Jeeves,' I said, 'I have begun to feel absolutely haunted.'

'Sir?'

'This woman dogs me. I never seem to get a moment to myself. Old Sippy was supposed to come here to make a study of the Cambridge colleges, and she took me round about fifty-seven this morning. This afternoon I went to sit in the garden, and she popped up through a trap and was in my midst. This evening she cornered me in the morning-room. It's getting so that, when I have a bath, I wouldn't be a bit surprised to find her nestling in the soap dish.'

'Extremely trying, sir.'

'Dashed so. Have you any remedy to suggest?'

'Not at the moment, sir. Miss Pringle does appear to be distinctly interested in you, sir. She was asking me questions this morning respecting your mode of life in London.'

'What?'

'Yes, sir.'

I stared at the man in horror. A ghastly thought had struck me. I quivered like an aspen.

At lunch that day a curious thing had happened. We had just finished mangling the cutlets and I was sitting back in my chair, taking a bit of an easy before being allotted my slab of boiled pudding, when, happening to look up, I caught the girl Heloise's eye fixed on me in what seemed to me a rather rummy manner. I didn't think much about it at the time, because boiled pudding is a thing you have to give your undivided attention to if you want to do yourself justice; but now, recalling the episode in the light of Jeeves's words, the full sinister meaning of the thing seemed to come home to me.

Even at the moment, something about that look had struck me as oddly familiar, and now I suddenly saw why. It had been the identical look which I had observed in the eye of Honoria Glossop in the days immediately preceding our engagement – the look of a tigress that has marked down its prey.

'Jeeves, do you know what I think?'

'Sir?'

I gulped slightly.

'Jeeves,' I said, 'listen attentively. I don't want to give the impression that I consider myself one of those deadly coves who exercise an irresistible fascination over one and all and can't meet a girl without wrecking her peace of mind in the first half-minute. As a matter of fact, it's rather the other way with me, for girls on entering my presence are mostly inclined to give me the raised eyebrow and the twitching upper lip. Nobody, therefore, can say that I am a man who's likely to take alarm unnecessarily. You admit that, don't you?'

'Yes, sir.'

'Nevertheless, Jeeves, it is a known scientific fact that there is a particular style of female that does seem strangely attracted to the sort of fellow I am.'

'Very true, sir.'

'I mean to say, I know perfectly well that I've got, roughly speaking, half the amount of brain a normal bloke ought to possess. And when a girl comes along who has about twice the regular allowance, she too often makes a bee line for me with the love light in her eyes. I don't know how to account for it, but it is so.'

'It may be Nature's provision for maintaining the balance of the species, sir.'

'Very possibly. Anyway, it has happened to me over and over again. It was what happened in the case of Honoria Glossop. She was notoriously one of the brainiest women of her year at Girton, and she just gathered me in like a bull pup swallowing a piece of steak.'

'Miss Pringle, I am informed, sir, was an even more brilliant scholar than Miss Glossop.'

'Well, there you are! Jeeves, she looks at me.'

'Yes, sir?'

'I keep meeting her on the stairs and in passages.'

'Indeed, sir?'

'She recommends me books to read, to improve my mind.'

'Highly suggestive, sir.'

'And at breakfast this morning, when I was eating a sausage, she told me I shouldn't, as modern medical science held that a four-inch sausage contained as many germs as a dead rat. The maternal touch, you understand; fussing over my health.'

'I think we may regard that, sir, as practically conclusive.'

I sank into a chair, thoroughly pipped.

'What's to be done, Jeeves?'

'We must think, sir.'

'You think. I haven't the machinery.'

'I will most certainly devote my very best attention to the matter, sir, and will endeavour to give satisfaction.'

Well, that was something. But I was ill at ease. Yes, there is no getting away from it, Bertram was ill at ease.

Next morning we visited sixty-three more Cambridge colleges, and after lunch I said I was going to my room to lie down. After staying there for half an hour to give the coast time to clear, I shoved a book and smoking materials in my pocket, and climbing out of a window, shinned down a convenient water-pipe into the garden. My objective was the summer-house, where it seemed to me that a man might put in a quiet hour or so without interruption.

It was extremely jolly in the garden. The sun was shining, the crocuses were all to the mustard and there wasn't a sign of Heloise Pringle anywhere. The cat was fooling about on the lawn, so I chirruped to it and it gave a low gargle and came trotting up. I had just got it in my arms and was scratching it under the ear when there was a loud shriek from above, and there was Aunt Jane half out of the window. Dashed disturbing.

'Oh, right-ho,' I said.

I dropped the cat, which galloped off into the bushes, and dismissing the idea of bunging a brick at the aged relative, went on my way, heading for the shrubbery. Once safely hidden there, I worked round till I got to the summer-house. And, believe me, I had hardly got my first cigarette nicely under way when a shadow fell on my book and there was young Sticketh-Closer-Than-a-Brother in person.

'So there you are,' she said.

She seated herself by my side, and with a sort of gruesome playfulness jerked the gasper out of the holder and heaved it through the door.

'You're always smoking,' she said, a lot too much like a lovingly chiding young bride for my comfort. 'I wish you wouldn't. It's so bad for you. And you ought not to be sitting out here without your light overcoat. You want someone to look after you.'

'I've got Jeeves.'

She frowned a bit.

'I don't like him,' she said.

'Eh? Why not?'

'I don't know. I wish you would get rid of him.'

My flesh absolutely crept. And I'll tell you why. One

of the first things Honoria Glossop had done after we had become engaged was to tell me she didn't like Jeeves and wanted him shot out. The realization that this girl resembled Honoria not only in body but in blackness of soul made me go all faint.

'What are you reading?'

She picked up my book and frowned again. The thing was one I had brought down from the old flat in London, to glance at in the train – a fairly zippy effort in the detective line called *The Trail of Blood*. She turned the pages with a nasty sneer.

'I can't understand you liking nonsense of this –' She stopped suddenly. 'Good gracious!'

'What's the matter?'

'Do you know Bertie Wooster?'

And then I saw that my name was scrawled right across the title page, and my heart did three back somersaults.

'Oh – er – well – that is to say – well, slightly.'

'He must be a perfect horror. I'm surprised that you can make a friend of him. Apart from anything else, the man is practically an imbecile. He was engaged to my Cousin Honoria at one time, and it was broken off because he was next door to insane. You should hear my Uncle Roderick talk about him!'

I wasn't keen.

'Do you see much of him?'

'A goodish bit.'

'I saw in the paper the other day that he was fined for making a disgraceful disturbance in the street.'

'Yes, I saw that.'

She gazed at me in a foul, motherly way.

'He can't be a good influence for you,' she said. 'I do wish you would drop him. Will you?'

'Well –' I began. And at this point old Cuthbert, the cat, having presumably found it a bit slow by himself in the bushes, wandered in with a matey expression on his face and jumped on my lap. I welcomed him with a good deal of cordiality. Though but a cat, he did make a sort of third at this party; and he afforded a good excuse for changing the conversation.

'Jolly birds, cats,' I said.

She wasn't having any.

'Will you drop Bertie Wooster?' she said, absolutely ignoring the cat *motif*.

'It would be so difficult.'

'Nonsense! It only needs a little will-power. The man surely can't be so interesting a companion as all that. Uncle Roderick says he is an invertebrate waster.'

I could have mentioned a few things that I thought Uncle Roderick was, but my lips were sealed, so to speak.

'You have changed a great deal since we last met,' said the Pringle disease reproachfully. She bent forward and began to scratch the cat under the other ear. 'Do you remember, when we were children together, you used to say that you would do anything for me?'

'Did I?'

'I remember once you cried because I was cross and wouldn't let you kiss me.'

I didn't believe it at the time, and I don't believe it now. Sippy is in many ways a good deal of a chump, but surely even at the age of ten he cannot have been such a priceless ass as that. I think the girl was lying, but that didn't make the position of affairs any better. I edged away a couple of inches and sat staring before me, the old brow beginning to get slightly bedewed.

And then suddenly – well, you know how it is, I mean. I suppose everyone has had that ghastly feeling at one time or another of being urged by some overwhelming force to do some absolutely blithering act. You get it every now and then when you're in a crowded theatre, and something seems to be egging you on to shout 'Fire!' and see what happens. Or you're talking to someone and all at once you feel, 'Now, suppose I suddenly biffed this bird in the eye!'

Well, what I'm driving at is this, at this juncture, with her shoulder squashing against mine and her black hair tickling my nose, a perfectly loony impulse came sweeping over me to kiss her.

'No, really?' I croaked.

'Have you forgotten?'

She lifted the old onion and her eyes looked straight into mine. I could feel myself skidding. I shut my eyes. And then from the doorway there spoke the most beautiful voice I had ever heard in my life:

'Give me that cat!'

I opened my eyes. There was good old Aunt Jane, that queen of her sex, standing before me, glaring at me as if I were a vivisectionist and she had surprised me in the middle of an experiment. How this pearl among women had tracked me down I don't know, but there she stood, bless her dear, intelligent old soul, like the rescue party in the last reel of a motion picture.

I didn't wait. The spell was broken and I legged it. As I went, I heard that lovely voice again.

'He shot arrows at my Tibby from a bow,' said this most deserving and excellent octogenarian.

For the next few days all was peace. I saw comparatively little of Heloise. I found the strategic value of that water-pipe outside my window beyond praise. I seldom left the house now by any other route. It seemed to me that, if only the luck held like this, I might after all be able to stick this visit out for the full term of the sentence.

But meanwhile, as they say in the movies –

The whole family appeared to be present and correct as I came down to the drawing-room a couple of nights later. The Prof, Mrs Prof, the two Exhibits and the girl Heloise were scattered about at intervals. The cat slept on the rug, the canary in its cage. There was nothing, in short, to indicate that this was not just one of our ordinary evenings.

'Well, well, well!' I said cheerily. 'Hullo-ullo-ullo!'

I always like to make something in the nature of an entrance speech, it seeming to me to lend a chummy tone to the proceedings.

The girl Heloise looked at me reproachfully.

'Where have you been all day?' she asked.

'I went to my room after lunch.'

'You weren't there at five.'

'No. After putting in a spell of work on the good old colleges I went for a stroll. Fellow must have exercise if he means to keep fit.'

'*Mens sana in corpore sano,*' observed the prof.

'I shouldn't wonder,' I said cordially.

At this point, when everything was going as sweet as a nut and I was feeling on top of my form, Mrs Pringle suddenly socked me on the base of the skull with a sandbag. Not actually, I don't mean. No, no. I speak figuratively, as it were.

'Roderick is very late,' she said.

You may think it strange that the sound of that name should have sloshed into my nerve centres like a half-brick. But, take it from me, to a man who has had any dealings with Sir Roderick Glossop there is only one Roderick in the world – and that is one too many.

'Roderick?' I gurgled.

'My brother-in-law, Sir Roderick Glossop, comes to Cambridge tonight,' said the prof. 'He lectures at St Luke's tomorrow. He is coming here to dinner.'

And while I stood there, feeling like the hero when he discovers that he is trapped in the den of the Secret Nine, the door opened.

'Sir Roderick Glossop,' announced the maid or some such person, and in he came.

One of the things that get this old crumb so generally

disliked among the better element of the community is the fact that he has a head like the dome of St Paul's and eyebrows that want bobbing or shingling to reduce them to anything like reasonable size. It is a nasty experience to see this bald and bushy bloke advancing on you when you haven't prepared the strategic railways in your rear.

As he came into the room I backed behind a sofa and commended my soul to God. I didn't need to have my hand read to know that trouble was coming to me through a dark man.

He didn't spot me at first. He shook hands with the prof and wife, kissed Heloise and waggled his head at the Exhibits.

'I fear I am somewhat late,' he said. 'A slight accident on the road, affecting what my chauffeur termed the –'

And then he saw me lurking on the outskirts and gave a startled grunt, as if I hurt him a good deal internally.

'This –' began the prof, waving in my direction.

'I am already acquainted with Mr Wooster.'

'This,' went on the prof, 'is Miss Sipperley's nephew, Oliver. You remember Miss Sipperley?'

'What do you mean?' barked Sir Roderick. Having had so much to do with loonies has given him a rather sharp and authoritative manner on occasion. 'This is that wretched young man, Bertram Wooster. What is all this nonsense about Olivers and Sipperleys?'

The prof was eyeing me with some natural surprise. So were the others. I beamed a bit weakly.

'Well, as a matter of fact –' I said.

The prof was wrestling with the situation. You could hear his brain buzzing.

'He said he was Oliver Sipperley,' he moaned.

'Come here!' bellowed Sir Roderick. 'Am I to understand that you have inflicted yourself on this household under the pretence of being the nephew of an old friend?'

It seemed a pretty accurate description of the facts.

'Well – er – yes,' I said.

Sir Roderick shot an eye at me. It entered the body somewhere about the top stud, roamed around inside for a bit and went out at the back.

'Insane! Quite insane, as I knew from the first moment I saw him.'

'What did he say?' asked Aunt Jane.

'Roderick says this young man is insane,' roared the prof.

'Ah!' said Aunt Jane, nodding. 'I thought so. He climbs down water-pipes.'

'Does what?'

'I've seen him – ah, many a time!'

Sir Roderick snorted violently.

'He ought to be under proper restraint. It is abominable that a person in his mental condition should be permitted to roam the world at large. The next stage may quite easily be homicidal.'

It seemed to me that, even at the expense of giving old Sippy away, I must be cleared of this frightful charge. After all, Sippy's number was up anyway.

'Let me explain,' I said. 'Sippy asked me to come here.'

'What do you mean?'

'He couldn't come himself, because he was jugged for biffing a cop on Boat-Race Night.'

Well, it wasn't easy to make them get the hang of the story, and even when I'd done it it didn't seem to make them any chummier towards me. A certain coldness about expresses it, and when dinner was announced I counted myself out and pushed off rapidly to my room. I could have done with a bit of dinner, but the atmosphere didn't seem just right.

'Jeeves,' I said, having shot in and pressed the bell, 'we're sunk.'

'Sir?'

'Hell's foundations are quivering and the game is up.'

He listened attentively.

'The contingency was one always to have been anticipated as a possibility, sir. It only remains to take the obvious step.'

'What's that?'

'Go and see Miss Sipperley, sir.

'What on earth for?'

'I think it would be judicious to apprise her of the facts yourself, sir, instead of allowing her to hear of them through the medium of a letter from Professor Pringle. That is to say, if you are still anxious to do all in your power to assist Mr Sipperley.'

'I can't let Sippy down. If you think it's any good –'

'We can but try it, sir. I have an idea, sir, that we may find Miss Sipperley disposed to look leniently upon Mr Sipperley's misdemeanour.'

'What makes you think that?'

'It is just a feeling that I have, sir.'

'Well, if you think it would be worth trying – How do we get there?'

'The distance is about a hundred and fifty miles, sir. Our best plan would be to hire a car.'

'Get it at once,' I said.

The idea of being a hundred and fifty miles away from Heloise Pringle, not to mention Aunt Jane and Sir Roderick Glossop, sounded about as good to me as anything I had ever heard.

The Paddock, Beckley-on-the-Moor, was about a couple of parasangs from the village, and I set out for it next morning, after partaking of a hearty breakfast at the local inn, practically without a tremor. I suppose when a fellow has been through it as I had in the last two weeks his system becomes hardened. After all, I felt, whatever this aunt of Sippy's might be like, she wasn't Sir Roderick Glossop, so I was that much on velvet from the start.

The Paddock was one of those medium-sized houses

with a goodish bit of very tidy garden and a carefully rolled gravel drive curving past a shrubbery that looked as if it had just come back from the dry cleaner – the sort of house you take one look at and say to yourself, 'Somebody's aunt lives there.' I pushed on up the drive, and as I turned the bend I observed in the middle distance a woman messing about by a flower-bed with a trowel in her hand. If this wasn't the female I was after, I was very much mistaken, so I halted, cleared the throat and gave tongue.

'Miss Sipperley?'

She had had her back to me, and at the sound of my voice she executed a sort of leap or bound, not unlike a barefoot dancer who steps on a tin-tack halfway through the Vision of Salome. She came to earth and goggled at me in a rather goofy manner. A large, stout female with a reddish face.

'Hope I didn't startle you,' I said.

'Who are you?'

'My name's Wooster. I'm a pal of your nephew, Oliver.'

Her breathing had become more regular.

'Oh?' she said. 'When I heard your voice I thought you were someone else.'

'No, that's who I am. I came up here to tell you about Oliver.'

'What about him?'

I hesitated. Now that we were approaching what you might call the nub, or crux, of the situation, a good deal of my breezy confidence seemed to have slipped from me.

'Well, it's rather a painful tale, I must warn you.'

'Oliver isn't ill? He hasn't had an accident?'

She spoke anxiously, and I was pleased at this evidence of human feeling. I decided to shoot the works with no more delay.

'Oh, no, he isn't ill,' I said; 'and as regards having

accidents, it depends on what you call an accident. He's in chokey.'

'In what?'

'In prison.'

'In prison!'

'It was entirely my fault. We were strolling along on Boat-Race Night and I advised him to pinch a policeman's helmet.'

'I don't understand.'

'Well, he seemed depressed, don't you know; and rightly or wrongly, I thought it might cheer him up if he stepped across the street and collared a policeman's helmet. He thought it a good idea, too, so he started doing it, and the man made a fuss and Oliver sloshed him.'

'Sloshed him?'

'Biffed him – smote him a blow – in the stomach.'

'My nephew Oliver hit a policeman in the stomach?'

'Absolutely in the stomach. And next morning the beak sent him to the bastille for thirty days without the option.'

I was looking at her a bit anxiously all this while to see how she was taking the thing, and at this moment her face seemed suddenly to split in half. For an instant she appeared to be all mouth, and then she was staggering about the grass, shouting with laughter and waving the trowel madly.

It seemed to me a bit of luck for her that Sir Roderick Glossop wasn't on the spot. He would have been sitting on her head and calling for the strait-waistcoat in the first half-minute.

'You aren't annoyed?' I said.

'Annoyed?' She chuckled happily. 'I've never heard such a splendid thing in my life.'

I was pleased and relieved. I had hoped the news wouldn't upset her too much, but I had never expected it to go with such a roar as this.

'I'm proud of him,' she said.

'That's fine.'

'If every young man in England went about hitting policemen in the stomach, it would be a better country to live in.'

I couldn't follow her reasoning, but everything seemed to be all right; so after a few more cheery words I said good-bye and legged it.

'Jeeves,' I said when I got back to the inn, 'everything's fine. But I am far from understanding why.'

'What actually occurred when you met Miss Sipperley, sir?'

'I told her Sippy was in the jug for assaulting the police. Upon which she burst into hearty laughter, waved her trowel in a pleased manner and said she was proud of him.'

'I think I can explain her apparently eccentric behaviour, sir. I am informed that Miss Sipperley has had a good deal of annoyance at the hands of the local constable during the past two weeks. This has doubtless resulted in a prejudice on her part against the force as a whole.'

'Really? How was that?'

'The constable has been somewhat over-zealous in the performance of his duties, sir. On no fewer than three occasions in the last ten days he has served summonses upon Miss Sipperley – for exceeding the speed limit in her car; for allowing her dog to appear in public without a collar; and for failing to abate a smoky chimney. Being in the nature of an autocrat, if I may use the term, in the village, Miss Sipperley has been accustomed to do these things in the past with impunity, and the constable's unexpected zeal has made her somewhat ill-disposed to policemen as a class and consequently disposed to look upon such assaults as Mr Sipperley's in a kindly and broadminded spirit.'

I saw his point.

'What an amazing bit of luck, Jeeves!'

'Yes, sir.'

'Where did you hear all this?'

'My informant was the constable himself, sir. He is my cousin.'

I gaped at the man. I saw, so to speak, all.

'Good Lord, Jeeves! You didn't bribe him?'

'Oh, no, sir. But it was his birthday last week, and I gave him a little present. I have always been fond of Egbert, sir.'

'How much?'

'A matter of five pounds, sir.'

I felt in my pocket.

'Here you are,' I said. 'And another fiver for luck.'

'Thank you very much, sir.'

'Jeeves,' I said, 'you move in a mysterious way your wonders to perform. You don't mind if I sing a bit, do you?'

'Not at all, sir,' said Jeeves.

8 — Fixing it for Freddie

'Jeeves,' I said, looking in on him one afternoon on my return from the club, 'I don't want to interrupt you.'

'No, sir?'

'But I would like a word with you.'

'Yes, sir?'

He had been packing a few of the Wooster necessaries in the old kitbag against our approaching visit to the seaside, and he now rose and stood bursting with courteous zeal.

'Jeeves,' I said, 'a somewhat disturbing situation has arisen with regard to a pal of mine.'

'Indeed, sir?'

'You know Mr Bullivant?'

'Yes, sir.'

'Well, I slid into the Drones this morning for a bite of lunch, and found him in a dark corner of the smoking-room looking like the last rose of summer. Naturally I was surprised. You know what a bright lad he is as a rule. The life and soul of every gathering he attends.'

'Yes, sir.'

'Quite the little lump of fun, in fact.'

'Precisely, sir.'

'Well, I made inquiries, and he told me that he had had a quarrel with the girl he's engaged to. You knew he was engaged to Miss Elizabeth Vickers?'

'Yes, sir. I recall reading the announcement in the *Morning Post*.'

'Well, he isn't any longer. What the row was about he didn't say, but the broad facts, Jeeves, are that she has scratched the fixture. She won't let him come near her, refuses to talk on the phone, and sends back his letters unopened.'

'Extremely trying, sir.'

'We ought to do something, Jeeves. But what?'

'It is somewhat difficult to make a suggestion, sir.'

'Well, what I'm going to do for a start is to take him down to Marvis Bay with me. I know these birds who have been handed their hat by the girl of their dreams, Jeeves. What they want is complete change of scene.'

'There is much in what you say, sir.'

'Yes. Change of scene is the thing. I heard of a man. Girl refused him. Man went abroad. Two months later girl wired him "Come back, Muriel." Man started to write out a reply; suddenly found that he couldn't remember girl's surname; so never answered at all, and lived happily ever after. It may well be, Jeeves, that after Freddie Bullivant has had a few weeks of Marvis Bay he will get completely over it.'

'Very possibly, sir.'

'And, if not, it is quite likely that, refreshed by sea air and good simple food, you will get a brainwave and think up some scheme for bringing these two misguided blighters together again.'

'I will do my best, sir.'

'I knew it, Jeeves, I knew it. Don't forget to put in plenty of socks.'

'No, sir.'

'Also of tennis shirts not a few.'

'Very good, sir.'

I left him to his packing, and a couple of days later we started off for Marvis Bay, where I had taken a cottage for July and August.

I don't know if you know Marvis Bay? It's in Dorsetshire; and, while not what you would call a fiercely exciting spot, has many good points. You spend the day there bathing and sitting on the sands, and in the evening you stroll out on the shore with the mosquitoes. At nine p.m. you rub ointment on the wounds and go to bed. It was a simple, healthy life, and it seemed to suit poor old Freddie absolutely. Once the moon was up and the breeze sighing in the trees, you couldn't drag him from that beach with ropes. He became quite a popular pet with the mosquitoes. They would hang round waiting for him to come out, and would give a miss to perfectly good strollers just so as to be in good condition for him.

It was during the day that I found Freddie, poor old chap, a trifle heavy as a guest. I suppose you can't blame a bloke whose heart is broken, but it required a good deal of fortitude to bear up against this gloom-crushed exhibit during the early days of our little holiday. When he wasn't chewing a pipe and scowling at the carpet, he was sitting at the piano, playing 'The Rosary' with one finger. He couldn't play anything except 'The Rosary', and he couldn't play much of that. However firmly and confidently he started off, somewhere around the third bar a fuse would blow out and he would have to start all over again.

He was playing it as usual one morning when I came in from bathing: and it seemed to me that he was extracting more hideous melancholy from it even than usual. Nor had my sense deceived me.

'Bertie,' he said in a hollow voice, skidding on the fourth crotchet from the left as you enter the second bar and producing a distressing sound like the death-rattle of a sand-eel, 'I've seen her!'

'Seen her?' I said. 'What, Elizabeth Vickers? How do you mean, you've seen her? She isn't down here.'

'Yes, she is. I suppose she's staying with relations or something. I was down at the post office, seeing if there were any letters, and we met in the doorway.'

'What happened?'

'She cut me dead.'

He started 'The Rosary' again, and stubbed his finger on a semi-quaver.

'Bertie,' he said, 'you ought never to have brought me here. I must go away.'

'Go away? Don't talk such rot. This is the best thing that could have happened. It's a most amazing bit of luck, her being down here. This is where you come out strong.'

'She cut me.'

'Never mind. Be a sportsman. Have another dash at her.'

'She looked clean through me.'

'Well, don't mind that. Stick at it. Now, having got her down here, what you want,' I said, 'is to place her under some obligation to you. What you want is to get her timidly thanking you. What do you want –'

'What's she going to thank me timidly for?'

I thought for a while. Undoubtedly he had put his finger on the nub of the problem. For some moments I was at a loss, not to say nonplussed. Then I saw the way.

'What you want,' I said, 'is to look out for a chance and save her from drowning.'

'I can't swim.'

That was Freddie Bullivant all over. A dear old chap in a thousand ways, but no help to a fellow, if you know what I mean.

He cranked up the piano once more, and I legged it for the open.

I strolled out on the beach and began to think this thing over. I would have liked to consult Jeeves, of course, but Jeeves had disappeared for the morning. There was no doubt that it was hopeless expecting Freddie to do anything for himself in this crisis. I'm not saying that dear old Freddie hasn't got his strong qualities. He is good at polo, and I have heard him spoken of as a coming man at snooker-pool. But apart from this you couldn't call him a man of enterprise.

Well, I was rounding some rocks, thinking pretty tensely, when I caught sight of a blue dress, and there was the girl in person. I had never met her, but Freddie had sixteen photographs of her sprinkled round his bedroom, and I knew I couldn't be mistaken. She was sitting on the sand, helping a small, fat child to build a castle. On a chair close by was an elderly female reading a novel. I heard the girl call her 'aunt'. So, getting the reasoning faculties to work, I deduced that the fat child must be her cousin. It struck me that if Freddie had been there he would probably have tried to work up some sentiment about the kid on the strength of it. I couldn't manage this. I don't think I ever saw a kid who made me feel less sentimental. He was one of those round, bulging kids.

After he had finished his castle he seemed to get bored with life and began to cry. The girl, who seemed to read him like a book, took him off to where a fellow was selling sweets at a stall. And I walked on.

Now, those who know me, if you ask them, will tell you that I'm a chump. My Aunt Agatha would testify to this effect. So would my Uncle Percy and many more of my nearest and – if you like to use the expression – dearest. Well, I don't mind. I admit it. I *am* a chump. But what I do say – and I should like to lay the greatest possible stress on this – is that every now and then, just when the populace has given up hope that I will ever show any real human intelligence – I get what it is idle to pretend is not an inspiration. And that's what happened now. I doubt if the idea that came to me at this juncture would have occurred to a single one of any dozen of the largest-brained blokes in history. Napoleon might have got it, but I'll bet Darwin and Shakespeare and Thomas Hardy wouldn't have thought of it in a thousand years.

It came to me on my return journey. I was walking back along the shore, exercising the old bean fiercely, when I saw the fat child meditatively smacking a jelly-fish with a spade. The girl wasn't with him. The aunt wasn't with him. In fact, there wasn't anybody else in sight. And the solution of the whole trouble between Freddie and his Elizabeth suddenly came to me in a flash.

From what I had seen of the two, the girl was evidently fond of this kid: and, anyhow, he was her cousin, so what I said to myself was this: If I kidnap this young heavyweight for a brief space of time: and if, when the girl has got frightfully anxious about where he can have got to, dear old Freddie suddenly appears leading the infant by the hand and telling a story to the effect that he found him wandering at large about the country and practically saved his life, the girl's gratitude is bound to make her chuck hostilities and be friends again.

So I gathered up the kid and made off with him.

Freddie, dear old chap, was rather slow at first in getting on to the fine points of the idea. When I appeared at the cottage, carrying the child, and dumped him down in the sitting-room, he showed no joy whatever. The child had started to bellow by this time, not thinking much of the thing, and Freddie seemed to find it rather trying.

'What the devil's all this?' he asked, regarding the little visitor with a good deal of loathing.

The kid loosed off a yell that made the windows rattle, and I saw that this was a time for strategy. I raced to the kitchen and fetched a pot of honey. It was the right idea. The kid stopped bellowing and began to smear his face with the stuff.

'Well?' said Freddie, when silence had set in.

I explained the scheme. After a while it began to strike him. The careworn look faded from his face, and for the first time since his arrival at Marvis Bay he smiled almost happily.

'There's something in this, Bertie.'

'It's the goods.'

'I think it will work,' said Freddie.

And, disentangling the child from the honey, he led him out.

'I expect Elizabeth will be on the beach somewhere,' he said.

What you might call a quiet happiness suffused me, if that's the word I want. I was very fond of old Freddie, and it was jolly to think that he was shortly about to click once more. I was leaning back in a chair on the veranda, smoking a peaceful cigarette, when down the road I saw the old boy returning, and, by George, the kid was still with him.

'Hallo!' I said. 'Couldn't you find her?'

I then perceived that Freddie was looking as if he had been kicked in the stomach.

'Yes, I found her,' he replied, with one of those bitter, mirthless laughs you read about.

'Well, then –?'

He sank into a chair and groaned.

'This isn't her cousin, you idiot,' he said. 'He's no relation at all – just a kid she met on the beach. She had never seen him before in her life.'

'But she was helping him build a sand-castle.'

'I don't care. He's a perfect stranger.'

It seemed to me that, if the modern girl goes about building sand-castles with kids she has only known for five minutes and probably without a proper introduction at that, then all that has been written about her is perfectly true. Brazen is the word that seems to meet the case.

I said as much to Freddie, but he wasn't listening.

'Well, who is this ghastly child, then?' I said.

'I don't know. O Lord, I've had a time! Thank goodness you will probably spend the next few years of your life in Dartmoor for kidnapping. That's my only consolation. I'll come and jeer at you through the bars on visiting days.'

'Tell me all, old man,' I said.

He told me all. It took him a good long time to do it, for he broke off in the middle of nearly every sentence to call me names, but I gradually gathered what had happened. The girl Elizabeth had listened like an iceberg while he worked off the story he had prepared, and then – well, she didn't actually call him a liar in so many words, but she gave him to understand in a general sort of way that he was a worm and an outcast. And then he crawled off with the kid, licked to a splinter.

'And mind,' he concluded, 'this is your affair. I'm not mixed up in it at all. If you want to escape your sentence – or anyway get a portion of it remitted – you'd better go and find the child's parents and return him before the police come for you.'

'Who are his parents?'

'I don't know.'

'Where do they live?'

'I don't know.'

The kid didn't seem to know, either. A thoroughly vapid and uninformed infant. I got out of him the fact that he had a father, but that was as far as he went. It didn't seem ever to have occurred to him, chatting of an evening with the old man, to ask him his name and address. So, after a wasted ten minutes, out we went into the great world, more or less what you might call at random.

I give you my word that, until I started to tramp the place with this child, I never had a notion that it was such a difficult job restoring a son to his parents. How kidnappers ever get caught is a mystery to me. I searched Marvis Bay like a bloodhound, but nobody came forward to claim the infant. You would have thought, from the lack of interest in him, that he was stopping there all by himself in a cottage of his own. It wasn't till, by another inspiration, I thought to ask the sweet-stall man that I got on the track. The sweet-stall man, who seemed to have seen a lot of him, said that the child's name was Kegworthy, and that his parents lived at a place called Ocean Rest.

It then remained to find Ocean Rest. And eventually, after visiting Ocean View, Ocean Prospect, Ocean Breeze, Ocean Cottage, Ocean Bungalow, Ocean Nook and Ocean Homestead, I trailed it down.

I knocked at the door. Nobody answered. I knocked again. I could hear movements inside, but nobody appeared. I was just going to get to work with that knocker in such a way that it would filter through these people's heads that I wasn't standing there just for the fun of the thing, when a voice from somewhere above shouted 'Hi!'

I looked up and saw a round, pink face, with grey whiskers east and west of it, staring down at me from an upper window.

'Hi!' it shouted again. 'You can't come in.'

'I don't want to come in.'

'Because – Oh, is that Tootles?'

'My name is not Tootles. Are you Mr Kegworthy? I've brought back your son.'

'I see him. Peep-bo, Tootles, Dadda can see 'oo.'

The face disappeared with a jerk. I could hear voices. The face reappeared.

'Hi!'

I churned the gravel madly. This blighter was giving me the pip.

'Do you live here?' asked the face.

'I have taken a cottage here for a few weeks.'

'What's your name?'

'Wooster.'

'Fancy that! Do you spell it W-o-r-c-e-s-t-e-r or W-o-o-s-t-e-r?'

'W-o-o –'

'I ask because I once knew a Miss Wooster, spelled
W-o- – '

I had had about enough of this spelling-bee.

'Will you open the door and take this child in?'

'I mustn't open the door. This Miss Wooster that I
knew married a man named Spenser. Was she any
relation?'

'She is my Aunt Agatha,' I replied, and I spoke with a
good deal of bitterness, trying to suggest by my manner
that he was exactly the sort of man, in my opinion, who
would know my Aunt Agatha.

He beamed down at me.

'This is most fortunate. We were wondering what to
do with Tootles. You see, we have mumps here. My
daughter Bootles has just developed mumps. Tootles
must not be exposed to the risk of infection. We could
not think what to do with him. It was most fortunate,
your finding the dear child. He strayed from his nurse. I
would hesitate to trust him to a stranger, but you are
different. Any nephew of Mrs Spenser's has my complete
confidence. You must take Tootles into your house. It
will be an ideal arrangement. I have written to my
brother in London to come and fetch him. He may be
here in a few days.'

'May!'

'He is a busy man, of course; but he should certainly
be here within a week. Till then Tootles can stop with
you. It is an excellent plan. Very much obliged to you.
Your wife will like Tootles.'

'I haven't got a wife!' I yelled; but the window had
closed with a bang, as if the man with the whiskers had
found a germ trying to escape and had headed it off just
in time.

I breathed a deep breath and wiped the old forehead.

The window flew up again.

'Hi!'

A package weighing about a ton hit me on the head and burst like a bomb.

'Did you catch it?' said the face, reappearing. 'Dear me, you missed it. Never mind. You can get it at the grocer's. Ask for Bailey's Granulated Breakfast Chips. Tootles takes them for breakfast with a little milk. Not cream. Milk. Be sure to get Bailey's.'

'Yes, but –'

The face disappeared, and the window was banged down again. I lingered a while, but nothing else happened, so, taking Tootles by the hand, I walked slowly away.

And as we turned up the road we met Freddie's Elizabeth.

'Well, baby?' she said, sighting the kid. 'So daddy found you again, did he? Your little son and I made great friends on the beach this morning,' she said to me.

This was the limit. Coming on top of that interview with the whiskered lunatic, it so utterly unnerved me that she had nodded good-bye and was half-way down the road before I caught up with my breath enough to deny the charge of being the infant's father.

I hadn't expected Freddie to sing with joy when he saw me looming up with child complete, but I did think he might have showed a little more manly fortitude, a little more of the old British bulldog spirit. He leaped up when we came in, glared at the kid and clutched his head. He didn't speak for a long time; but, to make up for it, when he began he did not leave off for a long time.

'Well,' he said, when he had finished the body of his remarks, 'say something! Heavens, man, why don't you say something?'

'If you'll give me a chance, I will,' I said, and shot the bad news.

'What are you going to do about it?' he asked. And it would be idle to deny that his manner was peevish.

'What can we do about it?'

'We? What do you mean, we? I'm not going to spend my time taking turns as a nursemaid to this excrescence. I'm going back to London.'

'Freddie!' I cried. 'Freddie, old man!' My voice shook. 'Would you desert a pal at a time like this?'

'Yes, I would.'

'Freddie,' I said, 'you've got to stand by me. You must. Do you realize that this child has to be undressed, and bathed, and dressed again? You wouldn't leave me to do all that single-handed?'

'Jeeves can help you.'

'No, sir,' said Jeeves, who had just rolled in with lunch; 'I must, I fear, disassociate myself completely from the matter.' He spoke respectfully but firmly. 'I have had little or no experience with children.'

'Now's the time to start,' I urged.

'No, sir; I am sorry to say that I cannot involve myself in any way.'

'Then you must stand by me, Freddie.'

'I won't.'

'You must. Reflect, old man! We have been pals for years. Your mother likes me.'

'No, she doesn't.'

'Well, anyway, we were at school together and you owe me a tenner.'

'Oh, well,' he said in a resigned sort of voice.

'Besides, old thing,' I said, 'I did it all for your sake, you know.'

He looked at me in a curious way, and breathed rather hard for some moments.

'Bertie,' he said, 'one moment. I will stand a good deal, but I will not stand being expected to be grateful.'

Looking back at it, I can see that what saved me from Colney Hatch in this crisis was my bright idea in buying up most of the contents of the local sweet-shop. By serving out sweets to the kid practically incessantly we managed to get through the rest of that day pretty satisfactorily. At eight o'clock he fell asleep in a chair; and, having undressed him by unbuttoning every button in sight and, where there were no buttons, pulling till something gave, we carried him up to bed.

Freddie stood looking at the pile of clothes on the floor with a sort of careworn wrinkle between his eyes, and I knew what he was thinking. To get the kid undressed had been simple – a mere matter of muscle. But how were we to get him into his clothes again? I stirred the heap with my foot. There was a long linen arrangement which might have been anything. Also a strip of pink flannel which was like nothing on earth. All most unpleasant.

But in the morning I remembered that there were children in the next bungalow but one, and I went there before breakfast and borrowed their nurse. Women are wonderful, by Jove they are! This nurse had all the spare parts assembled and in the right places in about eight minutes, and there was the kid dressed and looking fit to go to a garden party at Buckingham Palace. I showered wealth upon her, and she promised to come in morning and evening. I sat down to breakfast almost cheerful again. It was the first bit of silver lining that had presented itself to date.

'And, after all,' I said, 'there's lots to be argued in favour of having a child about the place, if you know what I mean. Kind of cosy and domestic, what?'

Just then the kid upset the milk over Freddie's trousers, and when he had come back after changing he lacked sparkle.

It was shortly after breakfast that Jeeves asked if he could have a word in my ear.

Now, though in the anguish of recent events I had rather tended to forget what had been the original idea in bringing Freddie down to this place, I hadn't forgotten it altogether; and I'm bound to say that, as the days went by, I had found myself a little disappointed in Jeeves. The scheme had been, if you recall, that he should refresh himself with sea-air and simple food and, having thus got his brain into prime working order, evolve some means of bringing Freddie and his Elizabeth together again.

And what had happened? The man had eaten well and he had slept well, but not a step did he appear to have taken towards bringing about the happy ending. The only move that had been made in that direction had been made by me, alone and unaided; and, though I freely admit that it had turned out a good deal of a bloomer, still the fact remains that I had shown zeal and enterprise. Consequently I received him with a bit of hauteur when he blew in. Slightly cold. A trifle frosty.

'Yes, Jeeves?' I said. 'You wished to speak to me?'

'Yes, sir.'

'Say on, Jeeves,' I said.

'Thank you, sir. What I desired to say, sir, was this: I attended a performance at the local cinema last night.'

I raised the eyebrows. I was surprised at the man. With life in the home so frightfully tense and the young master up against it to such a fearful extent, I disapproved of him coming toddling in and prattling about his amusements.

'I hope you enjoyed yourself,' I said in rather a nasty manner.

'Yes, sir, thank you. The management was presenting a super-super-film in seven reels, dealing with life in the wilder and more feverish strata of New York Society, featuring Bertha Blevitch, Orlando Murphy and Baby Bobbie. I found it most entertaining, sir.'

'That's good,' I said. 'And if you have a nice time this morning on the sands with your spade and bucket, you will come and tell me all about it, won't you? I have so little on my mind just now that it's a treat to hear all about your happy holiday.'

Satirical, if you see what I mean. Sarcastic. Almost bitter, as a matter of fact, if you come right down to it.

'The title of the film was *Tiny Hands*, sir. And the father and mother of the character played by Baby Bobbie had unfortunately drifted apart –'

'Too bad,' I said.

'Although at heart they loved each other still, sir.'

'Did they really? I'm glad you told me that.'

'And so matters went on, sir, till came a day when –'

'Jeeves,' I said, fixing him with a dashed unpleasant eye, 'what the dickens do you think you're talking about? Do you suppose that, with this infernal child landed on me and the peace of the home practically shattered into a million bits, I want to hear –'

'I beg your pardon, sir. I would not have mentioned this cinema performance were it not for the fact that it gave me an idea, sir.'

'An idea!'

'An idea that will, I fancy, sir, prove of value in straightening out the matrimonial future of Mr Bullivant. To which end, if you recollect, sir, you desired me to –'

I snorted with remorse.

'Jeeves,' I said, 'I wronged you.'

'Not at all, sir.'

'Yes, I did. I wronged you. I had a notion that you had given yourself up entirely to the pleasures of the seaside and had chucked that business altogether. I might have known better. Tell me all, Jeeves.'

He bowed in a gratified manner. I beamed. And, while we didn't actually fall on each other's necks, we gave each other to understand that all was well once more.

'In this super-super-film *Tiny Hands*, sir,' said Jeeves, 'the parents of the child had, as I say, drifted apart.'

'Drifted apart,' I said, nodding. 'Right! And then?'

'Came a day, sir, when their little child brought them together again.'

'How?'

'If I remember rightly, sir, he said, "Dadda, doesn't 'oo love mummie no more?"'

'And then?'

'They exhibited a good deal of emotion. There was what I believe is termed a cut-back, showing scenes from their courtship and early married life and some glimpses of Lovers Through the Ages, and the picture concluded with a close-up of the pair in an embrace, with the child looking on with natural gratification and an organ playing "Hearts and Flowers" in the distance.'

'Proceed, Jeeves,' I said. 'You interest me strangely. I begin to grasp the idea. You mean –?'

'I mean, sir, that, with this young gentleman on the premises, it might be possible to arrange a *dénouement* of a somewhat similar nature in regard to Mr Bullivant and Miss Vickers.'

'Aren't you overlooking the fact that this kid is no relation of Mr Bullivant or Miss Vickers?'

'Even with that handicap, sir, I fancy that good results might ensue. I think that, if it were possible to bring Mr Bullivant and Miss Vickers together for a short space of time in the presence of the child, sir, and if the child were to say something of a touching nature –'

'I follow you absolutely, Jeeves,' I cried with enthusiasm. 'It's big. This is the way I see it. We lay the scene in this room. Child, centre. Girl, l.c. Freddie up stage, playing the piano. No, that won't do. He can only play a little of "The Rosary" with one finger, so we'll have to cut out the soft music. But the rest's all right. Look here,' I said. 'This inkpot is Miss Vickers. This mug with "A Present from Marvis Bay" on it is the child. This penwiper is Mr Bullivant. Start with dialogue leading up to child's line. Child speaks line, let us say,

"Boofer lady, does 'oo love dadda?" Business of outstretched hands. Hold picture for a moment. Freddie crosses l. takes girl's hand. Business of swallowing lump in throat. Then big speech: "Ah, Elizabeth, has not this misunderstanding of ours gone on too long? See! A little child rebukes us!" And so on. I'm just giving you the general outline. Freddie must work up his own part. And we must get a good line for the child. "Boofer lady, does 'oo love dadda?" isn't definite enough. We want something more –'

'If I might make the suggestion, sir – ?'

'Yes?'

'I would advocate the words "Kiss Freddie?" It is short, readily memorized, and has what I believe is technically termed the punch.'

'Genius, Jeeves!'

'Thank you very much, sir.'

'"Kiss Freddie!" it is, then. But, I say, Jeeves, how the deuce are we to get them together in here? Miss Vickers cuts Mr Bullivant. She wouldn't come within a mile of him.'

'It is awkward, sir.'

'It doesn't matter. We shall have to make it an exterior set instead of an interior. We can easily corner her on the beach somewhere, when we're ready. Meanwhile, we must get the kid word-perfect.'

'Yes, sir.'

'Right! First rehearsal for lines and business at eleven sharp tomorrow morning.'

Poor old Freddie was in such a gloomy frame of mind that I decided not to tell him the idea till we had finished coaching the child. He wasn't in the mood to have a thing like that hanging over him. So we concentrated on Tootles. And pretty early in the proceedings we saw that the only way to get Tootles worked up to the spirit of the thing was to introduce sweets of some sort as a sub-motive, so to speak.

'The chief difficulty, sir,' said Jeeves, at the end of the first rehearsal, 'is, as I envisage it, to establish in the young gentleman's mind a connexion between the words we desire him to say and the refreshment.'

'Exactly,' I said. 'Once the blighter has grasped the basic fact that these two words, clearly spoken, result automatically in chocolate nougat, we have got a success.'

I've often thought how interesting it must be to be one of those animal-trainer blokes – to stimulate the dawning intelligence and all that. Well, this was every bit as exciting. Some days success seemed to be staring us in the eyeball, and the kid got out the line as if he had been an old professional. And then he would go all to pieces again. And time was flying.

'We must hurry up, Jeeves,' I said. 'The kid's uncle may arrive any day now and take him away.'

'Exactly, sir.'

'And we have no understudy.'

'Very true, sir.'

'We must work! I must say this child is a bit discouraging at times. I should have thought a deaf-mute would have learned his part by now.'

I will say this for the kid, though: he was a trier. Failure didn't damp him. Whenever there was any kind of sweet in sight he had a dash at his line, and kept saying something till he had got what he was after. His chief fault was his uncertainty. Personally, I would have been prepared to risk opening in the act and was ready to start the public performance at the first opportunity, but Jeeves said no.

'I would not advocate undue haste, sir,' he said. 'As long as the young gentleman's memory refuses to act with any certainty, we are running grave risks of failure.

Today, if you recollect, sir, he said "Kick Freddie!" That is not a speech to win a young lady's heart, sir.'

'No. And she might do it, too. You're right. We must postpone production.'

But, by Jove, we didn't! The curtain went up the very next afternoon.

It was nobody's fault – certainly not mine. It was just fate. Jeeves was out, and I was alone in the house with Freddie and the child. Freddie had just settled down at the piano, and I was leading the kid out of the place for a bit of exercise, when, just as we'd got on to the veranda, along came the girl Elizabeth on her way to the beach. And at the sight of her the kid set up a matey yell, and she stopped at the foot of the steps.

'Hallo, baby,' she said. 'Good morning,' she said to me. 'May I come up?'

She didn't wait for an answer. She just hopped on to the veranda. She seemed to be that sort of girl. She started fussing over the child. And six feet away, mind you, Freddie smiting the piano in the sitting-room. It was a dashed disturbing situation, take it from Bertram. At any minute Freddie might take it into his head to come out on the veranda, and I hadn't even begun to rehearse him in his part.

I tried to break up the scene.

'We were just going down to the beach,' I said.

'Yes?' said the girl. She listened for a moment. 'So you're having your piano tuned?' she said. 'My aunt has been trying to find a tuner for ours. Do you mind if I go in and tell this man to come on to us when he has finished here?'

I mopped the brow.

'Er – I shouldn't go in just now,' I said. 'Not just now, while he's working, if you don't mind. These fellows can't bear to be disturbed when they're at work. It's the artistic temperament. I'll tell him later.'

'Very well. Ask him to call at Pine Bungalow. Vickers is the name . . . Oh, he seems to have stopped. I suppose he will be out in a minute now. I'll wait.'

'Don't you think – shouldn't you be getting on to the beach?' I said.

She had started talking to the kid and didn't hear. She was feeling in her bag for something.

'The beach,' I babbled.

'See what I've got for you, baby,' said the girl. 'I thought I might meet you somewhere, so I bought some of your favourite sweets.'

And, by Jove, she held up in front of the kid's bulging eyes, a chunk of toffee about the size of the Albert Memorial!

That finished it. We had just been having a long rehearsal, and the kid was all worked up in his part. He got it right first time.

'Kiss Fweddie!' he shouted.

And the French windows opened and Freddie came out on to the veranda, for all the world as if he had been taking a cue.

'Kiss Fweddie!' shrieked the child.

Freddie looked at the girl, and the girl looked at him. I looked at the ground, and the kid looked at the toffee.

'Kiss Fweddie!' he yelled. 'Kiss Fweddie!'

'What does this mean?' said the girl, turning on me.

'You'd better give it him,' I said. 'He'll go on till you do, you know.'

She gave the kid the toffee and he subsided. Freddie, poor ass, still stood there gaping, without a word.

'What does it mean?' said the girl again. Her face was pink, and her eyes were sparkling in the sort of way, don't you know, that makes a fellow feel as if he hadn't any bones in him, if you know what I mean. Yes, Bertram felt filleted. Did you ever tread on your partner's dress at a dance – I'm speaking now of the days when women wore dresses long enough to be trodden on

– and hear it rip and see her smile at you like an angel and say, '*Please* don't apologize. It's nothing,' and then suddenly meet her clear blue eyes and feel as if you had stepped on the teeth of a rake and had the handle jump up and hit you in the face? Well, that's how Freddie's Elizabeth looked.

'*Well?*' she said, and her teeth gave a little click.

I gulped. Then I said it was nothing. Then I said it was nothing much. Then I said, 'Oh, well, it was this way.' And I told her all about it. And all the while Idiot Freddie stood there gaping, without a word. Not one solitary yip had he let out of himself from the start.

And the girl didn't speak, either. She just stood listening.

And then she began to laugh. I never heard a girl laugh so much. She leaned against the side of the veranda and shrieked. And all the while Freddie, the World's Champion Dumb Brick, standing there, saying nothing.

Well, I finished my story and sidled to the steps. I had said all I had to say, and it seemed to me that about here the stage-direction 'exit cautiously' was written in my part. I gave poor old Freddie up in despair. If only he had said a word it might have been all right. But there he stood speechless.

Just out of sight of the house I met Jeeves, returning from his stroll.

'Jeeves,' I said, 'all is over. The thing's finished. Poor dear old Freddie has made a complete ass of himself and killed the whole show.'

'Indeed, sir? What has actually happened?'

I told him.

'He fluffed in his lines,' I concluded. 'Just stood there saying nothing, when if ever there was a time for eloquence, this was it. He . . . Great Scott! Look!'

We had come back within view of the cottage, and there in front of it stood six children, a nurse, two loafers, another nurse, and the fellow from the grocer's.

They were all staring. Down the road came galloping five more children, a dog, three men and a boy, all about to stare. And on our porch, as unconscious of the spectators as if they had been alone in the Sahara, stood Freddie and his Elizabeth, clasped in each other's arms.

'Great Scott!' I said.

'It would appear, sir,' said Jeeves, 'that everything has concluded most satisfactorily, after all.'

'Yes. Dear old Freddie may have been fluffy in his lines,' I said, 'but his business certainly seems to have gone with a bang.'

'Very true, sir,' said Jeeves.

9 — Clustering Round Young Bingo

I blotted the last page of my manuscript and sank back, feeling more or less of a spent force. After incredible sweat of the old brow the thing seemed to be in pretty fair shape, and I was just reading it through and debating whether to bung in another paragraph at the end, when there was a tap at the door and Jeeves appeared.

'Mrs Travers, sir, on the telephone.'

'Oh?' I said. Preoccupied, don't you know.

'Yes, sir. She presents her compliments and would be glad to know what progress you have made with the article which you are writing for her.'

'Jeeves, can I mention men's knee-length underclothing in a woman's paper?'

'No, sir.'

'Then tell her it's finished.'

'Very good, sir.'

'And, Jeeves, when you're through, come back. I want you to cast your eye over this effort and give it the OK.'

My Aunt Dahlia, who runs a woman's paper called *Milady's Boudoir*, had recently backed me into a corner and made me promise to write her a few authoritative words for her 'Husbands and Brothers' page on 'What the Well-Dressed Man is Wearing'. I believe in encouraging aunts, when deserving; and, as there are many worse eggs than her knocking about the metrop, I had consented blithely. But I give you my honest word that if I had had the foggiest notion of what I was letting myself in for, not even a nephew's devotion would have kept me from giving her the raspberry. A deuce of a job it had been, taxing the physique to the utmost. I don't wonder now that all these author blokes have bald heads and faces like birds who have suffered.

'Jeeves,' I said, when he came back, 'you don't read a paper called *Milady's Boudoir* by any chance, do you?'

'No, sir. The periodical has not come to my notice.'

'Well, spring sixpence on it next week, because this article will appear in it. Wooster on the well-dressed man, don't you know.'

'Indeed, sir?'

'Yes, indeed, Jeeves. I've rather extended myself over this little bijou. There's a bit about socks that I think you will like.'

He took the manuscript, brooded over it, and smiled a gentle, approving smile.

'The sock passage is quite in the proper vein, sir,' he said.

'Well expressed, what?'

'Extremely, sir.'

I watched him narrowly as he read on, and, as I was expecting, what you might call the love-light suddenly died out of his eyes. I braced myself for an unpleasant scene.

'Come to the bit about soft silk shirts for evening wear?' I asked carelessly.

'Yes, sir,' said Jeeves, in a low, cold voice, as if he had been bitten in the leg by a personal friend. 'And if I may be pardoned for saying so – '

'You don't like it?'

'No, sir. I do not. Soft silk shirts with evening costume are not worn, sir.'

'Jeeves,' I said, looking the blighter diametrically in the centre of the eyeball, 'they're dashed well going to be. I may as well tell you now that I have ordered a dozen of those shirtings from Peabody and Simms, and it's no good looking like that, because I am jolly well adamant.'

'If I might – '

'No, Jeeves,' I said, raising my hand, 'argument is useless. Nobody has a greater respect than I have for your judgement in socks, in ties, and – I will go farther – in spats; but when it comes to evening shirts your nerve seems to fail you. You have no vision. You are prejudiced and reactionary. Hidebound is the word that suggests itself. It may interest you to learn that when I was at Le Touquet the Prince of Wales buzzed into the Casino one night with soft silk shirt complete.'

'His Royal Highness, sir, may permit himself a certain licence which in your own case – '

'No, Jeeves,' I said firmly, 'it's no use. When we Woosters are adamant, we are – well, adamant, if you know what I mean.'

'Very good, sir.'

I could see the man was wounded, and, of course, the whole episode had been extremely jarring and unpleasant; but these things have to be gone through. Is one a serf or isn't one? That's what it all boils down to. Having made my point, I changed the subject.

'Well, that's that,' I said. 'We now approach another topic. Do you know any housemaids, Jeeves?'

'Housemaids, sir?'

'Come, come, Jeeves, you know what housemaids are.'

'Are you requiring a housemaid, sir?'

'No, but Mr Little is. I met him at the club a couple of days ago, and he told me that Mrs Little is offering rich rewards to anybody who will find her one guaranteed to go light on the china.'

'Indeed, sir?'

'Yes. The one now in office apparently runs through the *objects d'art* like a typhoon, simoom, or sirocco. So if you know any – '

'I know a great many, sir. Some intimately, others mere acquaintances.'

'Well, start digging round among the old pals. And

now the hat, the stick, and other necessaries. I must be getting along and handing in this article.'

The offices of *Milady's Boudoir* were in one of those rummy streets in the Covent Garden neighbourhood; and I had just got to the door, after wading through a deep top-dressing of old cabbages and tomatoes, when who should come out but Mrs Little. She greeted me with the warmth due to the old family friend, in spite of the fact that I hadn't been round to the house for a goodish while.

'Whatever are you doing in these parts, Bertie? I thought you never came east of Leicester Square.'

'I've come to deliver an article of sorts which my Aunt Dahlia asked me to write. She edits a species of journal up those stairs. *Milady's Boudoir*.'

'What a coincidence! I have just promised to write an article for her, too.'

'Don't you do it,' I said earnestly. 'You've simply no notion what a ghastly labour – Oh, but, of course, I was forgetting. You're used to it, what?'

Silly of me to have talked like that. Young Bingo Little, if you remember, had married the famous female novelist, Rosie M. Banks, author of some of the most pronounced and widely read tripe ever put on the market. Naturally a mere article would be pie for her.

'No, I don't think it will give me much trouble,' she said. 'Your aunt has suggested a most delightful subject.'

'That's good. By the way, I spoke to my man Jeeves about getting you a housemaid. He knows all the hummers.'

'Thank you so much. Oh, are you doing anything tomorrow night?'

'Not a thing.'

'Then do come and dine with us. Your aunt is coming, and hopes to bring your uncle. I am looking forward to meeting him.'

'Thanks. Delighted.'

I mean it, too. The Little household may be weak on housemaids, but it is right there when it comes to cooks. Somewhere or other some time ago Bingo's missus managed to dig up a Frenchman of the most extraordinary vim and skill. A most amazing Johnnie who dishes a wicked *ragout*. Old Bingo has put on at least ten pounds in weight since this fellow Anatole arrived in the home.

'At eight, then.'

'Right. Thanks ever so much.'

She popped off, and I went upstairs to hand in my copy, as we boys of the Press call it. I found Aunt Dahlia immersed to the gills in papers of all descriptions.

I am not much of a lad for my relatives as a general thing, but I've always been very pally with Aunt Dahlia. She married my Uncle Thomas – between ourselves a bit of a squirt – the year Bluebottle won the Cambridgeshire; and they hadn't got half way down the aisle before I was saying to myself, 'That woman is much too good for the old bird.' Aunt Dahlia is a large, genial soul, the sort you see in dozens on the hunting field. As a matter of fact, until she married Uncle Thomas, she put in most of her time on horseback; but he won't live in the country, so nowadays she expends her energy on this paper of hers.

She came to the surface as I entered, and flung a cheery book at my head.

'Hullo, Bertie! I say, have you really finished that article?'

'To the last comma.'

'Good boy! My gosh, I'll bet it's rotten.'

'On the contrary, it is extremely hot stuff, and most of it approved by Jeeves, what's more. The bit about soft silk shirts got in amongst him a trifle; but you can take it from me, Aunt Dahlia, that they are the latest yodel and will be much seen at first nights and other occasions where Society assembles.'

'Your man Jeeves,' said Aunt Dahlia, flinging the article into a basket and skewering a few loose pieces of paper on a sort of meat hook, 'is a washout, and you can tell him I said so.'

'Oh, come,' I said. 'He may not be sound on shirtings –'

'I'm not referring to that. As long as a week ago I asked him to get me a cook, and he hasn't found one yet.'

'Great Scott! Is Jeeves a domestic employment agency? Mrs Little wants him to find her a housemaid. I met her outside. She tells me she's doing something for you.'

'Yes, thank goodness. I'm relying on it to bump the circulation up a bit. I can't read her stuff myself, but women love it. Her name on the cover will mean a lot. And we need it.'

'Paper not doing well?'

'It's doing all right really, but it's got to be a slow job building up a circulation.'

'I suppose so.'

'I can get Tom to see that in his lucid moments,' said Aunt Dahlia, skewering a few more papers. 'But just at present the poor fathead has got one of his pessimistic spells. It's entirely due to that mechanic who calls herself a cook. A few more of her alleged dinners, and Tom will refuse to go on paying the printers' bills.'

'You don't mean that!'

'I do mean it. There was what she called a *ris de veau à la financière* last night which made him talk for three-quarters of an hour about good money going to waste and nothing to show for it.'

I quite understood, and I was dashed sorry for her. My Uncle Thomas is a cove who made a colossal pile of money out in the East, but in doing so put his digestion on the blink. This has made him a tricky proposition to handle. Many a time I've lunched with him and found him perfectly chirpy up to the fish, only to have him turn blue on me well before the cheese.

Who was that lad they used to try to make me read at Oxford? Ship – Shop – Schopenhauer. That's the name. A grouch of the most pronounced description. Well, Uncle Thomas, when his gastric juices have been giving him the elbow, can make Schopenhauer look like Pollyanna. And the worst of it is, from Aunt Dahlia's point of view, that on these occasions he always seems to think he's on the brink of ruin and wants to start to economize.

'Pretty tough,' I said. 'Well, anyway, he'll get one good dinner tomorrow night at the Littles'.'

'Can you guarantee that, Bertie?' asked Aunt Dahlia earnestly. 'I simply daren't risk unleashing him on anything at all wonky.'

'They've got a marvellous cook. I haven't been round there for some time, but unless he's lost his form of two months ago Uncle Thomas is going to have the treat of a lifetime.'

'It'll only make it all the worse for him, coming back to our steak-incinerator,' said Aunt Dahlia, a bit on the Schopenhauer side herself.

The little nest where Bingo and his bride had settled themselves was up in St John's Wood; one of those rather jolly houses with a bit of garden. When I got there on the following night, I found that I was the last to weigh in. Aunt Dahlia was chatting with Rosie in a corner, while Uncle Thomas, standing by the mantelpiece with Bingo, sucked down a cocktail in a frowning, suspicious sort of manner, rather like a chappie having a short snort before dining with the Borgias: as if he were saying to himself that, even if this particular cocktail wasn't poisoned, he was bound to cop it later on.

Well, I hadn't expected anything in the nature of beaming *joie de vivre* from Uncle Thomas, so I didn't pay much attention to him. What did surprise me was the extraordinary gloom of young Bingo. You may say what you like against Bingo, but nobody has ever found him a depressing host. Why, many a time in the days of his bachelorhood I've known him to start throwing bread before the soup course. Yet now he and Uncle Thomas were a pair. He looked haggard and careworn, like a Borgia who has suddenly remembered that he has forgotten to shove cyanide in the *consommé*, and the dinner gong due any moment.

And the mystery wasn't helped at all by the one remark he made to me before conversation became general. As he poured out my cocktail, he suddenly bent forward.

'Bertie,' he whispered, in a nasty, feverish manner, 'I want to see you. Life and death matter. Be in tomorrow morning.'

That was all. Immediately after that the starting-gun went and we toddled down to the festive. And from that moment, I'm bound to say, in the superior interests of the proceedings he rather faded out of my mind. For good old Anatole, braced presumably by the fact of there being guests, had absolutely surpassed himself.

I am not a man who speaks hastily in these matters. I weigh my words. And I say again that Anatole had surpassed himself. It was as good a dinner as I have ever absorbed, and it revived Uncle Thomas like a watered flower. As we sat down he was saying some things about the Government which they wouldn't have cared to hear. With the *consommé pâté d'Italie* he said but what could you expect nowadays? With the *paupiettes de sole à la princesse* he admitted rather decently that the Government couldn't be held responsible for the rotten weather, anyway. And shortly after the *caneton Aylesbury à la broche* he was practically giving the lads the benefit of his whole-hearted support.

And all the time young Bingo looking like an owl with a secret sorrow. Rummy!

I thought about it a good deal as I walked home, and I was hoping he wouldn't roll round with his hard-luck story too early in the morning. He had the air of one who intends to charge in at about six-thirty.

Jeeves was waiting up for me when I got back.

'A pleasant dinner, sir?' he said.

'Magnificent, Jeeves.'

'I am glad to hear that, sir. Mr George Travers rang up on the telephone shortly after you had left. He was extremely desirous that you should join him at Harrogate, sir. He leaves for that town by an early train tomorrow.'

My Uncle George is a festive old bird who has made a habit for years of doing himself a dashed sight too well, with the result that he's always got Harrogate or Buxton hanging over him like the sword of what's-his-name. And he hates going there alone.

'It can't be done,' I said. Uncle George is bad enough in London, and I wasn't going to let myself be cooped up with him in one of these cure-places.

'He was extremely urgent, sir.'

'No, Jeeves,' I said firmly. 'I am always anxious to oblige, but Uncle George – no, no! I mean to say, what?'

'Very good, sir,' said Jeeves.

It was a pleasure to hear the way he said it. Docile the man was becoming, absolutely docile. It just showed that I had been right in putting my foot down about those shirts.

When Bingo showed up next morning I had had breakfast and was all ready for him. Jeeves shot him into the presence, and he sat down on the bed.

'Good morning, Bertie,' said young Bingo.

'Good morning, old thing,' I replied courteously.

'Don't go, Jeeves,' said young Bingo hollowly. 'Wait.'

'Sir?'

'Remain. Stay. Cluster round. I shall need you.'

'Very good, sir.'

Bingo lit a cigarette and frowned bleakly at the wallpaper.

'Bertie,' he said, 'the most frightful calamity has occurred. Unless something is done, and done right speedily, my social prestige is doomed, my self-respect will be obliterated, my name will be mud, and I shall not dare to show my face in the West End of London again.'

'My aunt!' I cried, deeply impressed.

'Exactly,' said young Bingo, with a hollow laugh. 'You have put it in a nutshell. The whole trouble is due to your blasted aunt.'

'Which blasted aunt? Specify, old thing. I have so many.'

'Mrs Travers. The one who runs that infernal paper.'

'Oh, no, dash it, old man,' I protested. 'She's the only decent aunt I've got. Jeeves, you will bear me out in this?'

'Such has always been my impression, I must confess, sir.'

'Well, get rid of it, then,' said young Bingo. 'The woman is a menace to society, a home-wrecker, and a pest. Do you know what's she's done? She's got Rosie to write an article for that rag of hers.'

'I know that.'

'Yes, but you don't know what it's about.'

'No. She only told me Aunt Dahlia had given her a splendid idea for the thing.'

'It's about me!'

'You?'

'Yes, me! Me! And do you know what it's called? It is called "How I Keep the Love of My Husband-Baby".'

'My what?'

'Husband-baby!'

'What's a husband-baby?'

'I am, apparently,' said young Bingo, with much bitterness. 'I am also, according to this article, a lot of other things which I have too much sense of decency to repeat even to an old friend. This beastly composition, in short, is one of those things they call "human interest stories"; one of those intimate revelations of married life over which the female public loves to gloat; all about Rosie and me and what she does when I come home cross, and so on. I tell you, Bertie, I am still blushing all over at the recollection of something she says in paragraph two.'

'What?'

'I decline to tell you. But you can take it from me that it's the edge. Nobody could be fonder of Rosie than I am, but – dear, sensible girl as she is in ordinary life – the moment she gets in front of a dictating machine she becomes absolutely maudlin. Bertie, that article must not appear!'

'But –'

'If it does I shall have to resign from my clubs, grow a beard, and become a hermit. I shall not be able to face the world.'

'Aren't you pitching it a bit strong, old lad?' I said. 'Jeeves, don't you think he's pitching it a bit strong?'

'Well, sir –'

'I am pitching it feebly,' said young Bingo earnestly. 'You haven't heard the thing. I have. Rosie shoved the cylinder on the dictating machine last night before dinner, and it was grisly to hear the instrument croaking out those awful sentences. If that article appears I shall be kidded to death by every pal I've got. Bertie,' he said, his voice sinking to a hoarse whisper, 'you have about as much imagination as a warthog, but surely even you can picture to yourself what Jimmy Bowles and Tuppy Rogers, to name only two, will say when they see me referred to in print as "half god, half prattling, mischievous child"?'

I jolly well could.

'She doesn't say that?' I gasped.

'She certainly does. And when I tell you that I selected that particular quotation because it's about the only one I can stand hearing spoken, you will realize what I'm up against.'

I picked at the coverlet. I had been a pal of Bingo's for many years, and we Woosters stand by our pals.

'Jeeves,' I said, 'you have heard?'

'Yes, sir.'

'The position is serious.'

'Yes, sir.'

'We must cluster round.'

'Yes, sir.'

'Does anything suggest itself to you?'

'Yes, sir.'

'What! You don't really mean that?'

'Yes, sir.'

'Bingo,' I said, 'the sun is still shining. Something suggests itself to Jeeves.'

'Jeeves,' said young Bingo in a quivering voice, 'if you see me through this fearful crisis, ask of me what you will even unto half my kingdom.'

'The matter,' said Jeeves, 'fits in very nicely, sir, with another mission which was entrusted to me this morning.'

'What do you mean?'

'Mrs Travers rang me up on the telephone shortly before I brought you your tea, sir, and was most urgent that I should endeavour to persuade Mr Little's cook to leave Mr Little's service and join her staff. It appears that Mr Travers was fascinated by the man's ability, sir, and talked far into the night of his astonishing gifts.'

Young Bingo uttered a frightful cry of agony.

'What! Is that – that buzzard trying to pinch our cook?'

'Yes, sir.'

'After eating our bread and salt, dammit?'

'I fear, sir,' sighed Jeeves, 'that when it comes to a matter of cooks, ladies have but a rudimentary sense of morality.'

'Half a second, Bingo,' I said, as the fellow seemed about to plunge into something of an oration. 'How does this fit in with the other thing, Jeeves?'

'Well, sir, it has been my experience that no lady can ever forgive another lady for taking a really good cook away from her. I am convinced that, if I am able to accomplish the mission which Mrs Travers entrusted to me, an instant breach of cordial relations must inevitably ensue. Mrs Little will, I feel certain, be so aggrieved with Mrs Travers that she will decline to contribute to her paper. We shall therefore not only bring happiness to Mr Travers, but also suppress the article. Thus killing two birds with one stone, if I may use the expression, sir.'

'Certainly you may use the expression, Jeeves,' I said cordially. 'And I may add that in my opinion this is one of your best and ripest.'

'Yes, but I say, you know,' bleated young Bingo. 'I mean to say – old Anatole, I mean – what I'm driving at is that he's a cook in a million.'

'You poor chump, if he wasn't there would be no point in the scheme.'

'Yes, but what I mean – I shall miss him, you know. Miss him fearfully.'

'Good heavens!' I cried. 'Don't tell me that you are thinking of your tummy in a crisis like this?'

Bingo sighed heavily.

'Oh, all right,' he said. 'I suppose it's a case of the surgeon's knife. All right, Jeeves, you may carry on. Yes, carry on, Jeeves. Yes, yes, Jeeves, carry on. I'll look in tomorrow morning and hear what you have to report.'

And with bowed head young Bingo biffed off.

He was bright and early next morning. In fact, he turned up at such an indecent hour that Jeeves very properly refused to allow him to break in on my slumbers.

By the time I was awake and receiving, he and Jeeves had had a heart-to-heart chat in the kitchen; and when Bingo eventually crept into my room I could see by the look on his face that something had gone wrong.

'It's all off,' he said, slumping down on the bed.

'Off?'

'Yes; that cook-pinching business. Jeeves tells me he saw Anatole last night, and Anatole refused to leave.'

'But surely Aunt Dahlia had the sense to offer him more than he was getting with you?'

'The sky was the limit, as far as she was concerned. Nevertheless, he refused to skid. It seems he's in love with our parlourmaid.'

'But you haven't got a parlourmaid.'

'We have got a parlourmaid.'

'I've never seen her. A sort of bloke who looked like a provincial undertaker waited at table the night before last.'

'That was the local greengrocer, who comes to help out when desired. The parlourmaid is away on her holiday – or was till last night. She returned about ten minutes before Jeeves made his call, and Anatole, I take it, was in such a state of elation and devotion and what-not on seeing her again that the contents of the Mint wouldn't have bribed him to part from her.'

'But look here, Bingo,' I said, 'this is all rot. I see the solution right off. I'm surprised that a bloke of Jeeves's mentality overlooked it. Aunt Dahlia must engage the parlourmaid as well as Anatole. Then they won't be parted.'

'I thought of that, too. Naturally.'

'I bet you didn't.'

'I certainly did.'

'Well, what's wrong with the scheme?'

'It can't be worked. If your aunt engaged our parlourmaid she would have to sack her own, wouldn't she?'

'Well?'

'Well, if she sacks her parlourmaid, it will mean that the chauffeur will quit. He's in love with her.'

'With my aunt?'

'No, with the parlourmaid. And apparently he's the only chauffeur your uncle has ever found who drives carefully enough for him.'

I gave it up. I had never imagined before that life below stairs was so frightfully mixed up with what these coves call the sex complex. The personnel of domestic staffs seemed to pair off like characters in a musical comedy.

'Oh!' I said. 'Well, that being so, we do seem to be more or less stymied. That article will have to appear after all, what?'

'No, it won't.'

'Has Jeeves thought of another scheme?'

'No, but I have.' Bingo bent forward and patted my knee affectionately. 'Look here, Bertie,' he said, 'you and I were at school together. You'll admit that?'

'Yes, but –'

'And you're a fellow who never lets a pal down. That's well known, isn't it?'

'Yes, but listen –'

'You'll cluster round. Of course you will. As if,' said Bingo with a scornful laugh, 'I ever doubted it! You won't let an old school-friend down in his hour of need. Not you. Not Bertie Wooster. No, no!'

'Yes, but just one moment. What is this scheme of yours?'

Bingo massaged my shoulder soothingly.

'It's something right in your line, Bertie, old man; something that'll come as easy as pie to you. As a matter of fact, you've done very much the same thing before – that time you were telling me about when you pinched your uncle's Memoirs at Easeby. I suddenly remembered that, and it gave me the idea. It's –'

'Here! Listen!'

'It's all settled, Bertie. Nothing for you to worry about. Nothing whatever. I see now that we made a big mistake in ever trying to tackle this job in Jeeves's silly, roundabout way. Much better to charge straight ahead without any of that finesse and fooling about. And so –'

'Yes, but listen –'

'And so this afternoon I'm going to take Rosie to a matinee. I shall leave the window of her study open, and when ⬛ have got well away you will climb in, pinch the cylinder and pop off again. It's absurdly simple –'

'Yes, but half a second –'

'I know what you are going to say,' said Bingo, raising his hand. 'How are you to find the cylinder? That's what is bothering you, isn't it? Well, it will be quite easy. Not a chance of a mistake. The thing is in the top left-hand drawer of the desk, and the drawer will be left unlocked because Rosie's stenographer is to come round at four o'clock and type the article.'

'Now listen, Bingo,' I said. 'I'm frightfully sorry for you and all that, but I must firmly draw the line at burglary.'

'But, dash it, I'm only asking you to do what you did at Easeby.'

'No, you aren't. I was staying at Easeby. It was simply a case of having to lift a parcel off the hall table. I hadn't got to break into a house. I'm sorry but I simply will not break into your beastly house on any consideration whatever.'

He gazed at me, astonished and hurt. 'Is this Bertie Wooster speaking?' he said in a low voice.

'Yes, it is!'

'But, Bertie,' he said gently, 'we agreed that you were at school with me.'

'I don't care.'

'At school, Bertie. The dear old school.'

'I don't care. I will not –'

'Bertie!'

'I will not –'

'Bertie!'

'No!'

'Bertie!'

'Oh, all right,' I said.

'There,' said young Bingo, patting me on the shoulder, 'spoke the true Bertram Wooster!'

I don't know if it has ever occurred to you, but to the thoughtful cove there is something dashed reassuring in all the reports of burglaries you read in the papers. I mean, if you're keen on Great Britain maintaining her prestige and all that. I mean, there can't be much wrong with the morale of a country whose sons go in to such a large extent for housebreaking, because you can take it from me that the job requires a nerve of the most cast-iron description. I suppose I was walking up and down in front of that house for half an hour before I could bring myself to dash in at the front gate and slide round to the side where the study window was. And even then I stood for about ten minutes cowering against the wall and listening for police-whistles.

Eventually, however, I braced myself up and got to business. The study was on the ground floor and the window was nice and large, and, what is more, wide open. I got the old knee over the sill, gave a jerk which took an inch of skin off my ankle, and hopped down into the room. And there I was, if you follow me.

I stood for a moment, listening. Everything seemed to be all right. I was apparently alone in the world.

In fact, I was so much alone that the atmosphere seemed positively creepy. You know how it is on these occasions. There was a clock on the mantelpiece that ticked in a slow, shocked sort of way that was dashed unpleasant. And over the clock a large portrait stared at me with a good deal of dislike and suspicion. It was a portrait of somebody's grandfather. Whether he was Rosie's or Bingo's I didn't know, but he was certainly a grandfather. In fact, I wouldn't be prepared to swear that he wasn't a great-grandfather. He was a big, stout old buffer in a high collar that seemed to hurt his neck, for he had drawn his chin back a goodish way and was looking down his nose as much as to say, '*You* made me put this dam' thing on!'

Well, it was only a step to the desk, and nothing between me and it but a brown shaggy rug; so I avoided grandfather's eye and, summoning up the good old bulldog courage of the Woosters, moved forward and started to navigate the rug. And I had hardly taken a step when the south-east corner of it suddenly detached itself from the rest and sat up with a snuffle.

Well, I mean to say, to bear yourself fittingly in the face of an occurrence of this sort you want to be one of those strong, silent, phlegmatic birds who are ready for anything. This type of bloke, I imagine, would simply have cocked an eye at the rug, said to himself, 'Ah, a Pekingese dog, and quite a good one, too!' and started at once to make cordial overtures to the animal in order to win its sympathy and moral support. I suppose I must be one of the neurotic younger generation you read about in the papers nowadays, because it was pretty plain within half a second that I wasn't strong and I wasn't phlegmatic. This wouldn't have mattered so much, but I wasn't silent either. In the emotion of the moment I let out a sort of sharp yowl and leaped about four feet in a north-westerly direction. And there was a crash that sounded as though somebody had touched off a bomb.

What a female novelist wants with an occasional table in her study containing a vase, two framed photographs, a saucer, a lacquer box, and a jar of potpourri, I don't know; but that was what Bingo's Rosie had, and I caught it squarely with my right hip and knocked it endways. It seemed to me for a moment as if the whole world had dissolved into a kind of cataract of glass and china. A few years ago, when I legged it to America to elude my Aunt Agatha, who was out with her hatchet, I remember going to Niagara and listening to the Falls. They made much the same sort of row, but not so loud.

And at the same instant the dog began to bark.

It was a small dog – the sort of animal from which you would have expected a noise like a squeaking slate-pencil; but it was simply baying. It had retired into a corner, and was leaning against the wall with bulging eyes; and every two seconds it chucked its head back in a kind of pained way and let out another terrific bellow.

Well, I know when I'm licked. I was sorry for Bingo and regretted the necessity of having to let him down; but the time had come, I felt, to shift. 'Outside for Bertram!' was the slogan, and I took a running leap at the window and scrambled through.

And there on the path, as if they had been waiting for me by appointment, stood a policeman and a parlourmaid.

It was an embarrassing moment.

'Oh – er – there you are!' I said. And there was what you might call a contemplative silence for a moment.

'I told you I heard something,' said the parlourmaid.

The policeman was regarding me in a boiled way.

'What's all this?' he asked.

I smiled in a sort of saint-like manner.

'It's a little hard to explain,' I said.

'Yes, it is!' said the policeman.

'I was just – er – just having a look round, you know. Old friend of the family, you understand.'

'How did you get in?'

'Through the window. Being an old friend of the family, if you follow me.'

'Old friend of the family, are you?'

'Oh, very. Very. Very old. Oh, a very old friend of the family.'

'I've never seen him before,' said the parlourmaid.

I looked at the girl with positive loathing. How she could have inspired affection in anyone, even a French cook, beat me. Not that she was a bad-looking girl, mind you. Not at all. On another and happier occasion I might even have thought her rather pretty. But now she seemed one of the most unpleasant females I had ever encountered.

'No,' I said. 'You have never seen me before. But I'm an old friend of the family.'

'Then why didn't you ring at the front door?'

'I didn't want to give any trouble.'

'It's no trouble answering front doors, that being what you're paid for,' said the parlourmaid virtuously. 'I've never seen him before in my life,' she added, perfectly gratuitously. A horrid girl.

'Well, look here,' I said, with an inspiration, 'the undertaker knows me.'

'What undertaker?'

'The cove who was waiting at table when I dined here the night before last.'

'Did the undertaker wait at table on the sixteenth instant?' asked the policeman.

'Of course he didn't,' said the parlourmaid.

'Well, he looked like – By Jove, no. I remember now. He was the greengrocer.'

'On the sixteenth instant,' said the policeman – pompous ass! – 'did the greengrocer – ?'

'Yes, he did, if you want to know,' said the parlourmaid. She seemed disappointed and baffled, like a tigress that sees its prey being sneaked away from it. Then she brightened. 'But this fellow could easily have found that out by asking round about.'

A perfectly poisonous girl.

'What's your name?' asked the policeman.

'Well, I say, do you mind awfully if I don't give my name, because –'

'Suit yourself. You'll have to tell it to the magistrate.'

'Oh, no, I say, dash it!'

'I think you'd better come along.'

'But I say, really, you know, I am an old friend of the family. Why, by Jove, now I remember, there's a photograph of me in the drawing-room. Well, I mean, that shows you!'

'If there is,' said the policeman.

'I've never seen it,' said the parlourmaid.

I absolutely hated this girl.

'You would have seen it if you had done your dusting more conscientiously,' I said severely. And I meant it to sting, by Jove!

'It is not a parlourmaid's place to dust the drawing-room,' she sniffed haughtily.

'No,' I said bitterly. 'It seems to be a parlourmaid's place to lurk about and hang about and – er – waste her time fooling about in the garden with policemen who ought to be busy about their duties elsewhere.'

'It's a parlourmaid's place to open the front door to visitors. Them that don't come in through windows.'

I perceived that I was getting the loser's end of the thing. I tried to be conciliatory.

'My dear old parlourmaid,' I said, 'don't let us descend to vulgar wrangling. All I'm driving at is that there is a photograph of me in the drawing-room, cared for and dusted by whom I know not; and this photograph will, I think, prove to you that I am an old friend of the family. I fancy so, officer?'

'If it's there,' said the man in a grudging way.

'Oh, it's there all right. On, yes, it's there.'

'Well, we'll go to the drawing-room and see.'

'Spoken like a man, my dear old policeman,' I said.

The drawing-room was on the first floor, and the photograph was on the table by the fireplace. Only, if you understand me, it wasn't. What I mean is there was the fireplace, and there was the table by the fireplace, but, by Jove, not a sign of any photograph of me whatsoever. A photograph of Bingo, yes. A photograph of Bingo's uncle, Lord Bittlesham, right. A photograph of Mrs Bingo, three-quarter face, with a tender smile on her lips, all present and correct. But of anything resembling Bertram Wooster, not a trace.

'Ho!' said the policeman.

'But, dash it, it was there the night before last.'

'Ho!' he said again. 'Ho! Ho!' As if he were starting a drinking-chorus in a comic opera, confound him.

Then I got what amounted to the brain-wave of a lifetime.

'Who dusts these things?' I said, turning on the parlourmaid.

'I don't.'

'I didn't say you did. I said who did.'

'Mary. The housemaid, of course.'

'Exactly. As I suspected. As I foresaw. Mary, officer, is notoriously the worst smasher in London. There have been complaints about her on all sides. You see what has happened? The wretched girl has broken the glass of my photograph and, not being willing to come forward and admit it in an honest, manly way, has taken the thing off and concealed it somewhere.'

'Ho!' said the policeman, still working through the drinking-chorus.

'Well, ask her. Go down and ask her.'

'You go down and ask her,' said the policeman to the parlourmaid. 'If it's going to make him any happier.'

The parlourmaid left the room, casting a pestilential glance at me over her shoulder as she went. I'm not sure she didn't say 'Ho!' too. And then there was a bit of a lull. The policeman took up a position with a large beefy back against the door, and I wandered to and fro and hither and yonder.

'What are you playing at?' demanded the policeman.

'Just looking round. They may have moved the thing.'

'Ho!'

And then there was another bit of a lull. And suddenly I found myself by the window, and, by Jove, it was six inches open at the bottom. And the world beyond looked so bright and sunny and – Well, I don't claim that I am a particularly swift thinker, but once more something seemed to whisper 'Outside for Bertram!' I slid my finger nonchalantly under the sash, gave a hefty heave, and up she came. And the next moment I was in a laurel bush, feeling like the cross which marks the spot where the accident occurred.

A large red face appeared in the window. I got up and skipped lightly to the gate.

'Hi!' shouted the policeman.

'Ho!' I replied, and went forth, moving well.

'This,' I said to myself, as I hailed a passing cab and sank back on the cushions, 'is the last time I try to do anything for young Bingo!'

These sentiments I expressed in no guarded language to Jeeves when I was back in the old flat with my feet on the mantelpiece, pushing down a soothing whisky-and.

'Never again, Jeeves!' I said. 'Never again!'

'Well, sir –'

'No, never again!'

'Well, sir –'

'What do you mean, "Well, sir"? What are you driving at?'

'Well, sir, Mr Little is an extremely persistent young

gentleman, and yours, if I may say so, sir, is a yielding and obliging nature –'

'You don't think that young Bingo would have the immortal rind to try to get me into some other foul enterprise?'

'I should say that it was more than probable, sir.'

I removed the dogs swiftly from the mantelpiece, and jumped up, all of a twitter.

'Jeeves, what would you advise?'

'Well, sir, I think a little change of scene would be judicious.'

'Do a bolt?'

'Precisely, sir. If I might suggest it, sir, why not change your mind and join Mr George Travers at Harrogate?'

'Oh, I say, Jeeves!'

'You would be out of what I might describe as the danger zone there, sir.'

'Perhaps you're right, Jeeves,' I said thoughtfully. 'Yes, possibly you're right. How far is Harrogate from London?'

'Two hundred and six miles, sir.'

'Yes, I think you're right. Is there a train this afternoon?'

'Yes, sir. You could catch it quite easily.'

'All right, then. Bung a few necessaries in a bag.'

'I have already done so, sir.'

'Ho!' I said.

It's a rummy thing, but when you come down to it Jeeves is always right. He had tried to cheer me up at the station by saying that I would not find Harrogate unpleasant, and, by Jove, he was perfectly correct. What I had overlooked, when examining the project, was the fact that I should be in the middle of a bevy of blokes who were taking the cure and I shouldn't be taking it myself. You've no notion what a dashed cosy, satisfying feeling that gives a fellow.

I mean to say, there was old Uncle George, for instance. The medicine-man, having given him the once-over, had ordered him to abstain from all alcoholic liquids, and in addition to tool down the hill to the Royal Pump-Room each morning at eight-thirty and imbibe twelve ounces of warm crescent saline and magnesia. It doesn't sound much, put that way, but I gather from contemporary accounts that it's practically equivalent to getting outside a couple of little old last year's eggs beaten up in sea-water. And the thought of Uncle George, who had oppressed me sorely in my childhood, sucking down that stuff and having to hop out of bed at eight-fifteen to do so was extremely grateful and comforting of a morning.

At four in the afternoon he would toddle down the hill again and repeat the process, and at night we would dine together and I would loll back in my chair, sipping my wine, and listen to him telling me what the stuff had tasted like. In many ways the ideal existence.

I generally managed to fit it in with my engagements to go down and watch him tackle his afternoon dose, for we Woosters are as fond of a laugh as anyone. And it was while I was enjoying the performance in the middle of the second week that I heard my name spoken. And there was Aunt Dahlia.

'Hallo!' I said. 'What are you doing here?'

'I came down yesterday with Tom.'

'Is Tom taking the cure?' asked Uncle George, looking up hopefully from the hell-brew.

'Yes.'

'Are you taking the cure?'

'Yes.'

'Ah!' said Uncle George, looking happier than I had seen him for days. He swallowed the last drops, and then, the programme calling for a brisk walk before his massage, left us.

'I shouldn't have thought you would have been able to

get away from the paper,' I said. 'I say,' I went on, struck by a pleasing idea. 'It hasn't bust up, has it?'

'Bust up? I should say not. A pal of mine is looking after it for me while I'm here. It's right on its feet now. Tom has given me a couple of thousand and says there's more if I want it, and I've been able to buy the serial rights of Lady Bablockhythe's *Frank Recollections of a Long Life*. The hottest stuff, Bertie. Certain to double the circulation and send half the best-known people in London into hysterics for a year.'

'Oh!' I said. 'Then you're pretty well fixed, what? I mean, what with the Frank Recollections and that article of Mrs Little's.'

Aunt Dahlia was drinking something that smelled like a leak in the gas-pipe, and I thought for a moment that it was that that made her twist up her face. But I was wrong.

'Don't mention that woman to me, Bertie!' she said. 'One of the worst.'

'But I thought you were rather pally.'

'No longer. Will you credit it that she positively refuses to let me have that article –'

'What!'

' – purely and simply on account of some fancied grievance she thinks she has against me because her cook left her and came to me.'

I couldn't follow this at all.

'Anatole left her?' I said. 'But what about the parlourmaid?'

'Pull yourself together, Bertie. You're babbling. What do you mean?'

'Why, I understood –'

'I'll bet you never understood anything in your life.' She laid down her empty glass. 'Well, that's done!' she said with relief. 'Thank goodness, I'll be able to watch Tom drinking his in a few minutes. It's the only thing that enables me to bear up. Poor old chap, he does hate it so! But I cheer him by telling him it's going to put him in shape for Anatole's cooking. And that, Bertie, is something worth going into training for. A master of his art, that man. Sometimes I'm not altogether surprised that Mrs Little made such a fuss when he went. But, really, you know, she ought not to mix sentiment with business. She has no right to refuse to let me have that article just because of a private difference. Well, she jolly well can't use it anywhere else, because it was my idea and I have witnesses to prove it. If she tries to sell it to another paper, I'll sue her. And, talking of sewers, it's high time Tom was here to drink his sulphur-water.'

'But look here –'

'Oh, by the way, Bertie,' said Aunt Dahlia, 'I withdraw any harsh expressions I may have used about your man Jeeves. A most capable feller!'

'Jeeves?'

'Yes; he attended to the negotiations. And very well he did it, too. And he hasn't lost by it, you can bet. I saw to that. I'm grateful to him. Why, if Tom gives up a couple of thousand now, practically without a murmur, the imagination reels at what he'll do with Anatole cooking regularly for him. He'll be signing cheques in his sleep.'

I got up. Aunt Dahlia pleaded with me to stick around and watch Uncle Tom in action, claiming it to be a sight nobody should miss, but I couldn't wait. I rushed up the hill, left a farewell note for Uncle George, and caught the next train for London.

'Jeeves,' I said, when I had washed off the stains of travel, 'tell me frankly all about it. Be as frank as Lady Bablockhythe.'

'Sir?'

'Never mind, if you've not heard of her. Tell me how you worked this binge. The last I heard was that Anatole loved that parlourmaid – goodness knows why! – so much that he refused to leave her. Well, then?'

'I was somewhat baffled for a while, I must confess, sir. Then I was materially assisted by a fortunate discovery.'

'What was, that?'

'I chanced to be chatting with Mrs Travers's housemaid, sir, and, remembering that Mrs Little was anxious to obtain a domestic of that description, I asked her if she would consent to leave Mrs Travers and go at an advanced wage to Mrs Little. To this she assented, and I saw Mrs Little and arranged the matter.'

'Well? What was the fortunate discovery?'

'That the girl, in a previous situation some little time back, had been a colleague of Anatole, sir. And Anatole, as is the too frequent practice of these Frenchmen, had made love to her. In fact, they were, so I understand it, sir, formally affianced until Anatole disappeared one morning, leaving no address, and passed out of the poor girl's life. You will readily appreciate that this discovery simplified matters considerably. The girl no longer had any affection for Anatole, but the prospect of being under the same roof with two young persons, both of whom he had led to assume – '

'Great Scott! Yes, I see! It was rather like putting in a ferret to start a rabbit.'

'The principle was much the same, sir. Anatole was out of the house and in Mrs Travers's service within half an hour of the receipt of the information that the young person was about to arrive. A volatile man, sir. Like so many of these Frenchmen.'

'Jeeves,' I said, 'this is genius of a high order.'

'It is very good of you to say so, sir.'

'What did Mr Little say about it?'

'He appeared gratified, sir.'

'To go into sordid figures, did he – '

'Yes, sir. Twenty pounds. Having been fortunate in his selections at Hurst Park on the previous Saturday.'

'My aunt told me that she – '

'Yes, sir. Most generous. Twenty-five pounds.'

'Good Lord, Jeeves! You've been coining the stuff!'

'I have added appreciably to my savings, yes, sir. Mrs Little was good enough to present me with ten pounds for finding her such a satisfactory housemaid. And then there was Mr Travers –'

'Uncle Thomas?'

'Yes, sir. He also behaved most handsomely, quite independently of Mrs Travers. Another twenty-five pounds. And Mr George Travers –'

'Don't tell me that Uncle George gave you something, too! What on earth for?'

'Well, really, sir, I do not quite understand myself. But I received a cheque for ten pounds from him. He seemed to be under the impression that I had been in some way responsible for your joining him at Harrogate, sir.'

I gaped at the fellow.

'Well, everybody seems to be doing it,' I said, 'so I suppose I had better make the thing unanimous. Here's a fiver.'

'Why, thank you, sir. This is extremely –'

'It won't seem much compared with these vast sums you've been acquiring.'

'Oh, I assure you, sir.'

'And I don't know why I'm giving it to you.'

'No, sir.'

'Still, there it is.'

'Thank you very much, sir.'

I got up.

'It's pretty late,' I said, 'but I think I'll dress and go out and have a bite somewhere. I feel like having a whirl of some kind after two weeks at Harrogate.'

'Yes, sir. I will unpack your clothes.'

'Oh, Jeeves,' I said, 'did Peabody and Simms send those soft silk shirts?'

'Yes, sir. I sent them back.'

'Sent them back!'

'Yes, sir.'

I eyed him for a moment. But I mean to say. I mean, what's the use?

'Oh, all right,' I said. 'Then lay out one of the gents' stiff-bosomed.'

'Very good, sir,' said Jeeves.

10 — Bertie Changes his Mind

It has happened so frequently in the past few years that young fellows starting in my profession have come to me for a word of advice, that I have found it convenient now to condense my system into a brief formula. 'Resource and Tact' – that is my motto. Tact, of course, has always been with me a *sine qua non*; while as for resource, I think I may say that I have usually contrived to show a certain modicum of what I might call *finesse* in handling those little *contretemps* which inevitably arise from time to time in the daily life of a gentleman's personal gentleman. I am reminded, by way of an instance, of the Episode of the School for Young Ladies near Brighton – an affair which, I think, may be said to have commenced one evening at the moment when I brought Mr Wooster his whisky and siphon and he addressed me with such remarkable petulance.

Not a little moody Mr Wooster had been for some days – far from his usual bright self. This I had attributed to the natural reaction from a slight attack of influenza from which he had been suffering; and, of course, took no notice, merely performing my duties as usual, until on the evening of which I speak he exhibited this remarkable petulance when I brought him his whisky and siphon.

'Oh, dash it, Jeeves!' he said, manifestly overwrought. 'I wish at least you'd put it on another table for a change.'

'Sir?' I said.

'Every night, dash it all,' proceeded Mr Wooster morosely, 'you come in at exactly the same old time

with the same old tray and put it on the same old table.
I'm fed up, I tell you. It's the bally monotony of it that
makes it all seem so frightfully bally.'

I confess that his words filled me with a certain
apprehension. I had heard gentlemen in whose
employment I have been speak in very much the same
way before, and it had almost invariably meant that they
were contemplating matrimony. It disturbed me,
therefore, I am free to admit, when Mr Wooster
addressed me in this fashion. I had no desire to sever a
connexion so pleasant in every respect as his and mine
had been, and my experience is that when the wife
comes in at the front door the valet of bachelor days goes
out at the back.

'It's not your fault, of course,' went on Mr Wooster,
regaining a certain degree of composure. 'I'm not
blaming you. But, by Jove, I mean, you must
acknowledge – I mean to say, I've been thinking pretty
deeply these last few days, Jeeves, and I've come to the
conclusion mine is an empty life. I'm lonely, Jeeves.'

'You have a great many friends, sir.'

'What's the good of friends?'

'Emerson,' I reminded him, 'says a friend may well be
reckoned the masterpiece of Nature, sir.'

'Well, you can tell Emerson from me next time you
see him that he's an ass.'

'Very good, sir.'

'What I want – Jeeves, have you seen that play called
I-forget-its-dashed-name?'

'No, sir.'

'It's on at the What-d'you-call-it. I went last night.
The hero's a chap who's buzzing along, you know, quite
merry and bright, and suddenly a kid turns up and says
she's his daughter. Left over from act one, you know –
absolutely the first he'd heard of it. Well, of course,
there's a bit of a fuss and they say to him "What-ho?"
and he says, "Well, what about it?" and they say, "Well,

what about it?'' and he says, ''Oh all right, then, if that's
the way you feel!'' and he takes the kid and goes off with
her out into the world together, you know. Well, what
I'm driving at, Jeeves, is that I envied that chappie. Most
awfully jolly little girl, you know, clinging to him
trustingly and what-not. Something to look after, if you
know what I mean. Jeeves, I wish I had a daughter. I
wonder what the procedure is?'

'Marriage is, I believe, considered the preliminary
step, sir.'

'No, I mean about adopting a kid. You can adopt kids,
you know, Jeeves. But what I want to know is how you
start about it.'

'The process, I should imagine, would be highly
complicated and laborious, sir. It would cut into your
spare time.'

'Well, I'll tell you what I could do, then. My sister will
be back from India next week with her three little girls.
I'll give up this flat and take a house and have them all
to live with me. By Jove, Jeeves, I think that's rather a
scheme, what? Prattle of childish voices, eh? Little feet
pattering hither and thither, yes?'

I concealed my perturbation, but the effort to preserve
my *sang-froid* tested my powers to the utmost. The
course of action outlined by Mr Wooster meant the
finish of our cosy bachelor establishment if it came into
being as a practical proposition; and no doubt some men
in my place would at this juncture have voiced their
disapproval. I avoided this blunder.

'If you will pardon my saying so, sir,' I suggested, 'I
think you are not quite yourself after your influenza. If I
might express the opinion, what you require is a few
days by the sea. Brighton is very handy, sir.'

'Are you suggesting that I'm talking through my hat?'

'By no means, sir. I merely advocate a short stay at
Brighton as a physical recuperative.'

Mr Wooster considered.

'Well, I'm not sure you're not right,' he said at length.
'I *am* feeling more or less of an onion. You might shove
a few things in a suitcase and drive me down in the car
tomorrow.'

'Very good, sir.'

'And when we get back I'll be in the pink and ready to
tackle this pattering-feet wheeze.'

'Exactly, sir.'

Well, it was a respite, and I welcomed it. But I began
to see that a crisis had arisen which would require adroit
handling. Rarely had I observed Mr Wooster more set on
a thing. Indeed, I could recall no such exhibition of
determination on his part since the time when he had
insisted, against my frank disapproval, on wearing
purple socks. However, I had coped successfully with
that outbreak, and I was by no means unsanguine that I
should eventually be able to bring the present affair to a
happy issue. Employers are like horses. They require
managing. Some gentlemen's personal gentlemen have
the knack of managing them, some have not. I, I am
happy to say, have no cause for complaint.

For myself, I found our stay at Brighton highly enjoyable,
and should have been willing to extend it, but Mr
Wooster, still restless, wearied of the place by the end of
two days, and on the third afternoon he instructed me to
pack up and bring the car round to the hotel. We started
back along the London road at about five on a fine
summer's day, and had travelled perhaps two miles
when I perceived in the road before us a young lady,
gesticulating with no little animation. I applied the
brake and brought the vehicle to a standstill.

'What,' inquired Mr Wooster, waking from a reverie,
'is the big thought at the back of this, Jeeves?'

'I observed a young lady endeavouring to attract our
attention with signals a little way down the road, sir,' I
explained. 'She is now making her way towards us.'

Mr Wooster peered.

'I see her. I expect she wants a lift, Jeeves.'

'That was the interpretation which I placed upon her actions, sir.'

'A jolly-looking kid,' said Mr Wooster. 'I wonder what she's doing, biffing about the high road.'

'She has the air to me, sir, of one who has been absenting herself without leave from her school, sir.'

'Hallo-allo-allo!' said Mr Wooster, as the child reached us. 'Do you want a lift?'

'Oh, I say, can you?' said the child, with marked pleasure.

'Where do you want to go?'

'There's a turning to the left about a mile farther on. If you'll put me down there, I'll walk the rest of the way. I say, thanks awfully. I've got a nail in my shoe.'

She climbed in at the back. A red-haired young person with a snub-nose and an extremely large grin. Her age, I should imagine, would be about twelve. She let down one of the spare seats, and knelt on it to facilitate conversation.

'I'm going to get into a frightful row,' she began. 'Miss Tomlinson will be perfectly furious.'

'No, really?' said Mr Wooster.

'It's a half-holiday, you know, and I sneaked away to Brighton, because I wanted to go on the pier and put pennies in the slot-machines. I thought I could get back in time so that nobody would notice I'd gone, but I got this nail in my shoe, and now there'll be a fearful row. Oh, well,' she said, with a philosophy which, I confess, I admired, 'it can't be helped. What's your car? A Sunbeam, isn't it? We've got a Wolseley at home.'

Mr Wooster was visibly perturbed. As I have indicated, he was at this time in a highly malleable frame of mind, tender-hearted to a degree where the young of the female sex was concerned. Her sad case touched him deeply.

'Oh, I say, this is rather rotten,' he observed. 'Isn't

there anything to be done? I say, Jeeves, don't you think
something could be done?'

'It was not my place to make the suggestion, sir,' I
replied, 'but, as you yourself have brought the matter up,
I fancy the trouble is susceptible of adjustment. I think
it would be a legitimate subterfuge were you to inform
the young lady's schoolmistress that you are an old
friend of the young lady's father. In this case you could
inform Miss Tomlinson that you had been passing the
school and had seen the young lady at the gate and taken
her for a drive. Miss Tomlinson's chagrin would no
doubt in these circumstances be sensibly diminished if
not altogether dispersed.'

'Well, you *are* a sportsman!' observed the young
person, with considerable enthusiasm. And she
proceeded to kiss me – in connexion with which I have
only to say that I was sorry she had just been devouring
some sticky species of sweetmeat.

'Jeeves, you've hit it!' said Mr Wooster. 'A sound,
even fruity, scheme. I say, I suppose I'd better know your
name and all that, if I'm a friend of your father's.'

'My name's Peggy Mainwaring, thanks awfully,' said
the young person. 'And my father's Professor
Mainwaring. He's written a lot of books. You'll be
expected to know that.'

'Author of the well-known series of philosophical
treatises, sir,' I ventured to interject. 'They have a great
vogue, though, if the young lady will pardon my saying
so, many of the Professor's opinions strike me personally
as somewhat empirical. Shall I drive on to the school,
sir?'

'Yes, carry on. I say, Jeeves, it's a rummy thing. Do
you know, I've never been inside a girls' school in my
life.'

'Indeed, sir?'

'Ought to be a dashed interesting experience, Jeeves,
what?'

'I fancy that you may find it so, sir,' I said.

We drove on a matter of half a mile down a lane, and, directed by the young person, I turned in at the gates of a house of imposing dimensions, bringing the car to a halt at the front door. Mr Wooster and the child entered, and presently a parlourmaid came out.

'You're to take the car round to the stables, please,' she said.

'Ah!' I said. 'Then everything is satisfactory, eh? Where has Mr Wooster gone?'

'Miss Peggy has taken him off to meet her friends. And cook says she hopes you'll step round to the kitchen later and have a cup of tea.'

'Inform her that I shall be delighted. Before I take the car to the stables, would it be possible for me to have a word with Miss Tomlinson?'

A moment later I was following her into the drawing-room.

Handsome but strong-minded – that was how I summed up Miss Tomlinson at first glance. In some ways she recalled to my mind Mr Wooster's Aunt Agatha. She had the same penetrating gaze and that indefinable air of being reluctant to stand any nonsense.

'I fear I am possibly taking a liberty, madam,' I began, 'but I am hoping that you will allow me to say a word with respect to my employer. I fancy I am correct in supposing that Mr Wooster did not tell you a great deal about himself?'

'He told me nothing about himself, except that he was a friend of Professor Mainwaring.'

'He did not inform you, then, that he was *the* Mr Wooster?'

'*The* Mr Wooster?'

'Bertram Wooster, madam.'

I will say for Mr Wooster that, mentally negligible though he no doubt is, he has a name that suggests almost infinite possibilities. He sounds, if I may elucidate my meaning, like Someone – especially if you have just been informed that he is an intimate friend of so eminent a man as Professor Mainwaring. You might not, no doubt, be able to say offhand whether he was Bertram Wooster the novelist, or Bertram Wooster the founder of a new school of thought; but you would have an uneasy feeling that you were exposing your ignorance if you did not give the impression of familiarity with the name. Miss Tomlinson, as I had rather foreseen, nodded brightly.

'Oh, *Bertram* Wooster!' she said.

'He is an extremely retiring gentleman, madam, and would be the last to suggest it himself, but, knowing him as I do, I am sure that he would take it as a graceful compliment if you were to ask him to address the young ladies. He is an excellent extempore speaker.'

'A very good idea,' said Miss Tomlinson decidedly. 'I am very much obliged to you for suggesting it. I will certainly ask him to talk to the girls.'

'And should he make a pretence – through modesty – of not wishing –'

'I shall insist.'

'Thank you, madam. I am obliged. You will not mention my share in the matter? Mr Wooster might think that I had exceeded my duties.'

I drove round to the stables and halted the car in the yard. As I got out, I looked at it somewhat intently. It was a good car, and appeared to be in excellent condition, but somehow I seemed to feel that something was going to go wrong with it – something serious – something that would not be able to be put right again for at least a couple of hours.

One gets these presentiments.

It may have been some half-hour later that Mr Wooster came into the stable-yard as I was leaning against the car enjoying a quiet cigarette.

'No, don't chuck it away, Jeeves,' he said, as I withdrew the cigarette from my mouth. 'As a matter of fact, I've come to touch you for a smoke. Got one to spare?'

'Only gaspers, I fear, sir.'

'They'll do,' responded Mr Wooster, with no little eagerness. I observed that his manner was a trifle fatigued and his eye somewhat wild. 'It's a rummy thing, Jeeves, I seem to have lost my cigarette-case. Can't find it anywhere.'

'I am sorry to hear that, sir. It is not in the car.'

'No? Must have dropped it somewhere, then.' He drew at his gasper with relish. 'Jolly creatures, small girls, Jeeves,' he remarked, after a pause.

'Extremely so, sir.'

'Of course, I can imagine some fellows finding them a bit exhausting in – er –'

'*En masse*, sir?'

'That's the word. A bit exhausting *en masse*.'

'I must confess, sir, that that is how they used to strike me. In my younger day, at the outset of my career, sir, I was at one time page-boy in a school for young ladies.'

'No, really? I never knew that before. I say, Jeeves – er – did the – er – dear little souls *giggle* much in your day?'

'Practically without cessation, sir.'

'Makes a fellow feel a bit of an ass, what? I shouldn't wonder if they usedn't to stare at you from time to time, too, eh?'

'At the school where I was employed, sir, the young ladies had a regular game which they were accustomed to play when a male visitor arrived. They would stare fixedly at him and giggle, and there was a small prize for the one who made him blush first.'

'Oh, no, I say, Jeeves, not really?'

'Yes, sir. They derived great enjoyment from the pastime.'

'I'd no idea small girls were such demons.'

'More deadly than the male, sir.'

Mr Wooster passed a handkerchief over his brow.

'Well, we're going to have tea in a few minutes, Jeeves. I expect I shall feel better after tea.'

'We will hope so, sir.'

But I was by no means sanguine.

I had an agreeable tea in the kitchen. The buttered toast was good and the maids nice girls, though with little conversation. The parlourmaid, who joined us towards the end of the meal, after performing her duties in the school dining-room, reported that Mr Wooster was sticking it pluckily, but seemed feverish. I went back to the stable-yard, and I was just giving the car another look over when the young Mainwaring child appeared.

'Oh, I say,' she said, 'will you give this to Mr Wooster when you see him?' She held out Mr Wooster's cigarette-case. 'He must have dropped it somewhere. I say,' she proceeded, 'it's an awful lark. He's going to give a lecture to the school.'

'Indeed, miss?'

'We love it when there are lectures. We sit and stare at the poor dears, and try to make them dry up. There was a man last term who got hiccoughs. Do you think Mr Wooster will get hiccoughs?'

'We can but hope for the best, miss.'

'It would be such a lark, wouldn't it?'

'Highly enjoyable, miss.'

'Well, I must be getting back. I want to get a front seat.'

And she scampered off. An engaging child. Full of spirits.

She had hardly gone when there was an agitated noise, and round the corner came Mr Wooster. Perturbed. Deeply so.

'Jeeves!'

'Sir?'

'Start the car!'

'Sir?'

'I'm off!'

'Sir?'

Mr Wooster danced a few steps.

'Don't stand there saying "sir?" I tell you I'm off. Bally off! There's not a moment to waste. The situation's desperate. Dash it, Jeeves, do you know what's happened? The Tomlinson female has just sprung it on me that I'm expected to make a speech to the girls! Got to stand up there in front of the whole dashed collection and talk! I can just see myself! Get that car going, Jeeves, dash it all. A little speed, a little speed!'

'Impossible, I fear, sir. The car is out of order.'

Mr Wooster gaped at me. Very glassily he gaped.

'Out of order!'

'Yes, sir. Something is wrong. Trivial, perhaps, but possibly a matter of some little time to repair.' Mr Wooster, being one of those easy going young gentlemen who will drive a car but never take the trouble to study its mechanism, I felt justified in becoming technical. 'I think it is the differential gear, sir. Either that or the exhaust.'

I am fond of Mr Wooster, and I admit I came very near to melting as I looked at his face. He was staring at me in a sort of dumb despair that would have touched anybody.

'Then I'm sunk! Or' – a slight gleam of hope flickered across his drawn features – 'do you think I could sneak out and leg it across country, Jeeves?'

'Too late, I fear, sir.' I indicated with a slight gesture the approaching figure of Miss Tomlinson, who was advancing with a serene determination in his immediate rear.

'Ah, there you are, Mr Wooster.'

He smiled a sickly smile.

'Yes – er – here I am!'

'We are all waiting for you in the large schoolroom.'

'But I say, look here,' said Mr Wooster, 'I – I don't know a bit what to talk about.'

'Why, anything, Mr Wooster. Anything that comes into your head. Be bright,' said Miss Tomlinson. 'Bright and amusing.'

'Oh, bright and amusing?'

'Possibly tell them a few entertaining stories. But, at the same time, do not neglect the graver note. Remember that my girls are on the threshold of life, and will be eager to hear something brave and helpful and stimulating – something which they can remember in after years. But, of course, you know the sort of thing, Mr Wooster. Come. The young people are waiting.'

I have spoken earlier of resource and the part it plays in the life of a gentleman's personal gentleman. It is a quality peculiarly necessary if one is to share in scenes not primarily designed for one's cooperation. So much that is interesting in life goes on apart behind closed doors that your gentleman's gentleman, if he is not to remain hopelessly behind the march of events, should exercise his wits in order to enable himself to be – if not a spectator – at least an auditor when there is anything of interest toward. I deprecate as vulgar and undignified the practice of listening at keyholes, but without lowering myself to that, I have generally contrived to find a way.

In the present case it was simple. The large schoolroom was situated on the ground floor, with commodious French windows, which, as the weather was clement, remained open throughout the proceedings. By stationing myself behind a pillar on the porch or veranda which adjoined the room, I was enabled to see and hear all. It was an experience which I should be sorry to have missed. Mr Wooster, I may say at once, indubitably excelled himself.

Mr Wooster is a young gentleman with practically every desirable quality except one. I do not mean brains, for in an employer brains are not desirable. The quality to which I allude is hard to define, but perhaps I might call it the gift of dealing with the Unusual Situation. In the presence of the Unusual, Mr Wooster is too prone to smile weakly and allow his eyes to protrude. He lacks Presence. I have often wished that I had the power to bestow upon him some of the *savoir-faire* of a former employer of mine, Mr Montague-Todd, the well-known financier, now in the second year of his sentence. I have known men call upon Mr Todd with the express intention of horsewhipping him and go away half an hour later laughing heartily and smoking one of his cigars. To Mr Todd it would have been child's play to speak a few impromptu words to a schoolroom full of young ladies; in fact, before he had finished, he would probably have induced them to invest all their pocket-money in one of his numerous companies; but to Mr Wooster it was plainly an ordeal of the worst description. He gave one look at the young ladies, who were all staring at him in an extremely unwinking manner, then blinked and started to pick feebly at his coat-sleeve. His aspect reminded me of that of a bashful young man who, persuaded against his better judgement to go on the platform and assist a conjurer in his entertainment, suddenly discovers that rabbits and hard-boiled eggs are being taken out of the top of his head.

The proceedings opened with a short but graceful speech of introduction from Miss Tomlinson.

'Girls,' said Miss Tomlinson, 'some of you have already met Mr Wooster – Mr *Bertram* Wooster, and you all, I hope, know him by reputation.' Here, I regret to say, Mr Wooster gave a hideous, gurgling laugh and, catching Miss Tomlinson's eye, turned a bright scarlet. Miss Tomlinson resumed: 'He has very kindly consented to say a few words to you before he leaves, and I am sure that you will all give him your very earnest attention. Now, please.'

She gave a spacious gesture with her right hand as she said the last two words, and Mr Wooster, apparently under the impression that they were addressed to him, cleared his throat and began to speak. But it appeared that her remark was directed to the young ladies, and was in the nature of a cue or signal, for she had no sooner spoken to them than the whole school rose to its feet in a body and burst into a species of chant, of which I am glad to say I remember the words, though the tune eludes me. The words ran as follows:

Many greetings to you!
Many greetings to you!
Many greetings, dear stranger,
Many greetings,
Many greetings,
Many greetings to you!
Many greetings to you!
To you!

Considerable latitude of choice was given to the singers in the matter of key, and there was little of what I might call co-operative effort. Each child went on till she had reached the end, then stopped and waited for the stragglers to come up. It was an unusual performance, and I, personally, found it extremely exhilarating. It seemed to smite Mr Wooster, however, like a blow. He recoiled a couple of steps and flung up an arm defensively. Then the uproar died away, and an air of expectancy fell upon the room. Miss Tomlinson directed a brightly authoritative gaze upon Mr Wooster, and he blinked, gulped once or twice, and tottered forward.

'Well, you know –' he said.

Then it seemed to strike him that this opening lacked the proper formal dignity.

'Ladies –'

A silvery peal of laughter from the front row stopped him again.

'Girls!' said Miss Tomlinson. She spoke in a low, soft voice, but the effect was immediate. Perfect stillness instantly descended upon all present. I am bound to say that, brief as my acquaintance with Miss Tomlinson had been, I could recall few women I had admired more. She had grip.

I fancy that Miss Tomlinson had gauged Mr Wooster's oratorical capabilities pretty correctly by this time, and had come to the conclusion that little in the way of a stirring address was to be expected from him.

'Perhaps,' she said, 'as it is getting late, and he has not very much time to spare, Mr Wooster will just give you some little word of advice which may be helpful to you in after-life, and then we will sing the school song and disperse to our evening lessons.'

She looked at Mr Wooster. He passed a finger round the inside of his collar.

'Advice? After-life? What? Well, I don't know –'

'Just some brief word of counsel, Mr Wooster,' said Miss Tomlinson firmly.

'Oh, well – Well, yes – Well –' It was painful to see Mr Wooster's brain endeavouring to work. 'Well, I'll tell you something that's often done *me* a bit of good, and it's a thing not many people know. My old Uncle Henry gave me the tip when I first came to London. "Never forget, my boy," he said, "that, if you stand outside Romano's in the Strand, you can see the clock on the wall of the Law Courts down in Fleet Street. Most people who don't know don't believe it's possible, because there are a couple of churches in the middle of the road, and you would think they would be in the way. But you can, and it's worth knowing. You can win a lot of money betting on it with fellows who haven't found it out." And, by Jove, he was perfectly right, and it's a thing to remember. Many a quid have I –'

Miss Tomlinson gave a hard, dry cough, and he stopped in the middle of a sentence.

'Perhaps it will be better, Mr Wooster,' she said, in a cold, even voice, 'if you were to tell my girls some little story. What you say is, no doubt, extremely interesting, but perhaps a little –'

'Oh, ah, yes,' said Mr Wooster. 'Story? Story?' He appeared completely distraught, poor young gentleman. 'I wonder if you've heard the one about the stockbroker and the chorus-girl?'

'We will now sing the school song,' said Miss Tomlinson, rising like an iceberg.

I decided not to remain for the singing of the school song. It seemed probable to me that Mr Wooster would shortly be requiring the car, so I made my way back to the stable-yard, to be in readiness.

I had not long to wait. In a very few moments he appeared, tottering. Mr Wooster's is not one of those inscrutable faces which it is impossible to read. On the contrary, it is a limpid pool in which is mirrored each passing emotion. I could read it now like a book, and his first words were very much on the lines I had anticipated.

'Jeeves,' he said hoarsely, 'is that damned car mended yet?'

'Just this moment, sir. I have been working on it assiduously.'

'Then, for heaven's sake, let's go!'

'But I understood that you were to address the young ladies, sir.'

'Oh, I've done that!' responded Mr Wooster, blinking twice with extraordinary rapidity. 'Yes, I've done that.'

'It was a success, I hope, sir?'

'Oh, yes. Oh, yes. Most extraordinarily successful. Went like a breeze. But – er – I think I may as well be going. No use outstaying one's welcome, what?'

'Assuredly not, sir.'

I had climbed into my seat and was about to start the engine, when voices made themselves heard; and at the first sound of them Mr Wooster sprang with almost incredible nimbleness into the tonneau, and when I glanced round he was on the floor covering himself with a rug. The last I saw of him was a pleading eye.

'Have you seen Mr Wooster, my man?'

Miss Tomlinson had entered the stable-yard, accompanied by a lady of, I should say, judging from her accent, French origin.

'No, madam.'

The French lady uttered some exclamation in her native tongue.

'Is anything wrong, madam?' I inquired.

Miss Tomlinson in normal mood was, I should be disposed to imagine, a lady who would not readily confide her troubles to the ear of a gentleman's gentleman, however sympathetic his aspect. That she did so now was sufficient indication of the depth to which she was stirred.

'Yes, there is! Mademoiselle has just found several of the girls smoking cigarettes in the shrubbery. When questioned, they stated that Mr Wooster had given them the horrid things.' She turned. 'He must be in the garden somewhere, or in the house. I think the man is out of his senses. Come, mademoiselle!'

It must have been about a minute later that Mr Wooster poked his head out of the rug like a tortoise.

'Jeeves!'

'Sir?'

'Get a move on! Start her up! Get going and *keep* going!'

I applied my foot to the self-starter.

'It would perhaps be safest to drive carefully until we are out of the school grounds, sir,' I said. 'I might run over one of the young ladies, sir.'

'Well, what's the objection to that?' demanded Mr Wooster with extraordinary bitterness.

'Or even Miss Tomlinson sir.'

'Don't!' said Mr Wooster wistfully. 'You make my mouth water!'

'Jeeves,' said Mr Wooster, when I brought him his whisky and siphon one night about a week later, 'this is dashed jolly.'

'Sir?'

'Jolly. Cosy and pleasant, you know. I mean, looking at the clock and wondering if you're going to be late with the good old drinks, and then you coming in with the tray always on time, never a minute late, and shoving it down on the table and biffing off, and the next night coming in and shoving it down and biffing off, and the next night – I mean, gives you a sort of safe, restful feeling. Soothing! That's the word. Soothing!'

'Yes, sir. Oh, by the way, sir –'

'Well?'

'Have you succeeded in finding a suitable house yet, sir?'

'House? What do you mean, house?'

'I understood, sir, that it was your intention to give up the flat and take a house of sufficient size to enable you to have your sister, Mrs Scholfield, and her three young ladies to live with you.'

Mr Wooster shuddered strongly.

'That's off, Jeeves,' he said.

'Very good, sir,' I replied.

The P G Wodehouse Society (UK)

The P G Wodehouse Society (UK) was formed in 1997 and exists to promote the enjoyment of the works of the greatest humorist of the twentieth century.

The Society publishes a quarterly magazine, *Wooster Sauce*, which features articles, reviews, archive material and current news. It also publishes an occasional newsletter in the *By The Way* series which relates a single matter of Wodehousean interest. Members are rewarded in their second and subsequent years by receiving a specially produced text of a Wodehouse magazine story which has never been collected into one of his books.

A variety of Society events are arranged for members including regular meetings at a London club, a golf day, a cricket match, a Society dinner, and walks round Bertie Wooster's London. Meetings are also arranged in other parts of the country.

Membership enquiries

Membership of the Society is available to applicants from all parts of the world. The cost of a year's membership in 1998 was £15. Enquiries and requests for an application form should be addressed in writing to the Membership Secretary, Christine Hewitt, at 26 Radcliffe Road, Croydon, Surrey CRO 5QE, or write to the Editor of *Wooster Sauce*, Tony Ring, at 34 Longfield, Great Missenden, Bucks HP16 0EG.

You can visit their website at:
http://www.eclipse.co.uk/wodehouse